### "Well, did you need something, or not?"

Dare hadn't meant to sound so clipped, but he did succeed in wrenching Abby's gaze from his bare chest. Her aura shifted once more. Sharpened. Darkened.

She pulled an envelope from her back pocket and held it out. "Consider this a thank-you for getting rid of my boxes."

"That won't be necessary."

"What's the problem? You'll don a tux to scale the building but can't be bothered to suit up for an evening of Mozart?" A tiny dimple appeared as she smiled.

He shook his head again. Firmly. He tried to shut the door on the tickets as well as further argument when she tucked the envelope in his hand. He sucked in a sharp breath as her fingertips grazed his.

That was all it took.

Like the violin she carried to work, he was instantly, completely in tune—with *her*.

D0089623

Dear Reader,

No doubt your summer's already hot, but it's about to get hotter, because *New York Times* bestselling author Heather Graham is back in Silhouette Intimate Moments! *In the Dark* is a riveting, heart-pounding tale of romantic suspense set in the Florida Keys in the middle of a hurricane. It's emotional, sexy and an absolute edge-of-your-seat read. Don't miss it!

FAMILY SECRETS: THE NEXT GENERATION continues with *Triple Dare* by Candace Irvin, featuring a woman in jeopardy and the very special hero who saves her life. *Heir to Danger* is the first in Valerie Parv's CODE OF THE OUTBACK miniseries. Join Princess Shara Najran as she goes on the run to Australia— and straight into the arms of love. Terese Ramin returns with *Shotgun Honeymoon,* a wonderful—and wonderfully suspenseful—marriage-of-inconvenience story. Brenda Harlen has quickly become a must-read author, and *Bulletproof Hearts* will only further her reputation for writing complex, heartfelt page-turners. Finally, welcome back Susan Vaughan, whose *Guarding Laura* is full of both secrets and sensuality.

Enjoy them all, and come back next month for more of the most exciting romance reading around—only from Silhouette Intimate Moments.

Enjoy!

Leslie J. Wainger
Executive Editor

Please address questions and book requests to:
Silhouette Reader Service
U.S.: 3010 Walden Ave., P.O. Box 1325, Buffalo, NY 14269
Canadian: P.O. Box 609, Fort Erie, Ont. L2A 5X3

# Triple Dare
## CANDACE IRVIN

Silhouette®

INTIMATE MOMENTS™
Published by Silhouette Books
America's Publisher of Contemporary Romance

If you purchased this book without a cover you should be aware
that this book is stolen property. It was reported as "unsold and
destroyed" to the publisher, and neither the author nor the
publisher has received any payment for this "stripped book."

Special thanks and acknowledgment are given
to Candace Irvin for her contribution to the
FAMILY SECRETS: THE NEXT GENERATION series.

**SILHOUETTE BOOKS**

ISBN 0-373-27381-9

TRIPLE DARE

Copyright © 2004 by Harlequin Books S.A.

All rights reserved. Except for use in any review, the reproduction
or utilization of this work in whole or in part in any form by any
electronic, mechanical or other means, now known or hereafter
invented, including xerography, photocopying and recording, or in
any information storage or retrieval system, is forbidden without
the written permission of the editorial office, Silhouette Books,
233 Broadway, New York, NY 10279 U.S.A.

All characters in this book have no existence outside the imagination of
the author and have no relation whatsoever to anyone bearing the same
name or names. They are not even distantly inspired by any individual
known or unknown to the author, and all incidents are pure invention.

This edition published by arrangement with Harlequin Books S.A.

® and TM are trademarks of Harlequin Books S.A., used under license.
Trademarks indicated with ® are registered in the United States Patent
and Trademark Office, the Canadian Trade Marks Office and in other
countries.

Visit Silhouette Books at www.eHarlequin.com

**Printed in U.S.A.**

## CANDACE IRVIN

As the daughter of a librarian and a sailor, it's no wonder Candace says her two greatest loves are reading and the sea. After spending several exciting years as a U.S. naval officer sailing around the world, she decided it was time to put down roots and give her other love a chance. To her delight, she soon learned that writing romance was as much fun as reading it. A finalist for both the coveted RITA® Award and the Holt Medallion, as well as a two-time *Romantic Times* Reviewers' Choice Award nominee, Candace believes her luckiest moment was the day she married her own dashing hero, a former U.S. Army combat engineer with dimples to die for. The two now reside in the South, happily raising three future heroes and one adorable heroine—who won't be allowed to date until she's forty, at least.

Candace loves to hear from readers. You can e-mail her at candace@candaceirvin.com or snail-mail her c/o Silhouette Books, 233 Broadway, Suite 1001, New York, NY 10279.

For my dad, Ernest A. Phillips, Sr.
For everything.

# Prologue

He felt her even before he could see her.

Sometimes it happened like that.

And yet, it had never happened quite like this.

Every other time the emotions had ripped in, slicing straight through his skin until they were boring into his bones, wrenching him deep into the abyss before he could catch his breath. There he'd remain, trapped and tormented, until they'd run their course. But this time was different. *She* was different. And he was powerless to resist. He simply closed his eyes and stood there, more in than out of the elevator.

Several impatient passengers jostled past as they hurried out into the corridor before heading into the main lobby beyond. For once, the physical contact didn't faze him. He was too busy feeling. Absorbing. Measuring each and every one of his breaths against the heady, hypnotic awareness that continued to wash over him, through him, merging. Until gradually she became him. Just as he became her.

Completely.

Stunned, he jerked back into the elevator.

It didn't help.

He forced himself to step out. He forced another step, then another and another, until he, too, had reached the lobby. The others had begun to intrude again. The relentless crush of the city and beyond had returned as well. Years of practice allowed him to ratchet the intrusion down to a dull throb, just as some skill he'd never even known he possessed allowed him to remain completely focused upon *her.* She was twenty feet away, her lithe back to him, but he knew it was her. Just as surely as he felt her essence filling every inch of his being. He didn't need her to turn and face him. He already knew she was as beautiful on the outside as she was in her heart.

Still, he was driven to wait.

His reward came in the barest glimpse of a smooth, flushed cheek and a gently curving jaw as she turned to her companion and tucked a flowing tangle of dark curls behind an ear. One glance at the elderly woman who answered her wide smile and eager nod and suddenly he knew why she was there.

Just like that, the panic crashed in.

His heart began hammering within his chest, damned near fracturing his ribs as the doorman opened the building's main door for her. Perhaps it was for the best, because a moment later, the glass partition closed behind her, instantly severing the connection he'd felt clear down in his soul. But the knowledge punching in alongside the keening loss struck deeper.

She was the one.

She alone possessed the power to save or destroy him. But he had no way of knowing which until it was too late.

# Chapter 1

*Two months later*

It had taken her twelve months, a hundred and sixty-five concerts in almost as many cities scattered around the globe, but Abigail Pembroke finally had her life back. Unfortunately, the bulk of her former existence was still crammed inside the remaining two dozen boxes littering her brand-new living room.

Abby sighed as she studied the haphazard forest of cardboard. She should have taken the guys up on their offer to distribute the boxes around the apartment before they left. She might have, if the guilt hadn't already been biting in. Bad enough that she'd caved in to the temptation to escape her latest hotel room before the final concert of the summer series, she didn't need half the string section showing up for rehearsal tomorrow with strained backs. Not to mention she'd have had to open each box and root through its contents before she knew which room to place it in.

Her departure had been that hasty.

She'd been that humiliated.

Abby pushed the memory aside and used her scissors to slice through the tape sealing the next box. One look at the contents was all it took to make her regret not labeling *that* particular tangle of memories. She was still staring down at the rumpled lingerie she should have burned before she left for Milan when her CD player kicked in with one of her favorite Debussy sonatas for piano and violin.

Abby grinned. Leave it to a bunch of fiddle players to hook up the stereo first.

Her determination restored, Abby tossed the scissors aside and grabbed the cardboard flaps. Her arms protested as she jockeyed the waist-high box past the camelback sofa and coordinating armchair. The bottom of the box caught at the edge of the area rug, but once she'd freed it she was able to slide the box past the open kitchen and dining areas and down the hall without marring the hardwood floors. She shoved the box against the foot of her virgin bed and sighed.

Of all the furniture Marlena had helped her select, the towering iron four-poster had been the most extravagant.

She didn't care. What better way to start fresh?

Buoyed by the thought, she tucked a damp, unruly curl into her braid and reached inside the cardboard box. She dumped the scarlet teddy and matching robe at her feet and reached in the box again, this time snagging her telephone. Skirting the side of the still-naked mattress, she centered the phone atop her nightstand and frowned. The phone's cord didn't quite reach the outlet. Worse, the pink Cinderella casing and rotary dial looked as awkward and woefully out of place in her fancy new digs as she still felt.

*Dammit, don't.* Marlena was right. She had to move on. In more ways than one. She had Brian to think about. He was her complete responsibility now, whether he wanted to be or not. Abby pushed the latest round of painful memories aside and focused on her brother's beatific smile. His humbling joy when she'd told him she was going to move sooner and, hence, would have his room ready a whole week early. Brian might not want to move in with her, but he was definitely looking forward to resuming his weekly overnight visits. From the tight desperation in his hug when she'd left, he needed them, too. They both did.

Abby's gaze slipped to the phone she'd used to stave off the homesickness so many times. She had half a mind to set it atop that sleek coffee table her friend had steered her toward. But she wouldn't. Not because the old pink phone embarrassed her. She wanted it in here. She'd need it next to her in the coming months. Even if she couldn't use it to call home anymore.

Or maybe, especially.

A yawn sneaked up on her, forcing her to return her attention to the waiting box. It was nearly midnight. She had to be at Lincoln Center first thing in the morning and she'd yet to locate a blanket, much less a fitted sheet. Her gaze strayed to the oversized window on the far side of the room. She'd just have to put up with the muted glow bleeding in from the city. She'd already decided to hold off on hanging the drapes Marlena had designed until the contractor had a chance to install security bars on the windows. Unlike her, Brian was fascinated with heights. She'd lost both their parents now, she'd never survive if something happened to him.

Well, nothing *would*. The bars wouldn't be going on for two weeks. She'd just have to keep a closer eye on Brian than usual until then.

Abby retrieved the lingerie she'd dumped on the floor, wadding the outfit in her fist as she approached the window. Despite her healthy appreciation of heights, she couldn't help but be drawn in by the glittering rainbow stretching toward Central Park. The faint wail of a siren tugged her back to the present, the chores she had to finish before she could turn in. But as she started to turn away, something caught her eye.

She had seen pigeons perched on the ledges when Mrs. Laurens had shown her the place. Did the birds roost on the concrete sills during the night? It could be a problem. Brian adored birds as much as he did heights. The temptation might prove too much while she slept. Abby stepped closer to the window, her heart sinking as she caught another faint flutter. Except this time, she could have sworn it deliberately slid into the shadows. She took another step, stiffening as the next, even more subtle flash registered. Whatever it was was black, with a sliver of crisp white peeking out.

Definitely not feathers. Fabric.

Terror lashed through her. She darted sideways and instinctively switched off the string section's housewarming gift, knocking the floor lamp over in her haste. She had no idea if she'd cracked the stained-glass shade, but at least it hadn't shattered. Several moments passed before she risked inching back to the window. By the time she reached the soothing stillness of night, she felt as foolish as she must look. There was nothing there but a darkened, concrete sill where her overactive imagination had been.

What had she expected? A burglar?

If she'd still been in the cramped studio she'd rented before she'd left for Milan, sure. Located ten blocks up from the wrong side of Columbia University, her former walkup had been robbed twice in the three years she'd lived there. Fortunately, she and her Stradivarius had been on stage both times. Well, she wasn't on stage or in her old apartment now. It had taken a to-die-for offer from a symphony patron, a mountain of paperwork, a series of ignored phone calls from her ex and an unexpected stiletto to the back by a man she didn't even know, but she was finally safely ensconced in her sinfully huge six-room flat. Eighteen stories up.

New York City or not, no robber would climb that many stories. Would they?

But as Abby's eyes adjusted to the dark, she knew someone had. Without the light from the floor lamp interfering, she could clearly make out the fingers clinging to the far left of the shadowy ledge. Ten strong, distinctly masculine fingers. Someone was definitely out there.

Sweet heaven, what was she supposed to do? Her phone wasn't even hooked up.

*Wait.* The intercom connected to the main lobby—but the call switch was located at the front door. She should check the window first, make sure it was locked. She'd need the time to unlock her trunk and grab her violin. The Stradivarius was a work of art. Though insured for a cool three million, she'd never be able to replace it.

Fortunately, from this angle all she could make out were fingers; the man's head was completely obscured by the sill. That meant *he* couldn't see her either. Still, her heart resumed its frantic pace as she forced herself to inch close enough to the window to make sure. The brass latch pointed to the right. But did that mean the window was locked?

Before she could scrape enough courage together to check, the man's fingers shifted. Quivered.

Whoever the fool was, he was losing his grip!

Her hands shot up before she could stop them, her own fingers damp with sweat and quaking as she fumbled with the latch. She wrenched the window up and leaned out to grab the man's wrists before she could change her mind.

"Here, let me—"

"I'm fine." The terse growl reverberated through the air, filling her ears. "Now get back before you fall."

She stiffened in shock. But she obeyed.

She thought better of it when one of the man's hands slipped off the ledge—and a muffled curse followed. Before she could lunge forward, a pair of shoes sailed through the window, landing beside the fallen lamp with a thud. She caught a blur of black fabric next, straining against a set of impressive shoulders and equally powerful arms as the man levered himself up before smoothly vaulting into her bedroom. She stood there, gaping up at six-feet-plus of dark, towering muscle backlit against the glow of the city, as transfixed as she'd been the first time she'd been nudged out on stage at Avery Fisher Hall. Only she wasn't some gawky eight-year-old kid making her knee-knocking orchestral debut. She was a twenty-four-year-old woman and she was facing the would-be robber—or worse—who'd just violated her personal space.

The thought lodged in her throat, nearly choking her. Until his clothes sank in. His *tuxedo*. Despite the shadows, she could make out a complete tux, right down to the matching black cummerbund and loosened bow tie. Whoever this guy was, he was either the classiest criminal in New York—or the best-man-turned-escapee from the wedding reception from hell. Or was he the groom? Had the guy been jilted at the altar only to scale the building so he could jump off?

A sobering thought.

She pushed past it and forced herself to take stock of her situation. It didn't look good. A dead phone and an intercom that was not only on the opposite side of her apartment, but now also on the other side of that hulking form. Then again, the fallen lamp lay three feet away. The base might be slender, but it was made of solid metal.

She inched sideways.

Nothing. Her intruder either hadn't noticed or he didn't care. She darted the rest of the way before her courage fled, leaning down to scoop the lamp upright. Sweat slicked her fingers for the second time in as many minutes as she fumbled with the switch—and swallowed a curse. The three-way bulb had been damaged in the fall. At the lowest setting, all the lamp could muster was a feeble stream of light that did little more than highlight the man's inky, shoulder-length hair. The rest of his features were still cloaked by shadows, leaving her with an impression of barely suppressed strength, rigid control and a disturbing, almost erotic pull.

Burglars weren't sexy...were they?

Even odder, for some inexplicable reason her intruder appeared to be as dumbstruck by her presence as she was with his. Was this his first attempt at breaking and entering, then? Or was the man on drugs? Either way, she refused to be intimidated. If the man was going to attack her, he'd have done it already. Or was he simply resting up?

Stradivarius or not, she should have made a break for it while she had the chance.

Well, it was too late now. Abby tightened her grip on the lamp's base. "Well, do you plan on explaining yourself or should I call the police?"

*Brave words.*

She realized just how brave as the man slipped his hand into his tuxedo jacket. She forced herself not to flinch as it surfaced holding a wallet, not a gun or a knife. Her relief bled out as the man opened the wallet and withdrew a card. She couldn't make out the words, just the photo on a New York driver's license.

The ID was his.

"Darian Sabura. I'm sorry if I frightened you. I mean you no harm. Feel free to buzz Jerry. He'll vouch for me." The dark, smooth tones flowed across the shadows gliding over her flesh like the warm, mellow notes of a bass clarinet.

Abby forced herself to ignore the disturbing vibrations that quivered deep inside her. So he knew the doorman by name. It didn't prove anything. He could be trying to get her to drop her guard.

Or the lamp.

"Thanks, but I'm fine." For now. "As for the scare, I'll get over it." What she wouldn't do was return the favor. Bad enough the man knew where she lived. Even if he was on a first-name basis with the Tristan Court doorman, she wasn't about to give him a name to go with her address. Especially since he'd yet to explain himself. "So…are you going to tell me what you were doing outside my window?"

"Climbing."

She waited for more.

She waited in vain. Chatty, the man was evidently not. But even if he was on something, he didn't seem so out of it that he'd forgotten he'd offered his ID. She doubted he'd harm her now that she could identify him…unless he had no intention of letting her see morning. Curiosity edged out fear—but not by much. "Do you do this often?"

Again, she waited. Just when she thought he wouldn't answer, she caught his faint, almost embarrassed shrug.

"It's a…hobby of sorts."

A hobby? "As in, once or twice a week you don a tux, pick out a building and just…climb it?" Okay, so no drugs. The man was simply stark, raving nuts. With her luck, Mr. Darian Sabura hadn't picked the building at random. He probably lived here. She was about to ask when he cleared his throat.

"I should be leaving. I appreciate the shortcut, but I've taken up enough of your time—" The rest ended up muffled as he bent to retrieve something from the floor. It wasn't his shoes.

Humiliation seared through her as he held out the skimpy teddy and skimpier robe she'd tossed earlier. With everything that'd happened, she'd forgotten about them. She snatched the lingerie from his grasp with more force than she'd intended, causing the teddy to slip from her fingers. She managed to hook a finger into a slender strap before the teddy floated to the floor…but not before the crotch snagged on the man's cuff link. She'd never know how she managed to keep from diving under the bed as he calmly worked the scarlet lace free.

"Thanks."

He cleared his throat. "Yes, well, good night."

Relief rushed in as he turned toward her bedroom door, until she remembered— *His shoes.*

"Wait!"

The man might not know her name, but he knew where she lived. She had no intention of letting him leave behind a ready excuse for a future nighttime visit. She whirled around as he stopped, hooked his shoes off the floor. She caught up with him at the door—and promptly gasped. With the light streaming in from the living room, she could finally make out his features. He was older than she'd expected, thirty at least— and she knew him.

Okay, she didn't exactly *know* him.

Truth was, they hadn't even met.

But she had seen him, less than two weeks before. She'd just finished a late-afternoon meeting with her contractor and ridden the elevator back down to the ground floor. There, she'd spotted this man—this face—through the lobby's massive glass doors. In her own defense, he'd been impossible to miss. Not only had Darian roared up onto the sidewalk on a sleek, silver-and-maroon racing motorcycle, he'd taken the time to cuff a matching helmet from his head, revealing a clipped rugged jaw and a glorious tangle of black hair as he unstrapped a canvas backpack from his bike.

He wasn't lying. He did know the doorman.

Well enough for Jerry to store the bag behind the security desk for him as he roared off to wherever he was headed. It didn't matter. Darian Sabura was still a thief. Because he'd also managed to rob her twice now.

Of her breath.

And she hadn't gotten this close the first time.

He might have exchanged his sweat-stained T-shirt, worn leather boots and faded jeans for the sleek trappings suited to pungent cigars and the lofty private rooms of the Union Club, but this was still the face of a man who thrived in the great outdoors—the more rugged the better. His features bore the scars and weathering to prove it. From the fine lines around his eyes, the faint scar running the length of his entire right cheek and jaw, the nose that appeared once broken, not to mention the ghost of a serious tear that had once split the center of his bottom lip, she no longer doubted he'd been telling the truth about his unusual "hobby." Still, it wasn't the man's scars that had knocked the air from her lungs. Or even the memory of the fiercely honed muscles below.

It was his eyes. They were almost…haunted.

Dark green and framed with thick black lashes, his gaze held her entire body hostage. She couldn't move. All she could do was feel. *Him.* If the eyes were truly the mirrors of the soul, then somehow this man was holding back the weight of the entire world. And the strain was killing him.

He blinked.

The spell broke. A split second later, chagrin seared in. Darian Sabura might not be a criminal, and he might find sport in scaling the high-rises of the city, perhaps even the sheer cliffs and jagged mountain peaks of the world, but he was no Atlas. He was just a man. A man who was—

*Bleeding?* Abby dropped the shoes and touched his head.

He flinched.

She jerked her hand back. "I'm sorry. I didn't mean to hurt you."

He shook his head. "You didn't. I can't even feel it."

Surely he'd exaggerated?

No, she couldn't locate the exact source of the blood, but

she was able to follow the thin rivulet down the left side of his face. "Your shirt collar is nearly soaked with blood."

He shook his head. "It's okay."

"Nonsense. You may need stitches. Just let me—"

He jerked his head away before she could touch him again. "I said it's fine. I'm fine."

The heck he was. In a way his reaction reminded her of her brother's usual response to a stranger's touch. But with Brian the reaction stemmed from his innate shyness. Once her brother got to know a person, he loved to touch—better yet, hug. Often. It was one of the many blessings that came with her brother's Down's syndrome. She had the distinct impression this man rarely hugged, however, if ever.

She shook her head, exasperated by Darian's stubbornness. "Look, it's no trouble. I've already unpacked my first-aid kit in the kitchen. At least let me tape a bandage over that." The exchange she'd witnessed the other day with the doorman had done more than allay her lingering fears regarding possible criminal intent—it lent credence and meaning to Darian's statement of a minute ago: *I appreciate the shortcut.*

Had Spider Man simply been headed home?

She forced a shrug. "Leave if you want to, but don't blame me if the blood seeps into your tux on the way upstairs and stains it permanently."

He didn't reply. Instead, his stare captured hers. Probed. She had the distinct feeling he was searching for something. Whatever it was, she didn't think he'd been able to find it.

She was sure of it when he clipped a silent, almost resigned nod before spinning around and heading down the hall.

Bemused, she stepped out after him.

Two things struck her as Darian turned into the kitchen area instead of heading to the front door. One, he'd agreed to let her help, and two, he knew the layout of her apartment. Abby forced her racing pulse to slow. Yes, the man was gorgeous and, yes, she'd now lay odds he either lived in an identical apartment upstairs or knew someone who did. But even if that friend wasn't a woman, it didn't mean he was dating material. Not for her. She'd sworn off men after her fiasco of a breakup with Stuart. The only reason she'd returned to New York was to strengthen her bond with Brian. She certainly wasn't here to get involved again, especially with a man as strange as this one, with even stranger hobbies.

Her resolve restored, Abby hooked her arm into one of the padded barstools at the breakfast counter and followed Darian into the kitchen proper. She dumped the brass stool beside the sink. The lingerie she'd inadvertently brought along went straight into the trash compactor. She threw the switch for good measure before retrieving her first-aid kit from the nest of kitchen utensils still cradling it at the top of the closest box. By the time she turned, her reluctant patient was leaning against the opposite counter, his dark, disconcerting gaze tracking her every move.

He shifted his stare to the still-chumming compactor for a brief, pointed moment, then drew it back to her.

No way. She'd let the man into her kitchen. He was not getting into her head, let alone her foolish heart. She glanced at the stool and shrugged. "You're a giant. I'm not. I can't reach." He was six-two at least. At five-seven she was at a serious disadvantage if that cut was near his temple.

Her earlier suspicions regarding the man's aversion to chitchat were cemented as he crossed the modest galley kitchen and lowered his frame onto the stool, all without speaking. Or perhaps he'd been small-talked to death at whatever function he'd donned that tux for. She stuck out her hand, hoping to determine which. He simply stared. She redoubled her efforts, extending a genuine smile along with her hand. "Abigail Pembroke. My friends call me Abby. Given your hobby, I'm guessing yours call you Dare."

He didn't return her smile.

She must have shamed him into observing one of the tenets of etiquette, however, because his hand finally rose, slowly enveloping hers. His grip was warm and solid. His stare enveloped her as well.

"Dare will do…Abby."

Oh, Lordy. The mellow note had returned to his voice, once again causing the strings of interest to vibrate deep within her belly. She muted them quickly and tugged her hand from his grasp, turning to the sink to scrub the lingering heat from her fingers along with the dust from her boxes. Fortunately, Mrs. Laurens had left a bottle of liquid soap behind and Abby used that to help with the sterilizing part of her efforts. Abby caught the rustle of fabric as she reached for the last of the paper towels the elderly woman had left as well. Dare had obviously decided to remove the jacket to his tux. By the time she returned to that steady gaze and surprisingly still-snowy shirt, her nerves were firmly under control.

Or so she'd thought.

Sweet mercy. She stared. Shamelessly.

Two weeks ago and forty feet away, the man's chest had been ogle-worthy. Tonight, less than twelve inches away, it was downright riveting. The slightly crushed cotton of Dare's shirt enhanced every inch of his broad shoulders, thick, sinewy arms and fiercely honed chest—right down to the silk cummerbund banded about his waist. She followed the line of studs back to his loosened tie and the tantalizing V of flesh at the base of his throat. Flesh that still bore the slight sheen of his unorthodox exertion.

And his scent.

This close, it was impossible to evade. Not that she wanted to. Abby savored the earthy musk drifting into her lungs. No ripe, commercial colognes for this man. Dare's natural scent reflected his looks—dark and dangerous. Her second, slower whiff clogged in the middle of her throat as he cleared his. Expectantly.

She blushed.

Great. The man peeped into her window and *she* ended up pegged as the pervert. She purged his musk from her lungs along with her embarrassment, focusing instead on that sluggish, scarlet trickle as she stepped closer. Most of the blood appeared to have been soaked up by the dark waves that spilled past his right temple. She dumped the first-aid kit on the counter and smoothed the hair from his face.

He must have prepped himself better this time, because he managed to keep from stiffening.

She couldn't. "Oh my."

His brow lifted. The motion caused several fresh drops of blood to seep from the two-inch gash she'd located just past his temple. She wasn't a doctor, but even she knew the cut required more than a Band-Aid.

"You need stitches."

Unlike earlier in her bedroom, he offered no argument. Nor did he downplay her assessment. He simply shook his head. Firmly.

Abby studied the thin scar running the length of his outer right cheek and jaw, the one on his bottom lip. Neither showed evidence of stitches. She wouldn't be able to change his mind, then. Might as well do what she could. Popping open the first-aid kit, she rummaged through her meager supplies, culling a bottle of antibacterial wash, half a dozen squares of sterile gauze and her stash of slim butterfly bandages. She washed the gash as best she could, then used all seven of the butterfly strips to seal the slightly jagged edges together. Satisfied the strips would hold, she dampened the remaining squares of gauze with the antiseptic wash, then used the pads to clean the remaining blood from Dare's cheek.

The end result was surprisingly neat.

"There." She pitched the last of the gauze on the counter as he lifted his fingers to probe his cut.

Bandaged or not, that gash had to hurt.

She nodded to her kit. "I'm sorry. There should be a packet of ibuprofen in there but it's gone. I must have used it up before I moved."

"That's okay. You've done enough as it is. I appreciate all your help…and your concern."

She glanced at her watch as he stood, stunned as she realized he'd been there for nearly half an hour. It had felt like five minutes, ten tops. Even more disconcerting was that she was reluctant to see him go. She risked a teasing smile as he pushed the stool against the counter. "Glad to help. Just promise you'll take the elevator, okay? I'm out of bandages."

His lips actually quirked, then eased into a slow, mesmerizing smile. Somewhere along the way, she stopped breathing. She'd forgotten how.

She had the distinct impression Dare knew it.

To her disappointment, his smile faded. He opened his mouth as if to say something, then closed it. The haunted look that had struck her so deeply when she'd first spotted it in the doorway of her bedroom returned. His gaze seemed almost guarded now. *He* seemed guarded—against her. But that didn't make sense. What reason did he have to be threatened by her? They hadn't even met until tonight. Not really. Was it his head? Did it hurt worse than he'd said?

It must. Not only had his mood shifted, she could almost feel the energy draining out of him. He'd paled, too. "Look, why don't you sit back down?" She tipped her chin toward the breakfast counter and the forest of cardboard still cluttering the living room beyond. "It shouldn't take me more than a few minutes to locate the rest of my medical supplies. There's bound to be a bottle of ibuprofen in the mix."

"Thank you, but no. I have somewhere I need to be."

At this hour?

She swallowed her disbelief. Nutcase or not, she did not want the man leaving until she was sure he wouldn't pass out in the elevator—whether he was headed the one floor up or seventeen down. She tried teasing again. "Let me guess, you turn into a pumpkin at midnight."

This time, his lips didn't quirk. If anything, he became more guarded. "Something like that."

Disappointment seared in—so swiftly, she was forced to admit she was attracted to the man. But even if he was attracted to her, time limits meant only one thing. A woman. Wherever his apartment was located, there was a woman waiting inside it. Girlfriend, fiancé, wife—it didn't matter. She had no intention of playing second fiddle to anyone or anything ever again. Abby held fast to her resolve as Dare retrieved his jacket. She followed him out of the kitchen and around the boxes she had no idea how she was going to get rid of once they were empty and joined him in the apartment's tiny foyer. She unlocked both security bolts and opened the door.

Dare stepped into the dimly lit hall—and hesitated.

To her surprise, he turned back.

That haunted looked was *not* a figment of her imagination. It was real and it had returned. But damned if she could figure out what was causing it, much less the resignation that had crept in as well. Dare retrieved an ivory-colored business card from the inner pocket of his tux and held it out. "Put the boxes in the hall when you finish unpacking. Then call and leave a message on my machine. I'll have them removed."

She reached out, instinctively taking the card and skimming it. Two lines in, she stopped. Forced herself to reread. Not the phone number...the address. Dare lived upstairs all right. *All* the way up. She snapped her gaze to his, not even bothering to disguise the fury blistering in.

"You live in the *penthouse?*"

The haunting in his eyes intensified.

She didn't care. She no longer wondered what was behind it, either. She was too busy absorbing the shock. Two days after Greta Laurens had offered to sell her the apartment—and the very morning after she'd brought her brother by to make sure Brian also loved it—an unnamed resident had decided to exercise an obscure clause in Tristan Court's antiquated homeowners' agreement, one originally scripted by blue bloods at the turn of the century to keep so-called common folk from buying in. Abby received a formal, humiliating summons to appear before the building's residents' board, ostensibly to determine if she was suitable neighbor material. Though the board hadn't come out and said it, she knew darn well the color of her blood hadn't been the issue, but the genetic makeup of the rest of her cells.

Or rather, her brother's.

But that wasn't the worst of it.

This man—who hadn't even bothered to show up for that humiliating meeting—had instigated the entire, ugly mess. She didn't care if Dare *had* withdrawn his reservations by the time the board met, she should have left him clinging to the side of their building where she'd found him. Unfortunately, it was too late to rectify her mistake now. She did the next best thing. She slammed the door in his face.

# *Chapter 2*

Zeno Corza pocketed the compact binoculars he'd lifted from a pawnshop the night he'd hit town. Though his mark had already entered the apartment building, Zeno didn't cross the darkened street. Nor did he retrieve his cell phone and call in. It wasn't that he had nothing new to report.

He did.

But for all the boss's big words and bigger ideas, the guy wouldn't understand a change in plans, even a small one. He was too stuck on things going down his way. Well, the boss was also supposed to be big on results, too. Zeno was about to grab a couple of those. The brilliance of it was that he didn't have to stick out his own hand. All he had to do was tap an old acquaintance on the shoulder. Remind a certain someone that in the end, everyone's dirty little secrets leaked out.

Zeno clenched his fingers. The boss was wrong. He had brawn *and* brains.

Finesse.

Hell, after that fiasco in Chicago a couple of months ago, it wouldn't be hard to prove. Especially since New York was Zeno Corza's turf. Sure, he'd been busted while distributing his white-powder wares in the projects across town a couple years back—but he'd been smart enough to develop and then cash in a lucrative marker before his case even went to court, hadn't he? Zeno craned his neck toward the upper floors of the Tristan, grinning as the bank of windows he'd spent the better part of the past few days casing lit up. Time to retrieve his cell phone. Put his new and improved mission into motion. Prove to the boss for once and for all he was ready to move up in the organization.

And if the boss was right and he didn't have a way with words?

Well, there was always Sally.

Anticipation hummed in Zeno as he fingered the meticulously honed blade sheathed at the waist of his trousers. He'd named the old knife after the faithless bitch who'd once sworn to stick with him for life. In a way, she had. Part of her. After all these years, the blade's wooden handle still carried the stain of Sally's blood. Ironic when he thought about it.

That's all the boss had ordered him to get this time.

A single drop of blood. The rest was his to amuse himself with. Another reason Zeno knew he was smart—he'd come up with a lot of ways to amuse himself over the years....

Abby gently hung her brother's latest masterpiece on the wall and scrambled off the couch to admire the results of her handiwork. Not bad. The painting—a depiction of her new apartment building at sunset—was absolutely gorgeous.

She wasn't surprised.

For all her brother's difficulties with numbers and directions, Brian was an amazing impressionist. Tristan Court's stately turn-of-the-century facade was awash in soft reds, warm golds and a soothing burnt orange. Brian had even sketched in the impression of the doorman with a few strategic strokes of dark gray, highlighted with white. The phone rang as Abby reached out to adjust the bottom of the frame. Sighing, she turned to thread through the empty cardboard boxes still cluttering her living room, wondering if her uptight upstairs neighbor would revise his opinion of her brother if she showed him the painting.

She knew the answer before she reached the kitchen counter. She'd spent years dealing with the prejudices of strangers regarding Down's. Heck, getting to know Brian one-on-one for six months the year before hadn't even put a dent in her ex's carefully concealed, holier-than-thou bigotry.

And speak of the devil.

Abby glared at the name and number in her phone's caller ID window. It was Stuart Van Heusen, in the flesh—or rather, in her ear. *If* she picked up. Abby spun around and waded back through the boxes to retrieve her hammer. By the fourth ring she was tempted to send the tool sailing across the room and onto the phone. Her own prerecorded voice kicked in on the fifth shrill, only to cut out in mid-hello as Stuart decided against leaving a message and hung up.

Smart move.

She'd yet to return his first three calls.

Frankly, she still couldn't believe he'd had the nerve to show up at the concert hall that afternoon. Fortunately, she'd been onstage, halfway through rehearsal along with the other 105 members of the Philharmonic. By the time they'd finished, Stuart had given up and left. She'd been tempted to dial his cell number then, if only to tell him that the next time he stepped foot in her dressing room—assistant district attorney or not—she was going to have security escort him out. But then Marlena had arrived and her thoughts of Stuart had vanished as her friend practically bounded toward the stage.

At first Abby hadn't been able to tell if Marlena was heading for the violin or cello section—much less why. A cellist with the Philharmonic, Marlena's husband, Stephen, had taken Abby under his wing a decade ago when he learned the gangly new violinist had a twin with the same genetic condition as his infant son. But it was Marlena Abby had really bonded with. When Marlena and Stephen had decided to turn the upper floors of their apartment house into a group home for adults with Down's, Abby had been thrilled. So much so that when her brother had confessed two years ago that he wanted to follow her to New York to study art at a special school, she'd persuaded their dad to let Brian move into the house.

But Brian hadn't been doing well this past year. He'd taken their father's heart attack and subsequent death especially hard. It was the main reason Abby had bowed out of a second year with the string quartet tour and come home instead. When Marlena waved to her, she'd assumed something had happed to her brother. Fortunately, other than a cracked tooth, Brian was fine. Marlena had already taken him to the dentist that morning. The reason Marlena had been so animated was the item she'd stumbled across while in the waiting room.

Abby laid the hammer on the coffee table, her gaze drawn to the dog-eared magazine in the center. Like her, Marlena rarely purchased *Saucy*. Still, she hadn't been able to resist flipping through a free—though year-old—issue of the *Cosmo*-wanna-be rag. Marlena had stopped to chuckle over the feature "Snagging a Billionaire Bachelor," only to learn that, according to *Saucy,* there were ten such men in the U.S. alone. Number two was none other than Darian Sabura, the very man who'd climbed through Abby's window three days before!

Of all ten men, Dare was the only one who'd refused to be interviewed. Undaunted, the magazine had made up for the loss with a series of unauthorized photos, rumors and outright conjecture about Dare and his bachelor life. The raciest gossip concerned his parents. According to *Saucy*, the blood running through Dare's veins was bluer than Tristan Court's original residents combined, at least on his mother's side. As to his father's—evidently there'd been some speculation as to which man actually held that title. Especially when Dare's mother, Miranda, retired to her country home at the start of her pregnancy and saw no one until Dare was nearly a year old. As Dare matured, the rumors faded…until a falling-out between Dare and his father added an entirely new set to the mill—and the hint of a deeper, darker scandal, as well.

One that again concerned Dare's mother.

According to a police report *Saucy* had obtained from an unnamed homicide detective within the NYPD, Dare's mother had either fallen or been pushed off a subway platform when Dare was fifteen…or had she simply lost her balance due to the effects of the contents of the silver flask found in her purse?

Neither the detective nor *Saucy* would say, no doubt for fear of a lawsuit

Either way, Abby didn't blame Dare for refusing to comment. Nor could she begrudge him the lifestyle he'd pursued since his mother's death.

But his father apparently did.

Victor Sabura's blood might run more toward an earthy red, but his legal brilliance and relentless work ethic had made up for it among most of New York's wealthy upper crust. To Victor's disappointment, his son didn't appear to have inherited that same work ethic. Instead, Darian Sabura—aka Triple Dare, as he'd been dubbed by the extreme sports media—had spent his teens and early twenties honing skills more suited to recreational pursuits. Skiing, scuba, snowboarding, surfing, skydiving, auto racing, motocross, mountain climbing, Dare had mastered them all—in lieu of settling into a job. Any job.

Rumor had it Victor Sabura had washed his hands of his

adrenaline-addicted son years before and never looked back. If Abby was smart, she'd follow suit.

Except…she couldn't.

*Saucy*'s cameras might have been too far away to catch the shadows she'd seen in Dare's eyes, but Abby hadn't been. She could still see those dark emerald pools when she closed her eyes at night. She'd seen similar shadows darken her father's stare after her mother died when she and Brian were nine. She'd seen them dim her own gaze the year before, the night she'd gone to meet her future mother-in-law, only to have her heart and her pride bruised beyond humiliation. The shadows were still there the day she'd run away to Europe. They still darkened her brother's stare whenever they talked about their dad, letting her know Brian was still running from the man's death.

What was Dare running from—his bloodline? His mother's death?

Or something more?

And why did she care?

Abby told herself it was because Dare was her neighbor. One day he might be Brian's neighbor. For that reason alone, she should at least make an attempt to— Abby flinched as the phone pierced her reverie for the fourth time that night. She didn't bother checking the caller ID—she knew it was Stuart.

She snapped her gaze back to the magazine. To the envelope she'd used to mark the article on her new neighbor and his fellow billionaire bachelors. The envelope she'd been too chicken to deliver along with the man's shoes. That settled it. Anything was preferable to sitting here and listening to that phone ring. Even heading upstairs.

Dare stared at the glass door to his shower, desperate for the promised surcease a mere pace and a half away. And yet, as utterly drained as he was, he also knew he wouldn't be stepping inside. He couldn't.

Abby.

Dare closed his eyes as her essence swirled up into the penthouse, mingling with his as it had so often this past month whenever she'd stopped by to check on the progress of the re-modeling of her apartment below. Only this time, Abby was headed up along with it. He could feel her stepping into the stairwell at the eighteenth level and slowly ascending to his, her hesitance growing stronger with every step. Usually he needed to touch someone to read their emotions this deeply. That he could feel hers so strongly without physical contact still amazed him. It also had him wondering what it would be like to press his fingers to her flesh.

To truly touch her, inside *and* out.

Yes, Abby had tended to his latest wound in her kitchen three night ago. But his sense had been deliberately dulled at the time from the blessed numbing that came as a result of the adrenaline and the exertion of scaling a cliff or a mountain...or even a twenty-story turn-of-the-century apart-ment building without the aid and security of a rope. Had he known Abby would be moving into her place early, he still would have made the climb, though he'd have taken more care with his route. Specifically, he'd have chosen one that took him well around her bedroom window instead of straight through it.

Either way, the respite from the climb had lasted only so long. Which was why he'd left her apartment so abruptly.

By the time she'd finished her ministrations, his empathic sense had returned. He'd begun to feel the simmering emo-tions of those around him again, especially hers. Unfortu-nately, the endless procession of hands he'd been forced to shake at the party he'd recently left—and the utter onslaught of feeling that came with them—had left him drained. Vul-nerable. So he'd retreated up here and into his shower, shield-ing himself behind the one and only material he'd discovered could completely block out the crushing emotions of the city, so long as he remained entirely encased within it.

Glass.

If he was smart, he would seek out that same respite now, before Abby recovered her resolve and knocked on his door. Before he felt compelled to answer it. Despite her need to right things between them, he was once again in no shape to greet the one woman who could affect him this deeply without even trying. Dare sighed as he tugged his T-shirt off and dumped the dark blue cotton at his feet.

The night he'd entered Abby's window he'd caved in to his assistant's pleas and spent the evening attending yet another of those excruciating torture sessions Charlotte liked to call a fund-raiser. Unfortunately, Charlotte was right; they were also necessary. The reason the two of them were so effective at their calling—that of locating and assisting the battered women of the city—was threefold. The first involved his skill at locating those who truly needed them, women who for whatever reason could or would not seek help through the police or the city's more conventional programs and shelters. The second involved Charlotte's determination to see to the details of creating an entirely new identity, preferably one as far removed from the old as possible. And the third consisted of his own unerring ability to greet the potential benefactors Charlotte introduced him to and immediately discern who possessed the financial means and the conscience to donate what was needed—as well as the ability and desire to keep his or her assistance quiet indefinitely.

Unfortunately, this evening's task had fallen into the first phase of assistance—determining need. Specifically, Charlotte had needed him to vet a story. One that involved a child. An innocent slip of a girl.

The results had been unbearable.

So much so, he'd been compelled to embrace the girl.

He still wondered if he should have done it. It was always a risk. Though the mother hadn't argued, she hadn't understood either. Not really. He drew comfort from the fact that by the time Charlotte ensured that both mother and child were far away from the city, and safe, the mother would already have decided that what she thought she'd seen had really been her imagination. In time she would write off the results to repressed memory. If only he could repress his own memory—that unspeakable torment—as easily. Embracing anyone, much less a child, took so damned much out of him, there were days when he wondered why he chanced it. Why he didn't leave this damned city and its roiling emotions behind. Move to some remote corner of the earth and stay there forever.

But he knew.

For better or worse, he was as committed to helping the women they assisted as Charlotte was.

Dare also knew, even before he bent low to scoop his shirt off the floor and hook it about his neck, that he could no more resist the woman standing outside his apartment than he'd been able to deny that child. Especially since she'd finally strengthened her resolve enough to step up to his door to press the bell. Dare clamped his fingers about the ends of his shirt and turned his back on the utter peace the shower promised. He crossed his bedroom, then traveled the length of the apartment, surprised by the strength of her aura. Her inner essence was far easier to read now than it had been the day he'd first felt her in the lobby, and it continued to intensify with each step he took.

Was it her—or him? Or the evening's events?

He reached the door before he could decide, and opened it. A split second later Dare realized his mistake. Abby had changed her mind again and started to leave. Unfortunately, he'd been either too drained and distracted by the night's events or too consumed by her proximity to read the fluctuation in her emotions correctly. And now it was too late.

She turned back. "Oh, I thought—"

He waited.

She took in his partial state of undress and shook her head. "Never mind what I thought."

He stared at her fingers, mesmerized, as she tucked a stray dark brown curl into the loose braid that hung halfway down her back. Just as he'd wondered all too often of late what it would be like to reach out and touch her, he couldn't help but wonder what it would feel like to have those slender fingers soothing his flesh, as well. He must have stared too long, because her fingers trembled slightly as she lowered them. He didn't need to see her teeth nip at the corner of her bottom lip to know she was nervous. Nor did he need his sense.

Tension had already begun to clog the air between them, thickening it. She lowered her gaze and he finally noticed the contents of her left hand.

His shoes.

She held them up. "You forgot them."

Dare nodded. He hadn't even realized they were missing until he'd reached his apartment the other night. But by then his sense—both emotional and intellectual—had returned. He'd decided to wait, hoping she'd call and tell him she'd leave the shoes in the hall along with her boxes.

She'd done neither.

He hooked his fingers into the knotted laces, deftly retrieving the shoes without touching her. Still, he was forced to drop the shoes just inside the doorway, unnerved by the strength of the echo she'd left on the laces alone. He shifted his grip on the door and eased it shut. "Thank you."

"Wait."

He stopped. "Yes?"

Her pupils widened, causing her gaze to darken as the inner ring of brown crowded out the flecks of green. "I, ah, wondered if your offer regarding the boxes was still good."

He nodded. "Just leave them in the hall. They'll be gone by morning." Fortunately, she didn't ask how, or by whom.

But neither did she leave.

"Did you need something else?"

"No. Yes. That is, I'd like to—" Her gaze swept his features. Narrowed slightly. "Are you okay?"

"I'm fine."

"Are you sure? I mean, I hate to be rude, but you don't look so good. In fact, you're paler than you were the other night." Her stare shifted to his temple. Fortunately, the butterfly bandages she'd applied were obscured by his hair. "Is your cut—"

"It's healing properly." But more quickly than she'd ever believe possible. Truth be told, at the moment that cut was the only part of him that didn't feel as if he'd been kicked out of the side of a small plane at ten thousand feet sans parachute. "However, it has been a long day. I was about to step in the shower...." He trailed off deliberately, hoping she'd take the hint.

She didn't.

Worse, her gaze dropped to his chest. She stared.

Studied.

From the shift in her aura and growing fascination in those soft hazel eyes, he assumed she was merely tabulating the results of his dogged pursuit of motocross, auto racing, skydiving, as well as half a dozen other so-called extreme sports before he'd figured out that free climbing provided the most bang for the adrenaline-induced buck—or rather, the most effective dulling. But then he noticed her stare had settled on his left pectoral, directly over his heart.

He shifted his T-shirt as discreetly as he could and covered the tattoo.

"Well?" He hadn't meant to sound quite so clipped. But he had succeeded in wrenching her gaze from his chest. "Did you need something, or not?"

Her aura shifted once more. Sharpened. Darkened.

"Not." A moment later she smoothed her features. He felt her attempt to smooth her mood as well. To lighten it along with her heart. She retrieved a slim white envelope from the back pocket of her jeans and held it out. "Consider it a thank-you for getting rid of the boxes."

"That won't be necessary."

"Nonsense. I insist." When he still didn't take it, she nudged the envelope closer. "Contrary to my behavior the other night, I swear it's not a letter bomb. It's a pair of tickets for the symphony Saturday night. Bring a guest."

"I'm sorry, but I don't—"

"You're already going?"

He shook his head. *Not in this lifetime.*

"You already have plans?"

He should have lied but discovered he couldn't. "No."

"Then I don't understand. What's the problem? You'll don a tux to climb a building, but can't be bothered to suit up for an evening of Mozart?" A tiny dimple dipped in at the right of her lips as she smiled, attempting to tease him into accepting. "Trust me, contrary to certain rumors it's not a fate worse than death."

If she only knew.

He shook his head again. Firmly. Even as a recent addition to the orchestra, he doubted she'd had to pay for the tickets. Still, there was no sense in wasting them. He was about to shut the door on the tickets as well as further argument when she stepped forward to tuck the envelope in his hand. He sucked in his breath as her fingertips grazed his.

That was all it took.

Like that violin she'd carried to work these past two mornings, he was instantly, completely in tune—with her.

He jerked back instinctively.

A moment later he felt her suspicion as it seared into his heart. The knot of stinging tears followed again, in his own throat as well as hers. Her lips thinned as the profound disappointment and utter disgust locked in. "Don't worry, Mr. Sabura. It's not contagious."

She spun around as he struggled to recover.

"Abby!"

She stopped. But she refused to turn back.

He swallowed his shame. "It has nothing to do with Brian or his Down's syndrome. Now or regarding the board meeting. I swear."

Her braid shifted as she nodded. But she didn't believe him. Though common sense advised against it, something deep inside forced him to try again.

"Please…I never meant to hurt you."

*Well, you did.*

She hadn't said the words, but she might as well have. He could feel them. He still felt them, and her, as she stepped away from the door, bypassing the elevator on her right in favor of the stairs. Irony bit as Abby descended. He'd purchased all four of the apartments on the nineteenth floor years before to create a buffer from the rest of the building's inhabitants and the roiling emotions of their daily lives.

If anything, the empty floor now served to magnify the effect she had on him.

Now more than ever.

Resigned, he turned into his apartment and closed the door as she closed hers, two floors below. He crossed the length of his living room, then headed down the hallway, piercingly aware that she, too, was heading down her hall. But while Abby stopped shy of her bedroom, he forced himself to continue to his, to slump down at the edge of his bed and wait for the connection to ebb. Though the contact had been slight, he had no idea how long it would take. He only had the one experience to compare this—her—to. And yet, he already knew this woman and the inexplicable hold she had over him was completely different. Already it was stronger, and growing stronger with each passing day. Every hour.

Every *note*.

He lay back on his bed as Abby tucked her violin beneath her chin, retrieved her bow and began to play. Neither the nimble grace nor the haunting poise of her technique surprised him. She'd played with same breathtaking skill and uninhibited passion the night before. But this time, the connection she'd unwittingly forged between them outside his apartment door succeeded in pulling him in deeper. Suddenly, it was as if he was there in the room with her—*within* her. He could feel the soft, lilting melody she'd chosen as it breathed its magic into her heart, gradually easing her anger and disappointment until her soul finally stirred and took over. Within minutes, he no longer knew where he left off and she began. All he knew was that he was lost somewhere amid that gently soothing music and the utter beauty of her. He closed his eyes and gave himself up to both, slipping so smoothly and completely beneath her skin, it should have startled him. But it didn't.

Until it changed.

*He* changed. He wanted more. Needed it. For the first time in his life, craved it. Dare closed his eyes tighter, delved deep within himself and reached for her.

But the connection was gone.

He shot upright, clutching at the ends of his shirt as he sucked the air into his lungs, struggling to reorient himself to the bed, the room, his very self without her in it. But it was too late. The contact had been too brief. The bond had faded. All he was left with was this thrumming awareness of her. Though constant and bittersweet, it was once again too much—and yet, no longer enough.

Worse, for a moment he'd almost believed he could have more. That he could have her. But he couldn't.

Now least of all.

Six days after Abby's essence had first merged with his own in the lobby, he'd woken in the dead of night with the presence of another filling every inch of his heart. Only this time the essence hadn't eased in, it had stabbed straight through him, ripping him out of a sound sleep. At first Dare had been terrified the cry had come from her, perhaps even the brother he'd discovered Abby had. But it hadn't.

Nor had it come from anyone else he could locate.

By the time his thundering heart had slowed, there was nothing left but the mewling echo of pain—and the distinct impression that it had come from a young boy. A boy close to him. *Very* close. Dare had scoured the early-morning news, even walked the floors of his building and circled those surrounding his in hopes that if the cry had come from a child nearby, he'd be able to locate him. He'd even had Charlotte check the police stations and hospitals.

Their efforts had been for naught.

For once, no children nearby had been beaten or violated in their bodies or their hearts. But the echo had remained. Even now, if he concentrated hard enough, he could hear that cry— feel it—as if it were ripping through him anew. But even stranger and more disturbing was that he also knew the child was okay now. And he still sensed he and the boy were close.

Through *blood.*

He had to be mistaken. Perhaps Abby's presence in his life had skewed his sense, much like his mother's had at times growing up. As a child he'd felt his mother's pain on a daily basis, though some days it had cut deeper. He felt all too well the cold, emotionless void she'd received in place of her so-called husband, his so-called father. The bastard had cared so little for the two of them that for years he'd suspected the rumors that damned gossip magazine had actually printed before were true. That he and Victor Sabura didn't share the same DNA.

But they did.

No, he'd never been tested. Given his empathic sense, he hadn't needed to be. At fifteen he'd finally simply come out and asked the man. Demanded to know. Dare wasn't sure which had disappointed him more—hearing Victor admit they were related...or feeling the utter lack of subterfuge.

So why could he still feel that cry?

Had Victor fathered another child?

Or did that cry have something to do with the other, older brand still on his heart? The one *he'd* placed above it.

His tattoo.

Dare glanced down at his chest, only to stop shy of the half-inch mark as he spotted something else.

The envelope Abby had pushed on him.

It was still in his hand.

He retrieved the tickets and studied them. Not only was Abby the featured soloist this coming Saturday, but he was forced to admit to himself that he truly wanted to go.

But he could not.

He'd spent the past two months believing that cry had nothing to do with her. He was right...and he was wrong. That cry had been a harbinger of the storm that was to come. And he did not want Abby caught up inside it. Besides, there would be thousands of people in Avery Fisher Hall. The last time he'd been trapped within the same walls with that much raw, intense emotion from so many people—

He stood.

The mere memory propelled his feet into motion. Dare crossed the bedroom and entered the bath, where his respite still waited. He dropped the tickets and his shirt to the floor, not even bothering to shuck his jeans before he entered the eight-foot hexagonal chamber he'd commissioned years before. He closed the door firmly, sealing himself within the glass and sealing the entire world out, Abby Pembroke along with it. Only then did he strip off his jeans and toss them aside before turning into the steaming spray in an effort to cleanse her lingering essence from his mind and his heart.

While he still could.

"You were fantastic, hon! The star of the show."

Abby paused in the middle of removing her stage makeup to shoot a smile toward Marlena's reflection as her friend entered the dressing room. "Yeah, yeah. You say that to Stephen after every concert."

Marlena laughed as she closed the door. "True. But he's my husband, so I'm excused." Her grin turned wicked as she plopped down at the end of the padded bench. "Besides, I just tell the hulking lug that so I can get lucky later in bed."

Abby laughed so hard she dropped her tissue into the pot of cold cream. At five-ten with a wiry build, Stephen was no hulking lug, not even beside Marlena's petite build.

Her friend raked her fingers through her short blond curls and sighed. "I'm bushed—and I didn't even perform. You ready to go?"

"In a sec." Abby swung around on the bench. She'd already exchanged her black floor-length skirt and silk blouse for a peach T-shirt and faded jeans. She reached down for the worn leather flats that completed her postconcert ensemble, careful to keep her gaze on the carpet as she slipped the right shoe on. "I take it he didn't show up."

Silence.

By the time she glanced up, Marlena had crossed the dressing room and was studiously rearranging the bouquet of calla lilies currently overpowering the dressing-room table. Her friend fiddled with the flowers for several moments, then turned and sighed. "You really didn't think he'd come, did you?"

*No.*

Abby slipped into the other shoe. Five days might have

passed since she'd used Mr. Darian Sabura's shoes as an excuse to drop off that pair of tickets, but any hope she'd had the man would use them—and in the process, possibly change his tune regarding her brother—had vanished long before the final movement of tonight's symphony.

Marlena frowned as she plucked a spray of miniature peach orchids from the simple vase beside the lilies. "Honey, I know you had hopes of improving neighborly harmony, but it's time to face facts. The man's just not interested. Even if he had shown tonight, chances are he'd have taken one look at the genetic makeup of the rest of your guests and split."

As much as Abby would've liked to deny the assessment, she couldn't. "You're probably right."

"You know I am." Marlena turned and snagged the violin and case from the dressing-room table. She held them out. "Now, cheer up and pack. It's a big night. If not for you, for someone else I know."

Marlena was right about that, too—tonight was a big night. And not because of a successful solo—because of Brian. Abby grinned as she accepted the custom case her father had given her three Christmases ago. Her brother would be sleeping over for the first time since her return from Europe. Frankly, she couldn't wait to get him all to herself again. She popped the latches on the case and retrieved the cloth, carefully wiping the Stradivarius down before fitting the violin into its velvet bed. She slipped the horsehair bow into the empty slot and tucked the cloth inside. The moment she snapped the reinforced case shut and spun the combination lock, the door to the dressing room burst open.

Brian tumbled inside along with Marlena's son. Nathaniel raced over to his mom as her brother hauled Abby in for a hug. Brian's dark, upturned eyes danced behind his ever-present thick lenses as he grinned up at her. "You played very great tonight, Abby! The best. Everyone said so."

Abby laughed, her hand slipping up to ruffle his soft brown hair before she could stop it. Knowing Brian, she figured he'd grilled every single patron he could following the concert, too. "Thanks, bro. So, you up for a pizza and a sleepover?" She might have mastered the violin by six, but she still hadn't mastered the art of eating before a performance. Fortunately for her, Brian was up for Gino's pepperoni special 24/7, whether he'd eaten recently or not.

His grin split wide, letting her know tonight was no exception. "Let's go!"

Marlena held out her violin case and gym bag as she stood.

"Thanks." Abby took them as Stephen arrived just in time to follow Brian and Nathaniel right back out the door. She crossed the room to head out after them.

"Ab?"

She paused at the door. "Yeah?"

Marlena pointed to the flowers on the dressing-room table. "Are you really leaving those for the janitor?"

She shrugged. "Grab the miniature orchids if you like, but leave the lilies. Fred can dump those in the garbage, for all I care. Unless you want them, which I doubt."

Marlena frowned. "Don't tell me—"

"'Fraid so." She didn't care if Stuart *had* left his name off that bizarre pastoral postcard to get it past security. There were only so many people who knew callas were her favorite. Of those, only one who'd send a bouquet so huge it bordered on garish. And then there was the stunning arrogance of his note: "I have more of what you need." He'd even gone so far as to leave a cell number she didn't recognize at the bottom, no doubt in hopes she'd actually call.

She wouldn't.

In fact, she planned to apply for a new unlisted number herself come Monday morning. Right after she paid a visit to Stuart's mother. Until this evening, she'd assumed Stuart simply wanted to get back together to help his flagging campaign for city councilman. If she was wrong and the implied threat in that note was correct, changing her phone number wouldn't stop the harassment…but informing Katherine Van Heusen her precious son was trying to contact her again would.

Marlena grinned. "Atta girl. You're learning."

Her friend had no idea.

Abby sighed. "Yeah, well, hold your praise. I know three other guys who are going to come rushing back to harass us if we don't get a move on."

Marlena nodded as they hurried down the hall.

Fortunately, most of the symphony patrons had left. By the time she and Marlena made it to Lincoln Center's underground parking garage, Stephen's SUV was idling beside the curb. Marlena passed the orchids over as Stephen let Brian out of the car. "You sure you two wouldn't rather have a lift?"

Brian answered for her as he reached their side. "No way! We want to stop for *pizza*."

Marlena laughed. "Well at least let me take your bag. I'll bring it to the softball game tomorrow."

"Sounds good." Abby handed her bag to Marlena and the orchids to Brian, then waved to Nathaniel in the SUV before tucking the violin case beneath her left arm. She linked hands with her brother as they chatted and walked back down the hall toward the rear pedestrian exit that spilled out onto West Sixty-fifth. To her surprise, the street appeared darker than usual. As they turned left onto the sidewalk, she realized why. Either the grid that handled Lincoln Center was experiencing an electrical glitch or several of the halogen lamps along this side of the complex had dimmed enough to need replacing.

The effect was a bit spooky.

While traffic was still whizzing along Broadway at a decent clip, they were headed in the opposite direction, past Juilliard and the Walter Reade Theatre. Abby tightened her grip on Brian's hand as they turned toward Amsterdam. Several steps later she clamped down tighter as she caught sight of a parked limo twenty yards ahead on the opposite side of the street. More specifically, the broad-shouldered, suit-clad man leaning into the driver's window. To think she'd been impressed with Dare's silhouette that night in her room. This guy was twice as big. Worse, the vibes the gorilla gave off were twice as dangerous and even more unsettling.

In the wrong way.

But why? Other than the man's massive size, she had nothing to base the impression on.

Still, a voice deep inside her shouted *run*.

Even stranger, the voice wasn't hers.

Abby bit down on her lip. "Maybe we should have taken Marlena's offer for a ride tonight." They could still hail a cab on Broadway.

Brian shook his head stubbornly. "No way. I want Gino's!"

She tugged her gaze from the limo, ignoring the now bellowing voice inside her head. For goodness' sakes, Gino's was only two blocks away. "Okay, pizza it is."

The second she glanced back, she changed her mind. Glass shattered around their feet from the vase of orchids as she caught sight of a glinting blade. The brute had a knife—and he was using it. Abby shrieked as the thug ripped the limo door open to stab the driver again. She screamed as her brother bounded forward toward the attacker.

"Brian, no!"

The violin case crashed to her feet and she vaulted over it racing after Brian. Two steps later, the tip of her right shoe clipped the edge of a pothole and she fell to her knees. She was still scrambling to her feet in the middle of the street as Brian reached the limo. Abby screamed again, this time at the top of her lungs, as the thug spun around and grabbed her brother by his hair, bashing the side of his head into the passenger window with enough force to shatter the glass.

A split second later, tires squealed.

Abby froze, then jerked her gaze to her left. It was a mistake. She was instantly blinded by the twin headlights bearing down on her. Before she could move, a wall of solid muscle slammed into her from behind, mercifully wrenching her out of the way of the fishtailing car before tackling her to the far side of the street. Pain exploded inside her skull as her head smacked into the cement curb.

"You okay?" The man above her asked.

"Y-yes—"

"Good." He held her down. "Stay down."

She couldn't have disobeyed if she'd wanted to. Her vision was fuzzed and her balance was nonexistent. She crammed every ounce of strength she had into a single plea as the nausea threatened. "Please, help my broth—"

The limo roared to life, drowning out the rest.

It didn't matter. Her tackler had already jackknifed off her body and vaulted after the car. It happened so quickly, she never even saw the man's face. She had managed to place his voice, however. But by then it was too late.

She'd already passed out.

# Chapter 3

The second the limo peeled away, every muscle in Dare's body bellowed for him to whirl about, to sprint back up the street and haul Abby into his arms. To cradle her close and drag her out of the darkness that was swallowing her whole.

But he couldn't.

Abby was fine, dammit. He'd known it even as he'd felt her slip completely away from him and into the numbing void of unconsciousness. She'd taken quite a crack to her temple and had passed out from the shock.

Her brother had not.

Dare reached Brian's side, stunned by the intensity of his emotions. Brian was on his knees, his fingers clawing into the back of his neck as he rocked himself deeper and deeper into a fetal position in a desperate attempt to absorb the horror of what he'd seen. Dare had yet to touch him and already he could feel every nuance of roiling terror, the utter betrayal and confusion reverberating throughout Brian's soul. He reached out and touched Brian's shoulder.

Before Dare could draw his next breath, Brian whirled about, instantly accepting his silent offer. With no choice but to follow through, he bent and hefted Abby's brother into his arms, carrying him over the shattered glass and blood. He would need peace and quiet to absorb enough of Brian's horror to pull him from his shock and restore Brian's mind. As much peace as he could find in this place of violence and death. Dare stopped several yards up the street as two women rushed in to see what they could do about the man he'd left behind. He didn't bother telling the women their ministrations would be useless. Like Abby, the limo driver had already slipped into unconsciousness. But unlike her, the driver would not be recovering. And the moment Dare deepened his connection with Brian and absorbed the unexpected brunt and depth of Brian's frantic need, he was forced to admit—

There was a chance *he* might not recover.

She was lying on something cold. Hard.

Cement?

Abby forced her eyes open and struggled to focus amid the onslaught of flashing lights and the hazy sea of blue.

"Take it slow, Miss Pembroke."

A man's voice. One she didn't recognize. But he knew her name. She closed her eyes, then reopened them.

Her vision began to focus. She was lying on a sidewalk and there was a cop leaning over her, police lights strobing around her. She tried moving again. This time the cop helped her to sit up, tightening his grip as she succumbed to a sudden wave of dizziness.

"I've got you, ma'am."

"T-thank you. I—I'm okay now." She stared at the man's face as his hands fell away. It took a few seconds and her vision was still a bit fuzzed, but she was able to make out the rest of his features. Dark red hair. Eyes that matched the blue in his shirt and in those ruthless lights.

Young. A kid, really. In a way, he reminded her of—

She stiffened. "Oh my God, *Brian.* He's—"

"Fine." The cop patted her arms. "Your brother's okay, I promise. Physically. I have to warn you though, he was pretty shook up. Wouldn't let anyone but your neighbor near him."

Neighbor?

"Dare?" Uncertain, she'd breathed his name. Was he really here? Had he saved her from that car?

Saved Brian?

The cop nodded. He held out his hand, caught her fingers when she missed his grip and squeezed gently. "Officer Ryder, ma'am—John Ryder. My partner and I were on Broadway when we heard the crash. Unfortunately, it was over by the time we got here. Do you remember what happened?"

Crash?

Jarring, dichotic images stabbed through Abby's mind, assaulting her so deeply she'd swear Schoenberg himself had stitched them together, but none involved a crash. The limo, yes. That hulking thug. A bloodstained knife. Shattered glass.

Her brother's head.

She closed her eyes. It didn't help. "Brian…he tried to keep that man from—" She stopped, swallowed firmly. She dragged in a breath in an attempt to clear her head, but instead of fresh air, she ended up with the latent exhaust from the police cruiser six feet away. Her head throbbed harder. She raised her hand to try and stave off the latest wave of dizziness and discovered a lump at her temple. Something wet slicked the side of her face, too, soaking into the curls that'd been pulled free from her braid.

Sweat? Or blood?

*Brian.*

She didn't care if the world was still spinning, she had to get to Brian. She had to see for herself he was okay. She tried to stand, but the cop held her down. "Please, I n-need to see my brother."

"In a minute. But first—" Ryder withdrew a handkerchief from his pocket and pressed it against her throbbing temple for several moments, nodding as he pulled it away. "The paramedics are tied up at the moment. Don't worry, though, a second ambulance should be here soon." As if on cue, she caught the faint wail of a siren as he reached into another shirt pocket, this time retrieving a small notebook and a pen. The wailing grew louder as Ryder stuffed the handkerchief in his pocket and knelt beside her. "Ma'am, I know you're shook up, but I need to ask you a few questions. It's important if we hope to catch this guy. Mr. Sabura wasn't able to get a clear look at the perp. We were hoping you could describe him. His face, clothes, coloring? Any distinguishing features?"

The dizziness increased as she shook her head. The nausea and throbbing followed close behind.

She closed her eyes and counted to five.

The latter eased.

She kept her hand cupped to her brow as she opened her eyes. It helped with the dizziness, at least. "No. I mean, I didn't see him either. Not really. Dark hair, a dark suit, but I can't be sure. He was in the shadows. The guy was huge, though. Like he lifted weights or something—" She broke off as the wailing turned to deafening shriek. The promised additional ambulance was almost on top of them now. Seconds later, it turned off Amsterdam, mercifully killing its siren as it came to a stop somewhere off her right.

Panic ripped in as she heard a cop immediately bellow for the new paramedics—and a gurney.

For Brian?

She couldn't be sure. There was a police cruiser in the way.

Those incessant, blinding lights. "I'm sorry. I wish I could give you more, but I didn't see his face." Truth was, she hadn't even looked. She'd been focused on Brian.

Terrified.

"Did you get a look at the license plate, ma'am? Even a partial number would help narrow down the search."

"I'm sorry. I didn't see anything." Just that hideous knife. The limo's window.

Brian's head.

If hers felt like it was about to split open, how must his feel? "Please, I—I need to see my brother. *Now.*"

She must have sounded as desperate as she felt because the cop finally tucked his notebook away and helped her stand. As she looked around, she realized which crash the officer had been referring to. There was a van with a mobile food cart in tow jackknifed halfway up onto the sidewalk beside the Newhouse Theatre. The van's crushed front end was still married to the base of a steel streetlight.

God willing, the driver had fared as well as she.

Two uniformed cops ordered a group of gawkers back as a third officer unraveled a roll of yellow crime scene tape. He secured the tape to a pole as Ryder escorted her past the side of the van and down the street. Ten steps later, Abby felt glass crunching beneath her shoes. She assumed it was from the limo's shattered window, but she couldn't be sure. She couldn't see her brother yet, either. The staccato of lights from both ambulances and a pair of cruisers blocking traffic at the far intersection were playing havoc with her precarious vision as she drew closer.

Several steps later, her vision cleared. She immediately wished it hadn't.

The body.

Her stomach lurched as she stared down at the man her brother had tried in vain to save. She shifted her gaze in a desperate attempt to avoid the limo driver's distant, glassy stare only to spot his shredded shirt. It was saturated with blood. The excess had pooled beneath his jacket, spreading into the street…around a pair of glasses.

She'd recognize those thick lenses anywhere. They belonged to Brian.

Her legs buckled.

Evidently, Officer Ryder was more seasoned than he looked. He caught her before she could fall.

"Gotcha, ma'am."

Abby closed her eyes as the dizzying fog swirled in. It didn't help. Like the sight of her brother's head shattering that limo window, those bloodstained lenses were already burned into her brain. Her heart. By the time she regained her equilibrium, she swore the surrounding air had dropped thirty degrees. She shivered.

"Are you okay now, ma'am?"

No. She wasn't sure she'd ever be *okay* again.

She pulled herself together as best she could and nodded anyway. "W-where's my brother?"

"This way." Ryder snagged her elbow and nudged her toward the flashing lights. She followed automatically, only to stiffen several yards later as she spotted her brother's mussed hair through the open doors of a police cruiser. He was lying down across the rear seat, the top of his dark brown head toward her. Her violin was on the floorboard beside him, its steel case open as if someone had checked the Stradivarius to make sure it'd survived. Funny, for all she'd gone through to earn the right to play the thing, she'd forgotten all about it. All she could think about was her brother. The need to make sure he was okay.

She vaulted forward, leaving the cop in her wake as she scrambled across the remaining asphalt. But as she reached the cruiser and knelt beside the door, shock stopped her cold.

Brian was sleeping?

It would explain the thin blanket someone had tucked about her brother's body. Her surprise turned to apprehension as she smoothed the hair from his forehead. Her brother's breathing might appear deep and steady, but his cheeks were beyond pale. Flaccid. Was Brian asleep…or unconscious?

"Hey, bro. Wake up."

He didn't even stir.

She swallowed her panic and tried again. *"Brian?"*

"He's fine, ma'am. Just a bit dazed."

Abby turned to find a lanky paramedic, his tightly braided dreadlocks bunched securely at the base of his neck, rounding the rear of the cruiser. Her panic snapped back as the ebony-skinned man murmured something she couldn't quite make out to Ryder and shook his head.

Had Ryder downplayed her brother's condition?

Before she could ask, the cop turned and headed back into the crime scene.

Reassurance filled the paramedic's gaze as he lowered himself to her level. The man's lilting Caribbean accent soothed her even more, "Your brother's lucky Mr. Sabura arrived when he did, Ms. Pembroke. Brian has several cuts, along with swelling and bruising on his left shoulder. Fortunately none of those cuts require stitches."

"His shoulder? But…I thought he hit his head."

The paramedic shook his head. "It may have seemed so given the darkness and your angle of view, but I couldn't find any evidence of head trauma. One of the detectives told me that from the amount of glass present, the window was probably half open or less. Without the car he can't be sure—but that does mesh with your brother's injuries. Given the level of bruising, his shoulder bore the brunt of the attack."

Relief blistered in. With it, however, came more confusion

as she studied the steady rise and fall of her brother's chest. "I don't understand. How can he sleep at a time like this?"

"Shock. His Down's, too. The stabbing you two witnessed hit your brother especially hard. Brian was coherent when I arrived, but upset and extremely confused. Your brother appears to have blocked out the attack itself. Since he wasn't even in pain, he didn't understand why I wanted to examine him. Mr. Sabura managed to calm Brian down, but by the time I finished—" the paramedic shrugged "—his mind had simply shut down. His body followed. You'll want your doctor to look at him, but I'm certain a good night's sleep will help. Given a few days, he may be able to recall what happened."

"Thank God." Abby ran her fingers through her brother's hair. No bumps. Still— "You said he wasn't in any pain?" That didn't make sense. Even if he had struck his shoulder and not his head. "That monster smashed him into the window so hard the glass *shattered*."

He wasn't even sore?

The paramedic tugged his stethoscope from his neck as he shrugged. "The human body is amazing, Ms. Pembroke. I've seen people walk away from much worse. I've also seen them done in by less. If I were you, I would count it for the blessing it is and move on."

The man was right.

Abby stood, intent on doing just that. Unfortunately her own throbbing head chose that moment to combine with the returning dizziness. Her vision fuzzed as she swayed. For the second time that night her spine slammed into a wall of solid muscle behind her. But this time iron arms also banded about her chest before she could gasp, steadying her.

"Easy."

*Dare.*

Though he'd spoken but a single word, it was enough. She'd know that dark, smoky voice anywhere. Her vision had cleared, too—instantly. The pounding in her skull ceased. Even the ache in her ribs had faded. Just like that.

Because of him?

A fresh wave of chills swept through her at the thought, absurd though it was.

The paramedic took one look at the gooseflesh rippling down her arms and glanced above her head, toward Dare. "I need to get my bag. I'll be back in a sec."

She felt Dare's nod.

And then they were alone. The chills, the traffic crawling, the flashing emergency lights, a pair of passing cops, the growing crowd at the intersection beyond, even her slumbering brother—everything faded as the very essence of the man behind her, holding her, seemed to seep into her bones. It was as if Dare's body had somehow absorbed not only the physical pain of her injuries, but the terror in her heart as well. A soothing, mesmerizing warmth suffused her.

Lulling her.

It didn't make sense. She didn't care.

She was too busy relaxing into Dare's chest, into him.

She felt his breath drag in, deep and steady. Felt the solid thudding of his heart beneath her blouse, his hypnotic heat envelop the rest of her flesh. If the man hadn't chosen that moment to shift, to pull away ever so slightly, she wasn't sure she'd have found the strength to move.

Dare dropped his arms as she turned. He didn't step away from her as she'd expected, though. He hunkered down beside her instead, the sleeve of his tailored suit brushing her thighs as he reached into the car. She watched, stunned, as those callused fingers gently smoothed the hair from her brother's brow as if he was a child who needed comforting.

"He's doing great, Abby. He just needs time." Dare straightened and captured her eyes with that enigmatic emerald stare of his as he turned to fold his arms and lean against the quarter panel of the police cruiser. "Brian will be fine in the morning, I promise."

He meant it.

How could he be so sure? According to that article in *Saucy,* Darian Sabura had never even attended college, much less medical school. So why did she believe him?

Because she wanted to.

Somehow Abby managed to pull herself together, to shake off the bizarre spell this man had woven within her. This time *she* stepped away from him, putting two feet of desperately needed distance between them. To her surprise, the dizziness didn't return with the sudden motion. Neither did the ache in her head or chest. Heck, she hadn't even swayed.

But Dare had.

"Are you okay?"

He didn't answer. It didn't matter. The blood draining from his cheeks said it all. Dare closed his eyes as he ran his hands through his hair before dragging them down to knead his neck. Something was definitely off with the man. Had he taken a whack tonight himself? He didn't appear bruised.

By the time he folded his hands back about his chest, the fatigue appeared to have eased from his gaze. But it was still in his weary nod. "I'm fine, thank you. So is your brother. He is tired, however. He was inconsolable at first, but the EMTs and I managed to calm him. Unfortunately—as the EMT said—his mind and body simply shut down following his exam." Something she couldn't quite place flitted through the man's somber gaze. Bruised or not, it was not her imagination. She'd swear the man's body was on the verge of shutting down, as well.

From calming Brian?

Saving her?

It didn't make sense. Not given his hobbies. The man might not be bleeding from a cut on his temple as he had that night in her apartment, but he was definitely drained. But like that night, she'd lay odds he had no intention of discussing his health. She pushed the curiosity away and knelt to thread her fingers through her brother's hair. "Thank you for looking out for Brian. I can take him now." To be honest, though, she had no clue how she was going to manage. Brian might be two inches shorter than her, but he was twice as solid. She smoothed the hair from his forehead. "Hey, bro, time to wake up."

"*Don't.* Your brother needs rest." She stiffened as Dare's hand closed over hers. Not because of his touch, but because of the high-handedness of his order. Who did he think he was?

"I know what Brian needs. He's *my* brother." The moment the words lashed out, she regretted them.

Good Lord, she sounded like a spoiled brat arguing over a toy. This man had saved her life. Brian's, too. Shame seared her cheeks as she stared at the dusky fingers still clapped about her wrist. The same fingers she'd first spotted clinging to her windowsill exactly one week ago. She lifted her chin and studied the man she'd spent the past five days vilifying, if only in her mind. She had no idea why Dare had tried to keep her out of Tristan Court. It no longer mattered. She just knew she should have accepted his word outside his penthouse that night. Dare didn't give a damn about her brother's Down's.

Not the way Stuart and his scheming mother had.

"I'm sorry."

He shook his head. "It's okay."

"No, it's not." She drew her breath in deep, her gratitude in deeper—and forced herself not to extend her hand, much less give in the sudden urge to outright hug the man. "Mr. Sabura, I can never repay you for what you did for me. You saved my life. More important, you saved my brother's. I'll never forget that, or you. Thank you."

She understood then that Dare thrived on the challenges

and the adrenaline inherent in his intense recreational pursuits because he did not get off on adulation and glory. Even with the emergency lights still glancing off his cheeks, she could make out the deep flush on his cheeks. He seemed as much at a loss for words as she.

But she had feeling he didn't want to be. In fact, she could have sworn he had something he wanted to say. Desperately.

In the end, he simply cleared his throat. "You're welcome. I'm glad I was near enough to help."

Abby blinked.

Come to think of it, why was he here?

She must have been in shock, because for the first time that night she took in the man's dark tailored suit and really looked at it. At him. There was no way Dare had just happened by Lincoln Center, not tonight and not dressed like that. He was here because of her. The tickets she'd pushed on him. He must have decided to use them after all. But in the end, he hadn't. He couldn't have. Marlena would have noticed. The VIP seats she'd given Dare were on the opposite side of where Brian, Marlena and Nathaniel's had been.

So what had happened?

Abby studied the tinge of gray left behind as the flush faded from his cheeks, the exhaustion lingering in his eyes. The terse set to his lips. Had he taken ill at the last moment? Decided to wait outside in the fresh air?

For her?

She was about to throw conceit to the wind and ask when the paramedic returned with a shorter, dark-haired man in tow. From the gold badge hooked over the pocket of his rumpled suit, she could see the guy was plainclothes cop. Early forties, she'd guess. From the lines carved about his pinched, reedy face, not to mention reddened eyes and scruffed jaw, the cop was either overworked or he was already burned out from years of dealing with crime and death. She decided on the latter when he didn't bother shifting his foam cup of coffee from his right hand so he could extend it to her.

He didn't even glance at Dare. "I'm Detective Pike, Ms. Pembroke. Homicide. As soon as the paramedics have had a chance to look at you, I'll need you to come down to the station, fill out an official statement, answer a few questions."

"I'm sorry, Detective. I'm afraid I can't go anywhere with you. Not tonight. I need to get my brother home, into bed."

Pike shook his head. "I'm afraid I insist." He glanced into the cruiser, his impatience barely concealed beneath a swift sip of steaming coffee. "From what the EMT tells me, your brother's not going to be any help. Kid doesn't remember a thing. Though I suppose we could always try hypnosis."

"No."

The man shrugged. "Well, in that case, can't you call a friend? Or better yet, just drop him somewhere on the way?"

That was it. She'd had more than enough.

She might have misinterpreted Dare's feelings toward her brother and missed Stuart's altogether, but there was no mistaking this moron's. She didn't care if the man was overworked, she didn't care if he was the next chief of police. Abby stepped forward, smack into the detective's personal space. "*Drop* him? Just what do you think my brother is, a—"

Dare's fingers encircled her arm before she could finish, warm, calming. "Let it go, Abby. It's not worth it. Not tonight. Besides, he can't make you go anywhere."

Her anger ebbed. Dare was right.

She allowed him to nudge her back to the side of the cruiser. Dare, however, had remained well inside the detective's personal space. She had the distinct impression he and Pike knew each other. That they'd butted heads before. But that was absurd, wasn't it? As a homicide detective, Pike dealt with the underbelly of the city, not its upper crust.

She pushed the thought aside as that same homicide detective finally bowed beneath Dare's molten glare. "I'm sorry, Ms. Pembroke."

Abby crossed her arms, holding fast to her determination to get her brother home as quickly as possible. Despite Dare and the paramedic's assurances, she'd feel better after her brother's doctor examined him. "I meant what I said, Detective. I need to leave now. However, I'm perfectly willing to stop by your station in the morning to sign a statement." She gathered what little dignity she had left and waved off the paramedic as he stepped forward. "Thank you, but I'm fine. My head doesn't even hurt anymore. If I could just have my brother's glasses, we'll be leaving."

Before either could argue, Ryder, the officer who'd helped her as she regained consciousness, approached the cruiser. Ryder leaned in swiftly to whisper something to the detective, then nodded behind him to where another cop and a pair of scrambling paramedics jerked an occupied gurney to a stop just shy of the back of an ambulance to labor over their patient again.

The limo's driver? Or the van's?

Whoever it was, the frantic pace of treatment didn't bode well. Abby sent up a prayer for both men as Dare retrieved a slim cell phone from an inner coat pocket.

He captured her stare. "I've already called a cab. It'll be here any moment. I'll see you and your brother home." His tone left no room for argument.

She didn't mind. She was even grateful. Anything to get away from this place and that jerk of a detective.

Unfortunately that same jerk of a detective stepped closer. "Afraid not, Sabura. You can't talk yourself—or rather her—out of this one."

What was *that* about?

She had no idea. But Dare did. She was sure of it. The odd glint in the stare he'd shot the detective moments earlier returned, and it wasn't due to Pike's sarcastic familiarity. The men did know each other. But from the way their stares had locked, their past hadn't been forged through friendship.

Dare frowned. "Give it up, Pike. You can't hold her. She's not even a witness. Other than the knife, she didn't see a blessed thing."

True. But how did *he* know that?

She snagged Dare's arm. "What's going on?"

Pike shrugged. "That's what we'd like to know." He tipped his cup toward the gurney and the still laboring paramedics as the EMT answered a shouted summons to join the others. "According to that poor schmuck, you're more than just an accidental bystander, Ms. Pembroke."

She dug her nails into Dare's arm as she struggled to ward off the sudden dizziness that threatened.

Was he implying she *knew* the guy on that gurney?

That he knew her?

"That's impossible, Detective. I don't know anyone who drives a limo or a van."

Pike shook his head. "The vic wasn't driving when all hell broke loose. He was a passenger. In the limo."

She pulled her hand from Dare's arm.

It was a mistake. The fog swirled in faster.

Dare's arm returned immediately, encircling her. She sagged into his strength. "I—I don't understand. W-who—" Even with Dare's support, she still couldn't get the rest out.

Fortunately, Ryder read her mind and answered. "According to his ID, the man's name is Van Heusen, ma'am. He managed to speak before he lost consciousness. Not much, but he did say he'd been waiting in that limo—for you."

Dare caught her as she swayed. She swallowed firmly. "*S-Stuart* Van Heusen?"

"You do know him." Unfortunately, this statement didn't come from her enigmatic neighbor; it came from Pike.

She pulled herself from Dare's grasp and faced the detective reluctantly. "Yes. We…used to date. Before I left for Europe. But, uh, Stuart's phoned a few times since I returned—three or four calls over the past two weeks—but I never picked up." Thank God for caller ID.

"Why?"

Suspicion had darkened Pike's stare. She forced herself not to react to it. At least, not visibly. Given Stuart's family name—not to mention that Stuart was an assistant district attorney with the city—Pike probably knew Stuart or at least knew of him. But there was no way the detective could know the rest. Specifically, why she'd really broken off her relationship with Stuart. Nor would Pike ever find out. She'd kept her side of the bargain. She hadn't breathed a word to anyone. Not even Marlena. And she knew darn well Stuart's mother would never talk.

"Ms. Pembroke?"

"Yes?"

The last vestiges of his sorry excuse for politeness burned off. "I asked you a question. *Why* didn't you pick up?"

"Because I didn't want to talk to him."

The man's lips thinned. "All right. Let's try this from the opposite angle. Why did he want to talk to you?"

"I have no idea."

But she did. At the very least, she'd had her suspicions.

Stuart must have had his, too. And given who Stuart was, he'd undoubtedly investigated them—her—and uncovered the rest.

From the accusation now firing openly in Pike's gaze, it was clear the detective had his suspicions, as well. But before Pike could express them verbally, one of the paramedics bellowed for him. Frustration racked the man's entire stringy frame, but he spun around and followed Officer Ryder across the street. A terse conversation appeared to follow. It broke off as two of the paramedics heaved the gurney up into the rear of the ambulance. To her shock, Pike scrambled in alongside the EMTs, calling out, "All right, Ms. Pembroke. Take your brother home. But then you get to the station. Tonight!"

The door slammed shut behind him, leaving Abby in shock. What was that argument about? Was Stuart okay?

And if so…had he said anything?

Her heart began pounding in her chest. Sweat drenched her tattered blouse. She jerked backward and slammed into something hard. Solid. Warm.

Dare.

She'd forgotten all about her enigmatic neighbor. But as she inched away from the man's muscular chest before turning to face him, she had the distinct impression that Dare hadn't forgotten about her. Not for a moment. "Ready?"

She blinked.

He tipped his head toward the end of the street as one of the cops waved a cab through. The taxi stopped just shy of the remaining ambulance. "Our ride's here."

*Our* ride.

For a guy who'd recoiled from her mere touch the night before, he seemed awfully okay with the implications of that double-edged statement. Abby pushed the thought aside and followed Dare to the rear of the cruiser, only to receive another jolt of surprise at the sincere concern on Dare's face as he hefted her brother into his arms. Nothing left to do, she grabbed her violin and followed the men to the back of the cab. She had no idea where her purse was. At the moment she didn't care. She just wanted to get out of there.

She skirted her brother's dangling shoes and opened the taxi's rear door for Dare. But instead of depositing her brother on the seat as she'd expected, Dare eased into the back of the cab with Brian still cradled in his arms.

He glanced up at her. "Shut the door?"

She complied, hurrying around the rear of the cab to slide in on the opposite side. Before she could give the driver Marlena's address, Dare rattled it off.

"How did you—"

He shook his head as the taxi pulled away from the staccato of flashing lights. A moment later they were turning the corner and merging into nonstop traffic. "Relax, Abby. We'll be there in a few minutes. Until then, let's not disturb him, okay?"

*She* disturb Brian?

The two of them—together—had just rocked her to her core. Not only had her brother curled into Dare, Dare had relaxed, as well. He'd even closed his eyes. As the seconds ticked out, growing into a minute, then two, Abby started to wonder if Dare had sunk into a trance of some sort, right there in the back of the cab. If she didn't know any better, she'd swear Dare and her brother were sharing some silent, otherworldly connection. The occasional glow of the passing neon lights added to the eerie effect, washing their features in a rainbow of reds, oranges, golds and greens. Another few minutes of silence, broken only by the soft rock tune floating back from the front of the cab, and she was convinced that something was definitely going on with Dare. Either that or she'd hit her head harder than she'd thought. Though she didn't understand the connection at all, she was also inexplicably loathe to break it.

But why?

She had no idea. Nor did she have a chance to think about it. The cab had covered the blocks to Marlena and Stephen's in record time. Before long, they were pulling up beside the renovated apartment house. The front-porch light was already burning brightly. Before Abby could get out of the car, Marlena had thrown the front door open. She barreled down the steps with her husband in tow. Stephen rounded the cab to pay the driver and help Dare with Brian as Marlena grabbed her and pulled her into a long, bone-crushing hug.

"My God, I couldn't believe it when Mr. Sabura called! Thank the Lord you two are okay."

Abby pulled away to see Stephen preceding Dare—Brian still in his arms—up the front steps and into the house. She turned back to Marlena. "Dare called you? How on earth did he get your number?" Let alone Marlena's name.

"I don't know. I assumed you gave it to him." Marlena snagged her violin case before brushing the hair from Abby's forehead. She frowned as she spotted her skinned temple. "You need to get that cleaned."

Abby shook off her concern as they entered the house and started up the steps to the second floor. By the time they reached her brother's room, Dare had already laid Brian on his bed and begun removing his shoes.

"I'm fine," she said, but she was still confused. She hadn't given Dare the phone number or the address.

Had Brian? He'd memorized both, but how could he have been that coherent for Dare and then fallen asleep? Then again, what did she know about the human brain? She didn't even understand her own mind at the moment. Everything she thought she'd understood about Darian Sabura had been turned upside down in an instant. In fact, these past seven days since she'd opened that window and let him into her room were the antithesis of her entire relationship with Stuart. She'd swallowed Stuart Van Heusen's lies for months, only to discover she was horribly wrong about him.

But not as wrong as she'd been about Dare.

She knew that now. How could she not? One look at the man tucking her brother into his bed proved it. The genuine compassion and concern that radiated off Dare as he reached down to pull up Brian's blue comforter and smooth it beneath his chin floored her. Because it was real. She could tell from her friend's soft smile as they stepped quietly into the hall that Marlena was thinking the same thing.

"You were wrong about him, Abby. We both were."

"I know."

Marlena looped her arm through hers and sighed. "Oh, honey. I just thank God Mr. Sabura was there tonight."

"So do I. And it's Dare."

She and Marlena both started. Dare had come up on them so quietly they hadn't realized he'd followed them out.

Marlena recovered first and returned his smile.

Stephen clapped him on the back as he passed. "Thanks, Dare. I've called Dr. Chase as we discussed. He should be here soon. I'll go down and wait. Are you staying?"

To her surprise, Dare nodded. "I'll wait to hear what the doctor says, then I'll take Abby to the station."

"You don't have to—"

Marlena cut off her instinctive objection with a firm nod. "Yes, he does. Someone does. There's no telling how long it'll take. Stephen and I will stay here and take turns in Brian's room in case he sleepwalks."

Marlena was right.

Dare captured her gaze as she turned. "You're going to have to face Pike sometime. Might as well get it over with."

Unfortunately, Dare was right, too. She did have to deal with Pike. The sooner the better.

Abby caught the flare of compassion within those dark emerald-green eyes. It burned as steadily as Pike's suspicions had out on that street, as resolutely as it had for her brother, only now it burned for her. She could almost feel Dare willing her to relax, assuring her that everything would be okay, telling her to trust him.

Lean on him.

She wanted to. After everything that had happened tonight, everything she'd learned, she needed to. But how could she? He might not be the bigoted jerk she'd assumed he was. But she didn't even know him. Not really. So why was some strange sixth sense she hadn't even known she'd possessed telling her that she was about to get to know Dare—extremely well?

"You braying ass, I warned you not to disobey orders. Ever. And what do you do?" Zeno kept the cell phone sealed to his ear, the beads of sweat rolling down his face growing fatter and clammier as the boss ripped into him. "I told you to get one drop of blood. A hair, a sample of saliva. That's *it.* I did *not* tell you to kill anyone, did I?"

Now wait a minute, the boss had just said he wasn't supposed to kill—

Zeno clamped down on the qualifier lest he voice it. Now was not the time to argue. It was time to agree with everything the boss said. No matter what. It was the only way to save his hide. He fisted his fingers around the cell phone and lowered his voice as he turned into the alley wall. "I'm sorry, boss. I swear I didn't mean to kill him."

*Liar.*

"The driver was in the way, that's all." Hell, that much was true. Sort of. "I just thought—"

"That was your first mistake, Mr. Corza. You thought. Your second mistake was acting on that unique experience without consulting me. For if you had, I would have told you to do as you were *ordered.*"

"Y-yes, sir. But I—"

"I'm not interested in the rest of your feeble excuses. What I am interested in, Mr. Corza, is results. All I need to know is if you are capable of obtaining those results within my time frame. If not, I will simply send someone else to complete the job and of course to take care of y—"

"No, sir! I can do it. All of it."

"Good. Now, get off the phone and get what I want. And then clean up your filthy mess. If you don't…"

*Click.*

Zeno flinched as the boss hung up.

He wished to God that damned click had been some fancy form of mind game. But it wasn't. It was a promise, and he knew it. A promise he'd do anything in his power to make sure the boss decided not to follow through on.

Anything.

# Chapter 4

"I, uh, never thanked you."

Dare glanced up from the year-old issue of *Newsweek* and shifted it to the right of the wooden table. Abby sat catty-corner to him, tracing her fingers about the tattered edges of an equally ancient issue of *The New Yorker*. She'd been so silent since they'd been relegated to this sparse room, his own emotional equilibrium so taxed from the evening's events that he couldn't even be sure how long she'd been looking at him. By the time they'd reached the police station, his sense had shorted out. It had yet to return. And he'd been too exhausted to get his other senses to pick up the slack.

Namely sight. Despite the shadows flitting through those exhausted hazel depths, he had no idea what or whom Abby was referring to. So he guessed.

"Brian?"

Was she referring to his help in getting her brother settled, or to the fact that he'd waited with her until the doctor had finished his house call? Fortunately, Dr. Chase had confirmed that her brother's sleepiness was due to shock. What Abby didn't know was that if left undisturbed, by morning Brian would forget he'd even met Dare.

But when Abby knotted her fingers atop the magazine and shook her head, Dare realized she hadn't been referring to her brother at all.

"The trash."

He blinked. "I beg your—"

"The empty boxes? The bags of packing material? You got rid of it as promised—or you had someone do it." She flushed. "Anyway, I meant to head up and thank you."

But she hadn't been welcome.

She hadn't voiced it. But they both knew it was true.

He felt his own neck heat. "I am sorry."

There was something else they'd yet to discuss. Their original misunderstanding. Her brother's Down's. Dare shifted his stare to the far side of the interrogation room. To that taunting one-way mirror. Damn, but he did not want to be having this conversation here. Not with his most important sense still numb. And certainly not with Pike lounging on the other side of the mirror, watching every motion, sucking in every word. And Pike *was* watching.

According to the cop who'd escorted them into this room, Pike had already returned from the hospital. Despite being knocked seriously off kilter—not to mention the limits imposed by that oversized slab of glass—Dare would lay odds the detective had hurried up his perfunctory visit to Van Heusen's bedside simply so he could position himself on the other side of that one-way mirror the moment he and Abby arrived. Pike had to know Dare wouldn't leave Abby to his grilling. Not after having experienced the bastard's technique himself.

Dare shifted his face away from the mirror to keep Pike from experiencing maximum voyeuristic satisfaction. "Abby, your brother is a remarkable young man. You're damned fortunate to have him in your life."

He meant it.

Her father's recent death, her mother's years before—he'd learned of both during the link with her twin. Despite the losses, Abby had known love. The deep, unconditional kind. She still did. He'd seen it tonight in her and in her brother; he'd felt it. As devastating as events had been, the two still had each other. He'd spent his entire childhood yearning for that. Hell, even after his mother died and he'd walked away from her grave knowing the last person on the planet who'd felt anything for him was gone, he couldn't shake the fantasy that this constant, gnawing void wasn't supposed to be.

He'd wanted to believe it so badly he'd given in to the urge to carve that damned symbol over his heart.

Dare rubbed the tiny tattoo discreetly. He'd gotten it at seventeen. Flush with the triumph of reaching the summit of Everest for the first time, he'd felt the need to mark the occasion. Himself. He must have passed on two hundred suggestions at least—and then he'd seen the triquetra. At first he'd assumed he was drawn to the simplicity of the design, three interlocking circles within a triangle. But when the tattoo artist explained that the Celtic symbol represented trinity, he'd known there was more to it. At least in his mind. He'd had the strange idea that branding the triquetra over his heart would let someone, somewhere, know he was ready to be found.

He must have been drunk on the adrenaline of being among others for so long and *not* feeling the crush of their emotions, because he'd had it branded into his flesh that same night.

Naturally, no one had ever come for him.

He'd refused to have the tattoo removed. It served as a reminder of his foolishness. Unfortunately, it also served as a reminder of the void that was still there. A void so deep that years later even the combined latent emotions of the world wouldn't be able to fill it.

Nor did they displace the silence in the room now.

His unease grew as Abby tucked a limp curl into the braid that hung halfway down her back, becoming downright unbearable as she continued to avoid his stare. Instead, she focused on the magazine he'd been reading. Try as he might, he simply could not penetrate her aura. Like that night she'd let him in through her window, he had no idea what she was feeling. But the numbing that had resulted from that evening's climb and subsequent adrenaline rush had been deliberate.

Tonight's had not.

He would never forget the sheer terror that had ripped through him when he'd realized Abby was in danger. It was that damned dream he'd had in the flesh—that nightmare he'd woken from in the dead of night after she'd come into his life. Only now he was forced to wonder if that scream he'd heard in his soul, that gut-wrenching terror that accompanied it, had been *his*. Was that why he was still numb?

Or had his well simply run dry due to the unexpected strength of the bond with her brother? Perhaps he was still experiencing the effects of the concert he'd had no business even attempting to attend. But he'd been unable to refuse her invitation. He'd deliberately arrived late. Unfortunately, the raw emotion surging through Avery Fisher Hall had been too intense. The ensuing nausea had driven him back before he'd had a chance to claim his seat. He'd retreated to the men's room, hoping to acclimate himself in time to catch Abby's solo. He hadn't. He'd barely recovered in time to save her from that car and her brother from himself.

And now he couldn't even gauge her mood well enough to know what to say to get her to look at him.

Her gaze remained fused to the magazine.

*Damn.* Despite the voyeur behind that mirror, he dragged

his breath in deep and just spelled it out. "Abby, I swear to you, I don't give a damn about your brother's Down's. Nor does Brian have anything to do with my initial objections regarding your presence at the Tristan."

Though her gaze remained fused to the magazine, she spoke. Softly and with certainty. "I know. I figured that out tonight." He noticed she didn't ask for the real reason behind his initial objections. Nor did he offer it. Neither did he need his sense to feel her disappointment.

Another eternity seemed to pass, and then she sighed. "*He* did."

Stuart? Had her brother had something to do with her breakup with Stuart Van Heusen? Had the golden boy of the district attorney's office been unable to deal with her brother's condition? If so, he wasn't surprised. Even if he hadn't met Van Heusen's able assistant at a fund-raiser three months before and accidentally probed the woman's aura, he'd had his bubble burst long ago regarding the carefully masked, hypocritical natures of too many men—compliments of Detective Pike himself...and his own father. But then, he couldn't afford to share that with this woman either.

Especially here.

Dare clamped down on his anger and regret, and offered up the only thing he could. "I'm sorry."

A bitter smile twisted her lips as she finally glanced up. "Yeah, well, it's more than Stuart was."

He didn't understand.

He wanted to. But he knew better than to try to draw her out.

Unfortunately, Abby was too rattled from the night's events to guard her thoughts. Before he could warn her, she drew in her breath and faced him squarely. "We dated for almost a year. I thought he was serious, you know? Granted, I didn't have a lot of experience. In the beginning Stuart used to tease me that I too naive and too wrapped up in my music. He was right. Maybe that's why I fell for him so hard and so fast." She smoothed another stray curl into her braid and sighed. "You have to understand, Stuart Van Heusen was everything I wasn't. Older, sophisticated, financially secure. He was born into a world I only get to play in. Once I tuck my fiddle away, most men expect me to leave with it. If they do want me to stick around, it's usually without my clothes. I thought Stuart was different."

*Damn.* It was too late. If that last hadn't caught Pike's attention, nothing would. It sure as hell had captured his.

Dare caved in to the need. "He wasn't?"

She shook her head. "He was worse."

Worse?

His heart lurched. With the motion came the stirrings of emotions—none of which were his. Pain, anger and a perceived disgrace. The need to share the source with someone who just might understand. Someone she desperately hoped would refrain from judging her. He felt it all.

No doubt about it, the emotional brownout was easing.

The curse was returning. For the first time in a long time, he embraced it willingly. But the overall impression was still too vague. He reached out, instinctively closing his hand over hers. Just like that it strengthened, tearing through his pride as sharply as it had torn through hers. He stared directly into that exhausted, reddened gaze. "Stuart Van Heusen abused you. Deeply. Along with someone else."

But she hadn't been abused in the way he'd feared.

*Thank God.*

It wasn't until she'd snatched her hand from his grasp, that he even realized he'd voiced the discovery out loud. The first half, anyway. "What? I don't—" She broke off, swallowed firmly and immediately smoothed the shock in her facial features. It was too late. Like that night outside his apartment, their brief physical contact had tuned him to her so perfectly, he could feel the astonishment radiating from within her. By the time she licked her lips, the beginnings of suspicion had set in. "H-how could you know that?"

At least she hadn't denied it.

He shrugged. "I simply guessed." Though the age-old lie grated, it succeeded in placating her.

"Oh." She dampened her lips again. "It's not what you think. Stuart didn't betray me with another woman."

That wasn't what he thought. Much less was it what he now knew.

He wisely kept both to himself as she tugged her braid over her shoulder and worried her fingers over the elastic at the end. "There was another woman, though. His mother."

"She didn't approve of you?"

"No." The pain in her eyes as well as her heart belied the finality in that single word.

There was more.

But it was beyond his reach. Their touch had lasted seconds. Not nearly long enough for him to channel her feelings and use them to paint a more complete picture of the memory in his mind, much as her brother had used oils, brushes and a canvas to reproduce the Tristan. He needed more. Enough to know if he should head off the conversation in light of their greedy audience. An accidental brush would do. It often did. He pushed his magazine to the edge of the table and allowed it to fall, deliberately waiting until Abby reached down between them before he, too, reached out.

Unfortunately, their fingers did more than simply brush, they collided. Tangled. Held. He drew his breath in deep and received her essence along with it. Within seconds she'd enveloped him, filling every corner of his being, mingling with his very heart and soul—and she didn't even know it.

But when she inhaled sharply, he knew she felt it, too.

The pull.

It was inescapable. *She* was inescapable. Utterly captivating. And, God help him, he was powerless to resist.

He leaned closer—

Until a shallow cough rent the air.

They sprang apart.

It took several moments for the realization of what they'd almost done—along with *who* had interrupted it—to burn through the fog still swirling through his head.

"Pike."

The detective's hand was still on the knob of the door.

Why? How? There wasn't a shard of glass embedded within that slab of steel. So how had Pike been able to enter the room without Dare's internal radar registering the intrusion? But as the fog within his brain—his sense—finally dispersed, Dare knew. It was his mother all over again. Though rare, there were moments growing up when he'd felt his mother's pain so deeply it had obscured the emotions of others around him. Only this time, the effect was a hundred times more pronounced, a thousand times more dangerous. For Abby and him.

Especially around this man.

By the time he'd recovered, Pike had closed the door and stalked across the room, bypassing the closest chair in favor of the one at the far end of the table. It figured. Pike might not have believed his frantic explanation any more than his father had all those years ago, but like Victor Sabura, the detective had also been careful to keep outside Dare's reach whenever they'd had the misfortune to meet since.

Just in case.

The man nodded to Abby. "Ms. Pembroke. I apologize if I…interrupted something."

She flushed.

Dare burned. He shoved his anger down. Now wasn't the time to settle old scores. Too much was at stake. He might not be able to get a clear read on the man's intent, but they had enough history for him to know that something was amiss—and it wasn't good. It came in the form of the manila folder Pike had carried into the room and tossed atop the table in front of Abby. Dare clamped down on yet another curse.

Pike smiled. His twisted lips dripped with satisfaction as the detective tipped his graying temple toward the folder. "I thought you could use a more recent read."

Dare couldn't blame Abby for staring. Nor could he begrudge her the shock spreading through her. The sight of his name on the summary sheet chilled him to the bone as well—but for an entirely different reason.

The bastard had pulled his police record.

The damned thing had been sealed years before. Releasing it would have required a judge's signature—unless Pike had retained an illegal copy. Either way, he had obviously hoped to use his arrest history to knock Abby off balance, to scare her into giving up whatever it was that he thought she was withholding.

But there was more.

His curse finally ripped free as he realized what it was.

He turned to her, for the first time in his life not caring if the entire world knew him for the freak he was. He had to say it first. There was no way he could let Pike deliver the news. She'd sustained too many blows tonight as it was. He took her hand and did his best to prepare her mind and her heart before he delivered the blow. "Abby, Van Heusen's condition is worse than we thought. They don't think he's—"

The moment he felt her pull away, he released her. He no longer needed to touch her to know what she was feeling. Hell, he didn't even need the curse. The denial was etched within every inch of her face as she shot to her feet. She shook her head as she backed away from him, all the way to the wall.

*"No.* You're wrong. Stuart's fine. They got him to the hospital. He—" She swung her stare to Pike's. "Tell him he's wrong. Stuart is going to be *fine.*"

The detective remained silent.

*"Please."*

For the first time since Dare had known the man, he felt the pulse of genuine empathy beat within Pike's conscience. "I'm sorry, Ms. Pembroke. He's right. By the time we got Van Heusen to the hospital, he'd already coded twice. The paramedics revived him both times, but he's in a coma now. The doctors don't expect him to survive the night."

Dare stood as he felt the air surrounding Abby grow hot. Stifling. She was going to faint. Unfortunately, Pike headed for her side along with him.

Pike reached her first. "I've got her." The detective grabbed her upper arms and wrenched her away from him firmly. Deliberately. "You okay, Ms. Pembroke? Maybe you should lie down. We've got a cot in the back—"

*"No."*

The connection they'd forged prior to that near-kiss was stronger than he'd expected. Stronger even than on that night outside his door. One moment he was watching those soft thick lashes of hers as they flew wide and the next, it was as if he was inside her skin, as she struggled to focus her tunneled vision upon his face. Slowly but surely her circle of vision spread. Soon she could make out the white sleeves of his shirt, the dark blue of his tie, the hair spilling onto his shoulders, the shadow already rasping his cheeks and jaw. The moment she caught the quiet warning in his gaze, he relaxed. She knew what he was trying to tell her.

He needn't have worried.

She might be rattled, but she'd realized what Pike was attempting to do. The detective might have felt sorry for her, but he still intended to use her to his own end. Why else had he brought that damned folder with him? Despite its presence, she trusted Dare. He eased out his breath as she calmly extricated herself from Pike's grasp.

"I'm fine, Detective. Thank you. But I am tired. Upset."

Her hands shook as she preceded them back to the table and reclaimed her seat. "I'm sure you've heard by now I didn't see the man who attacked that driver—and Stuart—clearly. I wish I had. Maybe then—" She broke off, swallowed firmly and started again. "Please. If you could just give me my statement, I'll sign it. Then I'd like to go home."

Pike shook his head. "I'm afraid we've got more to cover than your version of tonight's events, Ms. Pembroke. For example, your relationship with Mr. Van Heusen."

The swift glance Abby shot toward the one-way mirror confirmed what Dare suspected. What Pike had been hoping for. Abby had been too upset during their conversation regarding Van Heusen to realize Pike had been eavesdropping. Dare had to hand it to her, though. Abby recovered well. She folded her hands primly in her lap. "What more do you need, Detective?"

Pike flicked his stare across the table. "You sure you want to have this conversation in front of him?"

"I trust Mr. Sabura not to repeat tales."

"Really? I mean, how well do you actually know the man? What he's like? What he's done?"

Dare slammed his hand on the table. "Dammit, Pike, cut to the chase. What do you want to know?"

The detective's mouth tightened as he was finally forced to focus on him. The man was ticked. Good. So was Dare. The bastard had been gunning for him for years. Until now, part of him had even respected it. But there was no way Dare would allow Pike to involve Abby in a vain attempt to even the score. And Pike did intend to try. Dare didn't need to read the depths of that blackened heart to know it, either. The thin smile Pike sketched as he claimed his chair said it all. Even at the age of fifteen, Dare had known that that narrow twist masked a streak of self-preservation a mile wide. Today the detective had used it to disguise his true intent.

The second folder.

He and Abby had been so consumed by the sight of the file Pike had tossed in front of her earlier, neither of them had realized there was another beneath it. Pike splayed the contents of the second folder out on the table. Abby's face stared up at them in the form of her photocopied New York State driver's license. Pike had scrawled a list of notes on the pages beneath. Several of the bullets were highlighted. Her Tristan address. The date she'd purchased the apartment and from whom; that she'd paid half a million dollars for it—with a note that the price was well under market value.

Fury blistered through Dare as Abby blanched.

The woman was a victim, dammit. And this ass was more concerned with scaring the daylights out of her so he could use that fear to try to lay the blame back on him. A hell of a way to exact revenge. "Dammit, Pike, this is—"

"One more word, Sabura, and I'll have you removed from the room."

The hell he would. "You can't."

Fury fired the detective's stare, smelting the rusted iron within. "You're not a lawyer and we both know it. Near as I can determine, you still don't even have a job."

If Pike had hoped to embarrass him, he'd failed. Dare leaned back in his chair and loosened his tie. "You're right, Detective. I'm not a lawyer. But I can call one, now, can't I? A damned good one." The comeback earned him a swallow. The distinct fist of fear. Dare claimed both, then offered his own thin smile in return, softening it as he turned to Abby. "You don't have to answer his questions. You're not under arrest. Even if he wanted to hold you, he's got nothing on you."

"Wrong." Pike slapped his palm on the table, wrenching

their attention back to him. "She said it herself at the scene. Or, rather, claimed it. Van Heusen was supposedly harassing her. Funny, I spoke to his mother at the hospital. Katherine Van Heusen seemed to think *she* might be harassing *him*."

"What?" Dare caught Abby as she lurched forward, pulling her back, steadying her. She swung her frantic stare to his. "That's a lie, Dare. Of all people, Kath—"

"Don't." He squeezed her arm. "Not another word." He had no idea what she'd planned on spilling, but it wasn't good.

Not for her.

Dare released her arm and turned back to Pike. "She's done, Pike. She didn't have a thing to do with what happened tonight and you know it. Every second of her evening can be accounted for."

"True. But yours can't."

This time Abby jackknifed to her feet. "You think *Dare* tried to kill Stuart?"

"It's one theory." Pike took the time to smooth the sleeves of his ill-fitting tweed jacket before he glanced up. "Maybe you're right. Maybe Van Heusen was harassing you. People have been known to fixate on public figures before—politicians, actors…musicians. And this guy's an ex. When you returned to the States, he decided he wanted you back. But you no longer wanted him. So you cried on ol' Triple D's shoulders. And Sabura offers to play white knight for the damsel in distress." Dare didn't bother objecting. If this was all Pike had, his house of cards was about to crumble.

He waited for Abby to pull the first one.

She did. "That's insane. I met Mr. Sabura a week ago. Why would I pour out my woes to a virtual stranger?"

Pike shrugged. "As I said, it's a theory."

She folded her arms across her T-shirt and locked them down. Her polite smile was just as tight. "Well, I hope you have another. A better one."

"Could be. You say you met the man a week ago. It may interest you to know Sabura's known about you for at least a month. Even tried to keep you out of your building."

This time her spine locked. "I was aware of that."

"And you don't mind?"

When she didn't turn, didn't even look at him, Dare was forced to straighten. Because of her aura. Because of the doubt that was beginning to creep in—into her. "I'm sure he had his reasons."

"Could be." Pike tapped the notes still splayed out in front of him. "Of course, it could also be that once Sabura failed to keep you out, he became fixated on you as well." Pike's black gaze flicked to him, then back to Abby. "It doesn't take much with the strange ones. Hell, Sabura probably has a whole fantasy life worked out for the two of you by now. He learns your post-concert routine and decides to hang out and bump into you *accidentally*. But he runs into Van Heusen instead. Figures out the guy's waiting for you, that you two used to be involved. Van Heusen might even have admitted that he wanted to rekindle the relationship. So Sabura panics and decides to take out the competition."

Just like that, Dare felt her doubt crumble. Abby actually smiled as she returned to her seat. "You make it sound like Dare has been stalking me, Detective."

"A man you just met—a man who lives in your new apartment building—just happens to be the one to save you from that van? To save your brother? You have to admit, it's awfully convenient. What the hell was he even doing there?"

"I already know why Mr. Sabura was there. I invited him. I gave him the tickets as a thank-you for helping me move in."

"So he told a cop on the scene. But he didn't use those tickets." The bastard broke eye contact with Abby and leveled that soulless stare on him. "One of the ushers remembers hooking up with Sabura just outside the hall ten minutes before intermission. Told Sabura he had to wait, Philharmonic policy. He must have waited too long because according to two guests I spoke to, Sabura never claimed his seat. So where was he?" That last was for him. When Dare refused to answer, Pike returned his stare to Abby. "Or did he forget to tell you he missed your solo?"

The doubt was back.

"No. I knew he wasn't there."

"So what happened, Ms. Pembroke?"

"He said he was ill. He was in the bathroom during the concert." It was the excuse he'd offered at Marlena's. Only now, where relief had filled her, the threads of doubt grew.

Pike tugged at them. "Ms. Pembroke, I'm sure this has happened before. I understand you were a child prodigy. Surely you've had admirers before who weren't quite…normal."

Like a disturbed voyeur who got his kicks climbing buildings in the dead of night and staring into windows. Her building. Her window. She didn't say it, but she was remembering. And the doubts were intensifying.

Dare's only hope was that she was fighting them. Abby wanted to believe in him, in the subconscious appeal he'd sent down the table. A table that looked far too much like another table in another interrogation room with a younger version of Pike sitting across from him. Dare focused his sense, used it to strengthen his plea.

Though she still wouldn't look at him, Abby grabbed onto the plea and held fast. "This is crazy. Detective, there was another man at that car. I saw him stab Stuart's driver. I wish to God I hadn't, but I did. That's the man I saw grab my brother and smash his shoulder into the limo's window, not Mr. Sabura."

Pike simply shrugged. "So he has friends. Associates. Given the quality of the batch, I'm sure one of them wouldn't have been opposed to helping out. Hell, I ought to know. I've arrested most of them. Sabura, too."

Silence clogged the air once more. The doubt returned as well. The suspicion. This time, Abby embraced both. Worse, though the effect from their touch had worn off, Dare could feel the surge of need within her. It was that strong. She desperately wanted to lower her stare. To open the other file Pike had left sitting on the table. He knew why.

Legally, Pike couldn't tell her a damned thing. But if she opened that file on her own? Why, then it was simply an oversight, wasn't it? One easily explained to Pike's superiors. After all, the bastard had had plenty of practice at this game over the years.

Starting with him.

The moment Dare felt her cave in to the urge to look, he spilled it. The only part he could.

"A friend and I were arrested for hot-wiring a car when we were kids. A police car. Bill's father was a cop. He got to go home. My father was out of town so I spent the weekend in a holding cell at Riker's Island." He tipped his head toward the file, deliberately daring her, even as he prayed she wouldn't take him up on it. "Go ahead, open it. Read it. I'm sure it's all there. Including the fact that I was guilty—we both were—but my father offered the department a generous restitution when he returned the following Monday. I pleaded no contest and was released that afternoon."

Only to have his entire world leveled the following night.

Dare fought the darkness and the pain, shored up his defenses. But the events of the evening had taken their toll on his psyche as well. The memory slipped through the cracks, slicing into his heart. His soul. By the time he succeeded in pushing it back, Abby's astonishment had eased. So had her suspicions.

She glanced at the file. "How old were you?"

"Fifteen."

Abby stiffened in her chair. "Fifteen? Isn't that too young for Riker's?"

"Hmm." His stare met Pike's. "It seems there was a clerical error." He severed his gaze and turned back to her. "It's okay. I survived."

Physically.

As for the rest? What had happened after? Pike would never repeat it. Not to Abby or anyone else. If he did, he'd have to explain his own actions. His own culpability. By the time the detective finished, Pike would end up sporting a straitjacket compliments of Bellevue…if the man didn't end up doing his own stint at Riker's first.

In the end, Pike didn't have to repeat anything. Abby made the connection herself. Part of it.

She turned to Pike. "And you were the arresting officer?"

Trapped, the detective shook his head. When the man refused to expound, Dare did it for him. She needed to know how far the man would go. "His mentor was. Pike was still green, along for the ride. Probably what saved his ass when the ax fell. His mentor, however, was asked to retire."

"Because *you* lied, Sabura."

Wrong. He'd told the truth. But no one had believed him. Not even his father. Not until it was too late. And even then, his father hadn't been able to accept it—much less him.

Just like his mom.

The echo of that pain slammed in so hard, Dare hadn't even realized Abby had had enough until she stood. He forced the memory deep into the prison of his mind. It wasn't until he stood alongside her that he realized his touch had succeeded. Her doubts were gone. She'd unconsciously read his heart and believed it. Believed in him. If only Abby had been back there then….

Pike glared across the table as he, too, stood. "We're not done, Ms. Pembroke."

"I'm afraid we are, Detective. Your theory has more holes in it than a bass clarinet. If you're looking for someone who had a reason to kill Stuart, try examining his cases. As I'm sure you know, the man is an assistant district attorney. Better yet, look into his politics. I'm sure you also know Stuart was running for city councilman this coming year. Either way, you can conduct your search without me. It's late and I'm tired. And you, sir, have a serious conflict of interest. I'll be happy to review my statement and sign it. But if your department needs any more information from me or my brother, they can send someone else. Is that clear?"

At 1:00 a.m., after the night Abby had had, she should have been barely able to stand. And yet, even with her deathly pale skin magnifying the bruises marring her cheek and jaw, the shadows beneath her eyes, she carried herself with the quiet grace of a queen as she returned Pike's stare.

Even so, the man refused to bow.

So Dare reached into the pocket of his coat and withdrew his cell phone, stabbing out a number he'd sworn he'd never use again—his father's. Dare paused over the send button. "Shall I?" For her, he would.

Pike growled. "Get the hell out of here. But I'm warning you—both of you—this isn't over."

That was the first accurate statement the detective had made since he'd walked in the room. Dare should have dealt with Pike long ago. But like Pike, he carried his own guilt.

It was time to put a stop to that, too.

Again, for her.

Dare opened the door and waited for Abby to precede him from the room. He closed the door on the seething detective, taking Abby's elbow as they entered the main portion of the station. Unfortunately, the touch was not to support her. It was for him. He was still too raw to deal with the onslaught of ugliness that began assaulting his psyche the moment they reached the noisy, oversized bay and its holding cell. He drew in Abby's essence, using the balm of her inner self to deflect the bulk of the filth as they traversed the room. It worked. He managed to pass half a dozen burned-out detectives, two murderers, a rapist, a child molester masquerading as a teacher and a wife-beating street cop before they reached the glass doors at the opposite end of the room. Relief seared in as he made it into the neon night without retching.

The crowded street—even at this hour—waited.

Fortunately, glass shielded him from most of the passersby. "Are you okay?"

He released Abby's arm as they stopped beside the curb, raising his hand to hail an oncoming cab. "I'm fine."

"You don't look fine. In fact, you look like you're about to pass out." She reached up, gasping as she pressed the backs of her slender fingers to his forehead. "You're burning up!"

He covered her fingers with his and drew them down as a cab stopped beside them. "It's okay. I'm at the tail end of a twenty-four-hour bug. It'll pass." Just as soon as he got her home. Reached his own apartment.

His shower.

Dare opened the passenger door, grateful when Abby slid across the rear seat. It saved him the exertion of rounding the cab. By the time he'd wedged his own body inside, she'd given the driver the Tristan's address. The cabbie nodded, then turned back to argue with the opening statements of a late-night radio talk-show host as the car pulled away from the curb. To Dare's surprise, Abby reached for his forehead, frowning as she smoothed the lingering sweat from his brow.

"Pike was wrong. You were ill. You still are. You should be home in bed treating that fever, not traipsing around the city with me." The passing glow from a neon sign enhanced the flush staining her own cheeks as she paused. "But I'm glad you did. Thank you."

He shook his head. "Nonsense. I should be thanking you. For your support in there with Pike. It…means a lot to me."

More than she'd ever know.

She didn't respond.

At least, not verbally. With the connection from her touch still humming through him, she didn't have to.

"Abby?"

More silence. But beneath it lay the distinct simmer of hesitation. And outright fear.

"Do you...want to talk about it?"

"No." Her fingers quivered as she reached up to tuck a stray curl behind her ear. "But I think I'm going to have to."

He focused his sense.

Pike. For all her calm assurance as they left, she was truly terrified of the man. Because of what the man had insinuated about him? "Hey, relax. Pike can't hurt me." The bastard had been trying to get something on him for years. But he couldn't. Because there was nothing there.

Nothing the man would testify to in court, anyway.

Dare shook his head. "Look, without a motive that so-called theory of his is nothing more than a dream." He'd never met her ex—*including* tonight. In fact, with his insides no longer scrambled, he'd finally realized Van Heusen had to have been stabbed into unconsciousness before he'd pushed Abby from the van's path and assured himself of her safety. Otherwise he'd have felt the man's presence as he left her side to check on the limo driver and then her brother. But he hadn't.

Or had he been too in tune with Abby?

Like he was now?

Dare could feel Abby's presence keenly. Her fear. If anything, it had intensified. Unable to stop himself, he reached across the darkened seat and snagged her chin, drawing that beautiful face to his. "Hey, it's okay. I know you don't know me well. But I swear, you can trust me. Tell me what's got you so scared. I'll help."

Shadows swirled within her eyes. Her heart.

Moments later, her bottom lip quivered. But it was several more minutes before her equally tremulous whisper followed. "I don't th-think you can help me. If Stuart d-dies, I don't think anyone can."

"Why not?"

He felt her draw her breath in deep, her courage in even deeper. "Do you remember when Pike asked me if I knew why Stuart had been trying to contact me...and I said no?"

"Yeah?"

"I lied."

# Chapter 5

The moment the words tumbled out, Abby regretted them. After all, it was one thing to know Dare was innocent of the crimes that had happened tonight; it was quite another to confess to the man that she'd perjured herself to the detective. Fortunately, Dare hadn't asked her to explain. Instead, he'd snapped his stare toward their cabdriver. His message had been clear. Don't explain that loaded confession until they arrived home.

Well, here they were.

Abby glanced past Dare's sleeve as the taxi stopped. The main entrance to the Tristan lay beyond. A moment later Dare was passing the driver a twenty, opening the taxi's door and standing outside. What were the odds he'd let her plead exhaustion and escape to her apartment alone?

She decided against waiting around to find out.

She scrambled out of the cab as smoothly as her legs allowed and hurried across the sidewalk. Unfortunately, the reflexes Dare had honed as a result of his unusual hobbies stood the man in good stead, allowing him to slam the taxi's door and catch up with her before the doorman could open the Tristan's.

Jerry grinned at the sight of the two of them together and tipped his hat. "Good evening, Ms. Pembroke. Mr. Sabura."

Despite everything that had happened that night, Abby managed to return the man's smile. "Evening, Jerry. I keep telling you, it's Abby."

"Yes, ma'am." His grin split wider as he followed them through the doors, showing off a set of blindingly white teeth that belied the man's years. Once inside the lobby, the doorman's smile faded. "Uh, sir?"

Dare stopped. "Yes?"

Jerry's faded blue gaze shifted toward his station. "I have that item you requested."

Dare nodded, then turned back to her. "Hang on a sec, okay?" Both men headed for the station before she could answer.

She should have escaped then.

But she couldn't.

Other than Marlena, Dare was the only one who might believe her version of her breakup with Stuart. Lord knew Pike wouldn't. Dare returned to her side all too quickly, slipping the key the doorman had handed him into his jacket pocket as he escorted her across the lobby to a waiting elevator. Abby had resigned herself to her fate as the doors closed. She had to tell someone. Preferably someone who would know what to do. If Dare didn't, perhaps his father would. Besides, she had a bottle of Tylenol in her apartment. The least she could do after all he'd done for her was make sure he took two for his fever.

Abby withdrew her keys from her purse as the elevator came to a stop. Moments later another door had opened and shut, this one to her apartment.

"Have a seat, I'll just be a moment."

She tossed her purse on the table by the intercom and took off across the dimly lit foyer before Dare could argue. Fortunately the man complied, heading for her couch as she made a beeline for her equally dim kitchen. By the time she'd returned to her living room with the pill bottle and a glass of water, Dare had switched the end-table lamp on low and removed his jacket and tie. He'd tossed both over the back of her armchair and stood staring at the painting hanging above her couch as she reached his side.

Brian's painting.

"Your brother's very good. He captured the Tristan and Jerry perfectly."

She nodded. "Brian's work is—"

Wait a minute. How did Dare know Brian had painted that? Surely the two hadn't taken the time to discuss art while she was unconscious? Brian had initialed the lower left edge of the canvas. But as usual, her brother's *BP* had ended up more as a cramped intricate swirl than as legible letters.

She stared at Dare.

He stared back.

She finally lowered her gaze to the thin scar running along the outer edge of his cheek and down into the square of his jaw. A man stubborn enough to pursue whatever goal Dare had been pursuing while he'd earned *that* wasn't going to cave beneath a simple stare from her, no matter how cool it was. She gave up and thrust the glass of water into his hand.

"Here."

She shook out two extra-strength tablets and pushed those on him as well, pointedly waiting for him to swallow both before she capped the bottle and accepted the glass back. Abby turned to set both on the coffee table, stiffening as she spotted the still-open issue of *Saucy*. She'd forgotten to tuck the magazine away before she left for the symphony that evening. Even in this low light, there was no way Dare could have missed it. Not when the naked, muscular torso clinging to the sheer cliff in the article's lead photograph was his. If your average picture was worth a thousand words, then that photo alone contained a million. And every one of them contradicted the information she'd gleaned about this man from secondhand gossip and biased police detectives alike.

So which story was real?

Which man?

She already knew the answer. She'd discovered it for herself outside Avery Fisher Hall earlier that evening. She set the Tylenol and glass beside the magazine and turned to check Dare's temperature.

As expected, he tensed.

"So how am I doing, nurse?"

She smiled easily for the first time that night. "Much better." Not only had his skin cooled since the station, he was no longer perspiring. "How do you feel?"

"Better than you."

She couldn't argue with the assessment. Nor did he have to be psychic to have made it. The tension simmering inside her, the flat-out fear—she couldn't deny either. Pike had gotten his wish. She was afraid of Dare. But not of what he would do to her. She was afraid of what he would think. She dragged her breath in deep, then blew it out.

It didn't help.

"Would you…like to have a seat? Coffee?" It seemed as good a stalling tactic as any.

He shook his head. "No coffee. But I will sit." Instead of claiming the armchair, Dare surprised her by not only joining her on the couch, but taking her hand in his. Either he'd gotten over his aversion to touching her, or he knew she wanted nothing more than to bolt from her apartment—and not because of him. She suspected it was the latter, especially when he squeezed her hand as gently as he had in the car.

"Why don't you start at the beginning?"

She would have, if she knew where the beginning was.

At the moment all she could see was the end. That hulking thug. His hideously gleaming knife. She'd spent most of the evening trying to block the sight of both from her mind. But now, sitting here in the soft shadows of her living room, the memories slammed in. The dizziness returned with them, as did the nausea. She closed her eyes against it all.

Especially the guilt.

Dare's low rumble filled her ears, steady and soothing. "It's okay. Take it slow."

But it *wasn't* okay. How could it ever be okay again? If she'd taken just one of those blasted phone calls, Stuart wouldn't have been lying in wait for her. Her eyes began to burn. Her heart followed. The worst part was, she couldn't even blame Katherine. Not really. Only herself.

"Abby?"

She purged her breath and just said it. "If Stuart dies…it's my fault. Part of what I told Pike was true. I was avoiding him. But…I also know why Stuart wanted to contact me." Shame seared in.

Abby pushed it aside.

If Dare could admit his sins, so could she. She drew strength from the thought, from him, and gathered the vestiges of her pride along with another set of memories she'd done her damnedest to block out. Only this set had been forged a year ago, just days before she'd agreed to fill in on the Hampton String Quartet and escaped to Europe. But even with compassion radiating off Dare, or perhaps because of it, she couldn't sit beside him while she recounted those sins.

She stood, rounded her coffee table and faced Dare from the opposite side. "You said start at the beginning. I guess that would be when I discovered Stuart had been lying to me since the day we met. I'm not sure how much attention you pay to the inner workings of the city and its politics, but Stuart was running for councilman in the upcoming election."

*If he survived.*

Fear snaked in, just as it had out on that street when she'd discovered Stuart had been attacked. Stuart might have turned out to be a jackass of the highest order, but she'd loved the man once. Until the night her illusions had come crashing down, she'd even entertained the idea of marriage and children. But even then, with the shock and the humiliation ricocheting through her, she hadn't wanted the man *dead*.

Abby crossed her arms to ward off the sudden chill that rippled down her flesh. "Anyway, Stuart hadn't yet tossed his hat into the ring when we were dating, but he was already lining up contributions and backers. I know, because he began bringing me to the city's round of pre-race political parties and dinners. That's when it happened. His mother found out he was escorting someone not of his social class and cut her tour of France short. The day Katherine landed in New York she phoned and asked if I'd like to have dinner…without her son. She called it a 'girls' night in.' You know, so we could get to know each other without Stuart around. Or so she claimed."

"In other words, the woman intended to warn you off."

Abby managed a nod.

He sighed. "She succeeded."

"Nope. She bought me off." She caught Dare's stare and held it. Or perhaps he was holding hers. She couldn't be sure. She did know that even in this low light, she could make out the odd torrent of emotions that had begun to churn through those shadowy pools. The anger and the pity—those she understood. But not the pain. She'd swear it was ripping through him as deeply as it had once ripped through her.

But that was impossible.

Unnerved, she forced herself to continue. "Katherine offered me a…choice. If I broke up with Stuart, I got a million dollars. If I didn't, she'd use her vast social connections to kill my career with the Philharmonic and any other orchestra in the country that could afford me. I was stunned. Furious. Beyond insulted. Until she produced this tape. And then—" Her voice broke. Try as she might, she couldn't finish it. But she could still feel it as if it had happened yesterday. The utter humiliation of it all. And darned if she didn't believe that Dare could feel that, too.

He stood. "What kind of tape? Video?"

She shook her head. "Audio. It was one of those microcassettes…a recording of Stuart and his mother. It turned out they'd had lunch earlier, though I doubt Katherine told Stuart I'd be stopping by for dinner later. They did discuss me, however. Brian, too. His Down's. Katherine was quite blunt with her objections, her description exceptionally vivid. Katherine was worried that my brother's genetic *stains* would transfer to her son. Initially to Stuart's budding political career and eventually to his future progeny. Her solution? Drop me immediately. Before either catastrophe had a chance to set. Stuart refused. But that just brought Katherine to dinner with the other half of the undesirable couple. Me."

Dare rounded the table, his fingers flexing at his sides as he stared down at her. She had the distinct impression he wanted to touch her. Hold her. How absurd was that?

She wrapped her arms tighter about her chest.

He shook his head. "I don't understand. Wasn't Katherine worried about the fallout to her son's political career?"

"You mean of dumping the retarded guy's sister so close to declaring his candidacy?"

This time Dare frowned. "I wouldn't have put it like that, but yes."

"Not really. Katherine admitted it was a risk. But it was one

she was willing to take. She was too afraid that I would succeed in weaving my wicked spell around her son. Plus, she
was positive there was enough time for Stuart to find a more
suitable companion by the time the election heated up. Especially if I kept my mouth shut and convinced him that I was
the one doing the dumping."

She paused to offer a bitter, glancing smile. "You see, it
turned out I was well liked by Stuart's main backer. The gen-
tleman's wife enjoyed my music. Not to mention Stuart was
unwilling to give up the PC advantage of having a fiancée who
had a brother with Down's. Though he did agree with Katherine that it would never be more than that. He wasn't willing to have his own children 'stained.' His exact words were,
'Don't worry, Mother. Once the election's over, Abby and her
brother will be out the door along with the placards and the
rest of the trash.'"

They were burned into her ears. Her heart.

She caught Dare's curse as she caved in to the tremors
threatening her legs, rounding the coffee table so she could
sink into the couch before they gave out altogether. She knew
what he was thinking. Ever since Pike had splayed the file
he'd started on her out on the table, she'd been thinking it, too.
She had no doubt that once Pike started digging he'd soon discover that not only was Dare innocent of everything that had
transpired tonight, he had no motive.

But she did.

It was a damned good thing Stuart Van Heusen was already
in the hospital. It saved Dare the trouble of hunting the jackal
down and putting him there himself. Either way, he'd be vis-
iting the man the moment he regained consciousness. But
until then, he had another bastard to deal with. Pike. The detective might not wield as much power and influence as Van
Heusen did, but Pike was far more dangerous.

Especially given the events of the night.

Abby's fears were correct. Her admission shed an entirely new light on the stabbings. Pike wouldn't care that it was the wrong color. Not if it radiated from someone close to Dare.

And Abby knew it.

Dare hadn't even needed his sense to discern that. He'd spotted the evidence with his eyes as Abby sank back into the couch. It was in that single, gut-wrenching tear. The tiny drop glistened in the lamplight, clinging to her lashes as she blinked. He could feel her desperately trying to keep it and the others behind it from slipping free. Eventually the heart-ache and the fear won. The tear slid down. Another followed, then another, until a gentle trickle formed.

He had to clench his fingers to keep from reaching out to soothe the damp trail left behind and use his unearthly gift to ease the ache in her soul. He didn't dare risk it. He'd already absorbed far more over the past several hours than he had in years. After the brownout he'd suffered at the station, he couldn't guarantee that he'd be able to pull back. Not with her. But when a second path of tears formed, the wave of desolation that came with it swamped him, because it was *his*.

His restraint crumbled.

He couldn't have stopped himself from sinking down onto the couch beside her if Pike himself had chosen that moment to knock down her door with a dozen armed cops in tow. Before Dare had realized what he'd done, he'd reached out and trailed his fingertips up her cheek. He caught the tears and smoothed them from her silken flesh, transfixed as he watched the moisture soak into his own skin. Humbled beyond words as he felt the absolute beauty of her inner essence soak into his. He drew his breath in deep as their hearts began to mingle. Their souls followed.

He knew she had no idea what was happening.

Not really.

To his relief, she didn't pull away. Instead, her soft hiccup filled the shadows around them. "You m-must think I'm a horrible person for accepting that money."

How could he?

He shook his head and caught a fresh tear. "Abby, you did it for your brother."

Her lashes flew wide. "How did you know—"

"It's in your face." *In your heart.*

Yes, she'd taken the bribe. But she'd done it for one reason and one reason alone. Brian. Dare smoothed his fingers along her jaw, savoring the smooth, tactile warmth of her flesh, even as he waited for her lingering emotions to finish shading in the hues of the memory. If he hadn't been seduced by this woman's spirit the moment he'd first felt it, he'd have caved in right here and now.

He dragged his gaze to her mouth, hypnotized by the flush staining the gentle bow of her lips. The longer he stared, the more he could feel and the deeper the connection became. Just as she had at the station, she felt it as well. Wanted it. And God help him, he wanted her, too. Temptation nudged him closer. So close, he could feel the wash of her breath teasing his mouth. Smell her soft, sweet scent. Taste the heady desire thrumming between them. His brain fogged. Before he realized what had happened, his heart had wrested control from his body and he leaned even closer.

Her lashes fluttered down.

A split second later, a sharp trill pierced the air.

Just as they had in that interrogation room, they sprang apart. Only this time, it wasn't Pike interrupting. It was the phone. Still as dazed as she, he followed her stare to the phone on the end table beside them. But the moment he spotted the name and number glowing softly in the caller ID window, the fog burned off.

"Abby, you need to get that."

He stood as she nodded numbly. Already knowing what was about to happen. What she was about to learn.

What he had been dreading.

She retrieved the cordless receiver by the third trill and brought the phone to her ear. "Hi, Marlena." A brief pause followed. The flush still staining her cheeks deepened. "No, Marlena, you didn't wake me. I just got home. Is everything okay?"

Dare didn't wait for the answer. He was too busy heading for the kitchen to search for something to help ease Abby's coming anguish. He already knew he couldn't risk touching her again tonight. That call proved it. There was only one reason Marlena would be phoning at this hour on this night.

He'd screwed up.

# Chapter 6

By the time Dare returned, Abby was staring at the floor, her soft hazel gaze as lifeless as the receiver clutched in her quaking hands. He could feel her attempting to marshal her strength, but it still took an eternity before she was able to drag her stare up to his. She was numb. She'd suffered one too many shocks tonight. And this one was solely his fault.

"H-he doesn't...r-remember me."

Dare closed his eyes.

He needn't have bothered. Her ragged whisper had still managed to slice in deep. Along with the regret. The guilt.

Dare set a pair of glasses down on the coffee table beside that damned magazine, and uncorked the bottle of cognac Mrs. Laurens had left behind in the pantry. It had been nearly a year since he'd accepted a drink from the same bottle—the night Greta Laurens had spotted him scaling their building. She'd let him in the same window Abby had, but unlike Abby, Greta had lived too many years to buy his "out for a midnight climb" excuse. He missed the woman, and her shrewd advice. He could have used it now as he poured out two cognacs and held one out to Abby.

"Here."

He waited for her to focus. When she didn't, he pushed the glass into her palm and waited for her fingers to close around it.

"Now drink."

She raised the glass without argument and downed the contents. A split second later, he felt the shock spearing through her as she straightened, first gasping and then damned near coughing her lungs up. He grabbed the empty glass from her flailing hand before it hit the table, setting it down gently as Abby succeeded in bringing her coughing under control. He forced himself to stand there—and not touch—as she wiped the tears from her eyes.

"I'm s-sorry, I don't…drink."

He'd gathered that.

At least she was breathing now. Feeling. But she was hurting, too. Dare sank down onto the couch beside her and refilled her glass. He carefully placed it back into her hand without touching her. "This time, sip."

She didn't; she simply stared into the glass.

"Abby, listen to me. Dr. Chase warned us this might happen, remember? He said there was a chance that when Brian woke, he still wouldn't remember the stabbing. It's normal. Especially given his Down's."

Liar.

Some loss was normal. Even then, the memories that were lost were usually limited to those immediately before and after the traumatic event. Not this.

Her gaze jerked to his. "I know what's normal for Brian, okay? He's *my* brother."

Damn. He wasn't helping. If anything, he was screwing this up even further. Hurting her more than he already had.

What made him think he could talk her through this anyway? He'd never had a flair with words—another reason why he avoided people. He might know how someone felt, often without even touching them, but damned if he'd ever been able to master the simple art of talking about those feelings, much less through them. So he relied on his touch.

He stared at his empty hands.

There was no chance of that succeeding with Abby now, was there? No chance of helping her through this pain. Pain that he had caused, whether he'd intended to or not. He reached out and retrieved his glass, filling the silence with a sip. Then a second. And a third. The twelve-year-old cognac might as well have been water for all he was able to taste it. But it gave him something to do. Something to hold. To look at.

"Dare?"

He snapped his gaze to where he'd wanted to be staring all along, to the one woman whose essence he couldn't have ceased seeking out if he'd tried—and he'd given up attempting to do that the moment he'd felt her soul cry out to his on that street tonight. There was no way he could abandon her now. Not with Pike involved. Regardless of the danger to himself, he was determined to see her through this.

If she let him.

She sighed. "Look, I'm sorry. I had no reason to snap at you. Especially about Brian."

"Abby—"

"Please, let me finish?"

He nodded.

"Thank you." She wrapped both hands around her glass. "Look, you've done so much for me. For Brian. I'm grateful for that—for you—no matter what that jerk of a detective thinks. It's just…I have to be honest. I'm scared. I know Dr. Chase warned us. I've even heard about traumatic amnesia before tonight. But, dammit, I didn't think he'd forget this much. I didn't think he'd forget *me*."

"I know." He nodded. "Exactly how much time has your brother lost?"

Her hand shook, nearly sending the cognac over the rim of the glass. "Almost a year."

He bit down on his curse.

But it made sense. When he'd hefted her brother up off that street and reached out to him emotionally, he'd been reacting on instinct, his desire to ease Brian's own fear and horror at what he'd witnessed. He hadn't counted on the depth of Brian's need or his trusting nature. Her brother wasn't like most adults. Because of his Down's, he didn't guard his emotions or his thoughts, nor was he suspicious or skeptical of others. Dare should have anticipated that. He would have if he hadn't spent half the evening holed up in the theatre's bathroom, attempting to absorb the combined emotional onslaught of nearly three thousand symphony patrons.

By the time he'd made it out to that street and forged his emotional link with her brother, he'd been too raw and too weak to break it. He'd accepted too much. The stabbing, as well as Brian's lingering confusion over why Abby had left New York the year before, his fears that regardless of her new apartment Abby would leave again. This time permanently.

Just as their father had.

Dare waited as Abby lifted her glass again, slowly but surely draining the contents. Despite her frown, he doubted she'd tasted the brandy any more than he had. Perhaps the cognac was a bad idea. He was sure of it when she held the glass out. He debated pouring a third measure.

Dammit, she wasn't his mother.

Tonight was an exception—for Abby and himself.

Dare pushed the past aside and refilled her glass, though he couldn't stop himself from skimping on what he intended to be her final round. Nor could he deny his relief when Abby merely sipped what little he'd given her, relief that was immediately supplanted by guilt as she spoke.

"Brian doesn't remember anything. My coming home, our dad. Nothing. He…still thinks I'm on tour."

This was not good.

But neither was it entirely unexpected. The moment his connection with Brian had locked in, he'd known Brian desperately wanted to forget the pain of his father's death. The loneliness. But their father had passed away while Abby was still in Europe. That meant Brian had lost the memory of her return to the city as well. Her purchase of this place. "You said Marlena phoned Dr. Chase. What did he say about the extent of the loss?"

"Same as you, give him time. The memories will probably come back. But—" Her hand shook as she brought the glass to her lips for another sip. Blindly. "He thinks I should stay away from Brian, at least for a while. Marlena agrees. They're worried that the shock of seeing me will bring everything back at once. They don't think Brian can handle that. I have to admit, neither do I." He reached out as she brought the cognac to her lips once more, deftly slipping the glass from her hand before she could down the remainder of the brandy.

She didn't protest.

She didn't do anything. She just sat there, staring at the coffee table as he set the glass beside the bottle.

"Abby?"

She finally turned to him, but she couldn't focus. It didn't matter. He could see clearly enough for the both of them, and his heart nearly split in two as he stared into her eyes.

"What am I going to do? I can't even see him, m-make sure he's okay. I can't see Marlena either, b-because she's got to be there for Brian. And what about Pike? You heard him.

Katherine's already spreading lies about me. And he believes her. If he finds out I took that money… God, I feel so—"

*Alone.*

He could have handled any emotion but that one. Especially in her. His restraint crumbled. Before he realized what he'd done, he'd drawn her into his arms until she was all but cradled against his chest. He didn't care. He couldn't have stopped himself if he'd tried. He smoothed back the stray wisps that had escaped her braid. "Shh. It's okay. I'm here, Abby. I'll be here as long as you need me."

He held her a good minute until finally he could feel the tension beginning to ease from her limbs, the fear from her heart. Another minute passed and both had faded completely. But the surcease hadn't come from him, not entirely. The cognac's numbing effects had merged with her exhaustion, as well as the horror of that stabbing, her fears that Pike would rake his filthy paws through her life, and now her renewed terror for her brother. He looked at her face. The soft, twin fans of her lashes. The steady rise and fall of her chest.

She was asleep.

Perhaps it was for the best.

How had he really thought this would all turn out?

Abby might need him now, but eventually he would have to extricate himself from her life. What alternative did he have? Even if she did believe him regarding the full brunt of his curse, she would never be able to deal with the fallout. She was a world-class musician. She thrived best on stage, weaving her lyrical spell for thousands of strangers at a time. It was part of who she was. Who *he* could never be. Much as he might want to, he would never fit into her life.

Not even on the periphery.

Dare glanced at his fingers as he smoothed a stray curl, only to discover they were trembling. The sight unnerved and yet fascinated him at the same time. He couldn't be sure if the physical reaction was due to the unique effect Abby had on his internal equilibrium or if it was due to the lingering effects of the brownout he'd suffered earlier. Perhaps a combination of both. Either way, the result was the same: he was having a hell of a time pulling away from her emotionally. Only once before had he absorbed so much of another's individual inner self so quickly. While he thanked God these circumstances were completely different, he was still unable to release her.

Or was he simply unwilling?

It was bad enough to admit his innate sense had consistently sought Abby out each time she'd returned to her apartment this past week and then monitored her moods. He didn't need to feel the complete voyeur. Especially with Pike's accusation still reverberating through his head.

*Pike.*

Abby was right. If Pike found out about that money, he'd head straight to the Van Heusen estate for the rest of the story. Dare would wager Katherine possessed a second recording—this one of her conversation with Abby. A recording that by now was already doctored to suit Katherine's interests and in the process, condemn Abby. The money Abby had accepted didn't concern him as much as the possibility of that second tape.

If it existed, he needed to know about it.

He needed to get his *hands* on it.

Fortunately, Pike had been right about one thing tonight. Dare did have several associates who'd enjoyed the detective's professional hospitality. He also had Charlotte. He needed to see Charlotte first thing in the morning anyway and return the key their last impromptu guest had left behind before she'd embarked on her new life, though he doubted the one who'd taken her place would use it. While he was at it, he'd ask his assistant to ensure that he was invited to another party. One where Katherine Van Heusen was sure to show. As for his associates, he'd be speaking to them as well. He had to. What if Pike was right about something else? What if the killer *had* been lying in wait for Abby? Pike would never be able to spot the man with his sights focused so intently on revenge. Even if tonight had been a random act of violence, the perp had to know there were witnesses. He'd be looking for those witnesses.

He'd be looking for *Abby*.

Dare glanced down as she shifted in his arms, his groin tightening instinctively as she snuggled deeper in his arms…in his lap. He should leave now, while she was out. Before he was tempted to stay. His body and his heart protested as he stood—but his mind recognized the retreat for the sane precaution it was. His fears gave him strength. One call to Jerry in the lobby and no one the doorman didn't recognize would make it past the lobby. Not that he'd need the backup. He would not be retreating to his shower tonight.

Not with that brute on the loose.

The brief climb would have to suffice.

Dare hefted Abby into his arms and skirted the coffee table. That blasted magazine. He forced himself to ignore the interview within—as well as his burning curiosity regarding Abby's reaction to the so-called legend it contained—as he carried her across the dimly lit living room, down the hall and into the darker shadows of her bedroom. He stopped at the side of a bed far too large for someone so petite. There, he managed to drag the comforter down and lay her on the ivory sheet without waking her. He removed her shoes and socks and drew the matching comforter up to her chin.

Lord, was she beautiful.

Yes, the sleep had restored her inner calm and her gentle strength. But it was more than that, it was much, much more. Not only had the cognac brought the soft hint of peaches back to her delicate jaw and cheeks, it had stained her lips a dark, intoxicating red. She resembled a fairy princess waiting for her lover's kiss. A lover he'd give anything to be for just one day. A kiss he'd give even more to share.

He froze as she shifted, staring at the errant wisp that had slipped down the side of her face to brush the corner of those mesmerizing lips. Though he knew better, he reached out as she stilled. But instead of smoothing the wisp aside as he'd intended, he wound the ringlet about his finger, savoring the feel of that cool silk against his flesh—until she stirred again. This time, her lips parted, sending the warm, seductive wash of her breath across his hand. Her lashes fluttered and he regained his senses. Instantly. He carefully eased the curl from his hand, the breath from his lungs, as she snuggled deeper into the pillow and back into sleep.

It was definitely time to leave before Pike's voyeuristic suspicions came to pass—at least in the privacy of his own mind. His dreams.

Dare turned and crept across the bedroom, stopping at the window he'd passed through the week before. He unlocked the latch and eased the pane up before removing his shoes. Though the oxfords sported laces, he didn't bother taking them with him. He'd be back in the morning. Instead, he slipped out of the window and closed it behind him as quietly as he could, finding his bearings and his grip through years of practice. He ignored the glowing lights of the city spread out beneath as he headed for and reached the window to his own bedroom.

Fortunately, his pane was already open, waiting.

Charlotte must have been by.

He thought about hanging out on the side of the building for a while. He climbed inside instead. Though the added time spent clinging to any ledge tended to increase the numbing effect, he already knew that tonight nothing short of a bound up Mount Everest could counteract the blitz of emotion ricocheting along his nerves—because these emotions were his.

For Abby.

Somehow, he had to find a way to block them—her—and soon. Before it was too late. But first—

Dare reached for his cell and cursed. He'd left the phone in his coat. In Abby's apartment.

Damn.

There was no way he would risk waking her, just as there was no way he would risk waiting until morning to arrange her security. He headed out of his bedroom and down the hall, into his office. As he reached for the phone on his desk, he noted even more evidence that Charlotte had been by. The mail. He flipped through the stack as he retrieved the cordless phone, immediately returning the receiver to its cradle as the third envelope caught his eye. The return address had been left blank. While that wasn't unusual given the niche he and Charlotte had carved out for themselves, the postmark was.

The letter had been franked in Florence, Italy.

Odd. He didn't know anyone there. Had one of the women they'd assisted over the past decade relocated again, this time on her own?

Curious, he retrieved his letter opener and slit the top of the envelope, his lungs damned near imploding as he tapped out an index card and scanned its single typed sentence: *He who seeks to destroy your heart also seeks you.*

Abby?

He slammed the suspicion aside. Forced his gut to stop clenching. It took a good five seconds, but he managed to persuade his lungs to accept its next, albeit searing, breath. *No way.* There was no conceivable way this card referred to Abby. He had feelings for her, yes. There was no way he could deny it. Not with the icy panic still hammering through his gut.

But she was *not* his heart. Not yet.

Besides, other than Pike and his flat-footed cronies, who would even know what Abby had seen tonight?

The man who'd attacked Van Heusen?

Even as the thought entered his brain, he discarded it. The envelope had been postmarked six days ago. Van Heusen had been stabbed mere hours ago. Unless the sender was psychic, there was no way he or she could know about Abby and her ex. Dare tossed the index card to his desk, only to have his lungs implode once more as the card fluttered end-over-end to land unlined side down in the center of his desk, a simple design facing him.

A triquetra?

He studied the black-and-white sketch of the trinity symbol bound by an even simpler circle, unable to move.

Impossible.

But it wasn't.

Nor did he need to wrench his shirt from his chest to prove it. But he did. He dumped his shirt on the floor and retrieved the card, sealing it to his skin—directly beside the trinity tattoo he'd never been able to fully explain even to himself since the moment he'd first seen it in that shop all those years ago and needed to brand it into his flesh. The sketch on the card and his tattoo were a dead-on match.

Right down to the size.

Someone wanted to get his attention—and he intended on finding out who. Even if it meant starting at the home of the one man he'd sworn he'd never speak to again.

His father.


Good Lord, what had happened to her head?

Abby rolled her face into her pillow as gingerly as she could. Unfortunately, turning just made the throbbing worse. If she didn't know any better, she'd swear some sadistic percussionist had decided to hammer out the final crescendoing notes of Tchaikovsky's "1812 Overture" on the inside of her skull. Desperate to kill the pain and the noise, she pushed up on her elbows only to freeze as her stomach bottomed out onto her mattress. A split second later, the explanation for it all sloshed in on a single, nauseating word.

*Hangover.*

But how? She clawed her way through the cobwebs in her brain, desperately trying to piece together whatever had led her to do something so stupid as drink. She remembered Dare returning from the kitchen with the bottle of cognac Greta Laurens had left in the pantry. He'd poured out several glasses. And she'd drunk every one of them.

But…why?

That thug. That knife.

*Brian.*

Abby jerked upright on the bed as the remainder of the nightmare crashed in all at once. She realized her mistake a moment later as the pounding in her head ratcheted straight into excruciating. She clapped her hands over her mouth as the contents of her stomach threatened yet again. Several slow, deep breaths later, the nausea ebbed. The pounding in her head had eased a bit, too. But the noise had grown louder, not softer and— Were those bells she could hear?

No, not bells. One bell. A doorbell.

Hers.

Was Dare checking up on her?

She pressed her fingers to her temple as she turned to the window and the grating rays of daylight. Dare's shoes were resting neatly at the baseboard. He'd left the window unlocked as well. Wouldn't he just climb in the same way he'd left?

That left Marlena—with news about Brian!

Abby lurched across the room with more hope than grace, shoving her snarled braid over her shoulder as she ping-ponged down the blessedly dim hallway and into the jarringly brighter living room.

In light of last night—that thug—she stopped just shy of

unlocking the door's twin bolts, just in case. The pounding in her head caught up with her as she stretched up to squint through the peephole.

Disappointment surged in along with a fresh wave of nausea as she realized her visitor wasn't Marlena.

It was a man.

His rugged features and strong jaw reminded her vaguely of Dare, but his skin wasn't nearly as dusky. No scars either. His eyes were attractive enough, but her own still refused to cooperate enough for her to make out the color. The guy's hair was easier—dark brown and clipped short. His suit was definitely black. Unfortunately, she'd also caught a brief flash of the gold shield that completed the detective's ensemble, along with his hoarse "—the door, ma'am. This is—" The rest was muffled by a series of sneezes until he got to "—Hook."

Great. Leave it to Pike to send a sick replacement.

Abby forced down her protesting stomach and opened the door—right into a full-blown coughing fit. She tried to step back, but ended up clinging to the door as the towering detective traded his badge for the handkerchief in his pocket. Good Lord, the man was six-four at least. Her dizziness returned as she craned her neck to keep his face in view. By the time the man had returned the handkerchief to his coat, his nose was red—and she was ready to pass out.

"I'm sorry, Ms. Pembroke. I caught a—"

"Cold. I can see that." She clutched her stomach as the roiling continued. "Look, Detective Hook, I'm sorry. I'm not myself this morning either. I had a rotten day yesterday and it's barely—" She lifted her wrist, but her watch was missing.

Dare? Or had she left it in her dressing room?

She could turn around, but she doubted she'd be able to see her wall clock from here. Not in this state. She craned her neck once more. "Exactly what time is it?"

"Almost eleven, ma'am."

Brown. His gaze was dark brown. Cold. Piercing. Just before the man snapped it past her shoulder to openly case her apartment. The moment that murky stare reached her coffee table, she felt the disapproval. She turned reluctantly and followed it all the way to the source.

The cognac bottle.

It was still open and less than half full now. One of her generous glasses sat in the middle of the table, damningly empty. Another hugged the base of the bottle with just enough cognac left inside for Hook to assume she'd already started out her day with a fresh hit.

Especially if he'd already gotten a rundown on her character from Pike.

Peachy. The latest installment of the Mod Squad hadn't even made it inside and she'd already been pegged as a flake and a lush.

She threw the door wide. "Come on in, Detective."

Might as well. The offer she'd planned on making—the one to meet him at the precinct later, after she'd had a chance to check on her brother, shower and pull her head together—wouldn't help now. She closed the door behind him.

"Have a seat." She started to nod toward the sofa until the jackhammering in her head turned vicious. She turned toward the kitchen to cover her wince. "You don't mind if I take a minute to start a pot of coffee, do you?"

"Not at all."

She rounded the breakfast bar and walked all the way to the back of the kitchen, using the concealing side panels of the wooden pantry to give her a few moments of respite from his penetrating look. There, she tucked in her wrinkled T-shirt and used her fingers to comb the worst of the rats from her hair, praying she didn't look as much like a murdering shrew as she suspected. Unable to do more, Abby rigged the coffeepot in record time. She downed three ibuprofen and headed back to her visitor. By the time she'd returned to the living room, New York's Finest was seated on her couch beside the cognac bottle, engrossed in the magazine she'd left on the table beside it.

She stopped behind the overstuffed reading chair she'd curled up in while reading that same magazine the day before, resisting the temptation to reach down over the back and retrieve the suit jacket Dare had left behind—so she could cling to it for support. "Detective Hook?"

No response.

She raised her voice. "Looking for a rich husband?"

He ignored the question as well as her sarcasm, but he glanced up. "That's him, isn't it? Your neighbor?"

She nodded. "Darian Sabura."

Odd. Surely Pike had briefed his fellow cop. Or had he?

"Detective, exactly why are you here?"

He set the magazine down. "I need to ask you a few follow-up questions regarding last night. It's standard procedure."

She didn't doubt it. Disappointment set in. "You're Pike's partner, then?"

"No."

The disappointment gave way to hope—for her and for Dare.

She must not have hid either feeling well because that dark brown stare took on a decidedly shrewd glint. Hook frowned. "You don't like Detective Pike, do you?"

Now, *there* was an understatement.

She turned the question back on him. "Do you?"

Either Hook had swallowed his own instinctive response or another bout of sneezing threatened. From the stall that followed, she gathered it was the former.

"Ms. Pembroke, I'm afraid I'm not—"

"—allowed to trash fellow members of the department?"

Another pause, but this time a wry smile made it through. "There is that."

Her earlier hope blossomed. If this guy did have a decent bead on his fellow detective, he might be willing to give Dare the benefit of doubt. Her, too. Maybe she could trust him.

For the moment.

Hook glanced at the chair. "Would you like to sit?"

She shook her head. "The coffee should be ready soon."

But that wasn't it. For some reason, she still felt more comfortable with the chair between them. She'd also finally caved in to the urge to reach down and retrieve the coat Dare had left behind, smoothing the black fabric over the back of the floral armchair as Hook slipped a slim spiral tablet and pen from his own coat pocket.

"Let's start with the attack itself. I understand you weren't able to remember much about the man who brandished that knife yesterday, but perhaps a night's sleep has helped. Do you remember anything more? About the man—or the knife or the limo?"

Other than the garish slash of scarlet-stained metal that continued to slice through her thoughts when she least expected it? Abby shook her head. "No."

He didn't believe her.

Worse, she had the distinct impression that like Pike, this detective was certain she was deliberately withholding something. Maybe it was the way his stare had narrowed, taking on a dark, almost violent edge, giving her the uneasy feeling the man seated on her couch was more than your average cop tracking down a lead—and making her wish there was more than the back of plush armchair and Dare's coat between them.

"So…you don't remember *anything* about the man? Anything at all?"

"No. I just told you that, and Officer Ryder and Detective Pike last night. I wish I had gotten a clear look at him, but I didn't." She'd been too busy staring at that knife. "I just know he was huge. Dark hair, dark suit. He seemed to radiate—"

*Evil.* Her head throbbed harder as the memory kicked back in. She wrapped Dare's jacket over her arms to ward off the chill that rippled through her as she tried to focus on it, to see past the gleaming edge of that knife. She got as far as the hilt before it vanished. "Wait…he had massive hands." She dropped her gaze instinctively. "A lot like yours."

A pregnant paused filled the room.

*Oh, way to go, Abby. Accuse the cop.*

That would get her out of the department's professional sights for sure. She was almost relieved when Hook sneezed.

At least it broke the silence.

"Bless you."

Hook tucked his handkerchief back into his coat pocket and retrieved his pen. "Thank you."

"So…how is Stuart doing?"

Another pause.

Again she had the impression he was waiting for something. But what?

He finally shook his head. Shrugged. "I'm afraid Van Heusen's still unconscious."

"I'm sorry to hear that, Detective."

Dammit, she was. But once again Hook didn't believe her. Not completely. It was in the man's hiked brow. The pointed skepticism beneath.

"Look, I don't know what Detective Pike told you, but I *am* sorry about what happened. More than you can know. No, I haven't seen Stuart in some time. And no, I don't even particularly like the man anymore, but I used to. There was a time when I even thought I loved him. I was wrong, but that doesn't change the fact that I could never, ever wish what I saw last night on anyone I'd cared about, no matter how our relationship ended." Just talking about it brought the memory of that blade slicing in. Nausea crashed in with it, and this surge wasn't fueled by an overindulgence in cognac. Her voice dropped to a whisper as she shuddered, "I still can't get the sight of that knife out my head."

Silence filled the air yet again. Only this time Abby had the feeling that Hook was withholding something. That the man was weighing whether or not he should tell her what it was.

"Is something wrong, Detective?"

He closed his notebook and set it on the table. He stared at her for several moments as he turned back. And then, "Who told you Van Heusen was stabbed?"

She blinked. Surely he wasn't implying—

But he was. He was also waiting for an answer. She swallowed yet another surge of acid that had nothing to do with that cognac. "I don't know. Someone must have." Or had she simply assumed Stuart had suffered the same fate as his driver? But if she had made the assumption on her own, no one had corrected her. Certainly not Pike. She finally rounded her reading chair and stood in front of it—three feet from that steady, heavy stare. "Let me get this straight. Are you telling me Stuart *wasn't* stabbed?"

More of that damnable silence. But this one was so dense, she'd have needed the very blade in question to slice through it. Abby tightened her grip on Dare's jacket as she waited for the detective to say something. Anything.

What the devil was that man thinking?

An eternity passed before Hook folded those massive hands of his together and provided another clue. "Ms. Pembroke, have you ever known Van Heusen to partake of illegal drugs?"

She fell into the chair. Literally.

Hook lunged forward. "Are you—"

She jerked her hands up, to ward off dizziness and him. "I'm okay." But she wasn't. The entire world was spinning. She clung to Dare's jacket, desperate to make it stop or at least slow down long enough for her drag in her breath.

"Ms. Pembroke?"

Abby kept her gaze fused to the jacket as the spinning eased. By the time it had stopped and she could make out the tiny threads woven into the coat, the implications had settled in as well. Was that what last night had been about? Drugs? She kept her stare on the coat as she shook her head numbly. "No. I never saw Stuart use drugs." The man was an assistant district attorney, for crying out loud. There was no way Stuart would jeopardize that, much less his precious family name for some drug-induced high. Or would he?

She finally looked up, met that iron stare. "Why are you asking me this? Did Stuart have drugs in his system? Or did you find the man who stabbed his driver? Does *he* sell drugs?"

"I'm afraid I'm not at liberty to answer."

That was it. The man was as bad as Pike. Digging into people's personal lives, ferreting out secrets and providing squat in return. She dug her fingers deeper into Dare's coat, hitting something solid in one of the inner pockets. His cell phone. She wrapped her fingers around it without looking. "You have some nerve, Detective. You come into my home and all but accuse someone I know—one of the city's most respected assistant district attorneys, no less—of abusing drugs and all you can offer in return is a lame 'no comment'?" Another one of those damned shrugs. She wasn't even surprised—until the next bomb exploded.

"What about blackmail?"

She tossed Dare's coat to the coffee table and jackknifed to her feet. "What *is* it with you people? First you accuse Dare of stalking the man, and now you think I was blackmailing him?" But he didn't. Or rather, he hadn't.

Not until that very moment.

Heck, she could all but see the man's mind turning this new possibility over. Examining it. But instead of voicing it, he tucked it away for later. Good God, she didn't need Pike around to cast the harsh light of suspicion on herself. She'd accomplished the ignoble feat all by herself.

Hook's slow drawl confirmed it. "Actually, Ms. Pembroke, I was wondering if someone else had reason to blackmail Van Heusen. Drugs, an old case…or something else entirely." Something he was now going to be digging that much deeper for. Something he now suspected had something to do with her.

He didn't say it. He didn't have to.

Unfortunately, *she* had to say something and soon.

Abby smoothed Dare's jacket over her arm as she rounded the chair. God willing, she could figure out how to control the damage she'd just wrought. She stepped up to the back of the chair and into her stage mindset, determined to give the best performance she'd ever given without a Tourte horsehair bow in one hand and the neck of an antique Alpine spruce violin in the other. "Detective, I don't know why someone would blackmail Stuart. But I suppose it's possible. He was an attorney and he was running for public office. As I told Detective Pike, I assume Stuart's made enemies. I'll be honest, he managed to offend me. I learned some ugly truths about Stuart the night I ended our relationship. But most of them had to do with prejudice. Are there more?" She offered a silent shrug in place of an answer.

Frankly, she'd wondered the same thing.

The night she'd met Stuart's mother, she could have sworn she wasn't the first woman Katherine had paid off. At the time it hadn't made sense. According to Stuart, he'd never gotten as serious with a woman before as he'd claimed to be with her. Or had that been another lie? In many ways her meeting with Katherine had been a lot like the one she'd had the night before with Pike, right down to the file of personal data that'd been dumped out on the table.

If anything, Katherine had been more thorough than Pike. It was all there: her previous salary with the Barrington Symphony, her family tree, how much her father—still alive at the time—*wasn't* worth financially, right down to the name of the boy who'd talked her out of her virginity the night she'd graduated from Juilliard. By the time Katherine was done spotlighting her modest beginnings, assuring her she was still the same insecure, country bumpkin who'd left Kansas at fourteen, Abby had believed her. For about two seconds.

That was when Katherine had made the mistake of dragging Brian into her tawdry assessment of Abby's life. She knew where she'd come from and she wasn't ashamed of it. And she sure as hell wasn't ashamed of Brian. Yes, she'd suffered the ups and downs—and, yes, the embarrassment and even jealousies—not uncommon to the siblings of Down's kids. But she'd gotten over it all. Including her own guilt over abandoning Brian for New York and the stage. She loved her brother. She wanted Brian in her life.

Somehow she didn't think that was going to be easy to accomplish from prison.

"Ms. Pembroke?"

She flinched. "I'm sorry, I didn't mean to ignore you. I've just…got a lot on my mind."

"That lot include your neighbor?"

What?

Oh, no. Don't tell her they were back to Dare. If they were, she wasn't upset, she was pissed. It must have shown because the man held up one of those paws.

"Take it easy, ma'am. I understand you moved in recently. Just wondering how much you know about Mr. Sabura."

That was it. She'd had enough. The guy looked nothing like Pike, but sounded exactly the same. Abby blessed the trio of ibuprofen tablets she'd taken earlier. They must have kicked in, because she managed to spin around without falling on her face. She stalked across the living room, turning as she reached her door. "Detective, I think it's time for you to leave."

The man stood. But he didn't move.

He leaned down and retrieved the issue of *Saucy* instead. He tipped his head to the cover shot of Dare. "I can understand your wanting to defend the man. I mean, Sabura saved your life. But I was also told he didn't want you to move in here. Though I suppose his reluctance makes sense."

Figures. Pike would have filled him in on that.

But who'd filled him in on the rest? The reason Dare had initially blocked her application. Even she didn't know that. But Hook did. There was no other reason for the satisfaction gleaming in the man's eyes. The man had lived up to his name, because he had her hooked and he knew it.

She folded her arms about Dare's jacket. "It does?"

His brow kicked up a notch.

"Okay, I'll bite. Why do his objections make sense?"

Those massive shoulders shrugged. "The other apartments."

The other what?

She might as well have shouted it because the man nodded. He rolled the magazine into a tube and waved it about the room—toward the ceiling. "Near as I can tell, he owns the penthouse, along with all four apartments upstairs."

Dare's coat fell to her feet.

He owned the entire nineteenth floor *and* the penthouse? She forced the shock down.

So Dare owned more real estate than one man could use. That wasn't a crime. He probably sublet the apartments. It made sense. That was probably why he'd tried to block her purchase, because he'd wanted this place for himself.

Hook shrugged. "Makes you wonder what he's doing with them—in them—doesn't it?"

She crossed her arms in a vain attempt to ward off a second wave of chills. There was no way she was retrieving that coat. "Maybe he just wants to keep the riffraff out." Her glare bounced right off Hook.

"Which riffraff would that be? You...or his known associates? You do know he was arrested, right?"

"Yes. He was fifteen. He and a friend hot-wired a car for heaven's sake. So it was a police car—big deal." Knowing Dare, he'd done it for the adrenaline. The thought succeeded in burning off the chill that had pierced her skin. "It was a prank that got out of control, Detective. One your buddies extracted their pound of flesh for when they threw him in Riker's Island. Personally, I think the cops were as much to blame as Dare and his friend. You guys should keep a better eye on the things."

Instead of offering a comeback, Hook unrolled the magazine, flipping through the pages as he spoke, "Actually, ma'am, it was a big deal. Well, the theft wasn't. You're right about that. The whole thing was supposed to be a prank. The other kid eventually admitted it was his idea. Sabura just got caught up in it." Hook stopped at the four-page spread on Dare and snapped his stare up, trapping hers. "But the crime Sabura got himself involved in after he got out of Riker's, now that was no prank. It was very, very serious."

Despite the fire burning in that stare, the chill was back, and this time it was spreading into her bones.

Abby licked her lips. "What crime was that?"

"Murder."

## Chapter 7

From the moment Dare began his search, it took three hours and forty-eight minutes to track his father down, roughly three hours and forty-four minutes longer than he'd possessed patience for. Especially given where Dare had managed to locate the man—specifically, at the town house Victor Sabura had rented for his current receptionist. Even more specifically, in the bed of said receptionist.

It appeared little had changed in Victor's life these past thirteen years.

Victor simply leaned against the walnut headboard, nodding to his companion as he smirked. "Angie, meet my son. I'd offer his name, but he won't be staying long."

Dare caved in to the latent humiliation emanating from the woman, leaning down to snag a blue silk robe from the carpet at his feet. He tossed it to the woman. "Leave."

She complied, silently donning the silk and knotting it about her waist as she slipped out from the sheets and hurried across the room. Dare waited until the door closed behind her before he pitched a larger swath of silk toward his father. "Get dressed. We need to talk."

Victor ignored him.

The man did have the decency to drag the robe about his waist as he rose from the bed and headed for what was undoubtedly the master bath. Five seconds later the sound of running water confirmed it.

Dare swallowed his curse.

Showers meant glass. He didn't have that long.

Abby might not have that long. Not with that bastard and his knife on the loose.

"Come on in the room. I'll be decent enough with the steam to appease even your antiquated sensibilities and you won't get another chance to grill me about last night."

Meaning Victor knew.

Hell, knowing the old man, the chief of police had probably phoned him personally. His father had become that successful over the past decade, mostly by winning the majority of the city's more heinous and lucrative cases for all the wrong reasons. For Abby's sake, Dare swallowed his distaste and entered the bathroom. Victor was right—the tempered glass had combined with the swirling steam to obscure a view no son wished to behold of his father, even a father he'd never respected.

Unfortunately, that same tempered glass obscured the rest.

The man's emotions.

Victor squashed a dime of liquid soap onto the reverse of the steamed glass at face level and rubbed out a large enough diameter for Dare to make out his father's Botox-enhanced features. "Spill it. What has the prodigal son so worried he had to interrupt his old man's Sunday-morning romp?"

Dare folded his arms across the T-shirt he'd dragged on that morning and leaned back against the marbleized bathroom counter. "You know damned well why I'm here."

"True." His father slicked the water from his face, his earlier smirk returning as he grabbed a can of shaving cream from the shower shelf, squirting out enough foam to cover stubble ten shades lighter than the rest of the hair some high-priced barber had dyed black. "She must be some piece for you to show up here."

"Not in the way you imply."

Crude laughter spilled over the top of the shower. "Let me guess—instead of feeling her up, you felt her *innocence*."

Dare let the comment slide. He had too much to lose if he opened his mouth now and reminded the bastard. He had even more to gain if he didn't.

Another laugh. "I thought so."

Dare stepped forward and glared through the glass. "Are you going to tell me what Pike and his department have on the thug who attacked Van Heusen, or not?"

The smirk spread as the razor scraped off another row of shaving cream. "Depends. You willing to trade?"

What? Dare might as well have inherited the empathic curse from his dad for all that he'd been able to keep his shock from showing as another strip of foam disappeared. "How about Mrs. Chang? I hear she's…lost her way home. I'd like to be able to put her husband's mind at ease. Care to help?"

Son of a b—

"Surely you didn't expect me help you out for nothing?"

"Why not, *Dad?* There's a first time for everything, even for a prodigal son." Dare ripped the shower door open—and stiffened. Because there wasn't a first time for him.

Not with Victor Sabura.

Because he *wasn't* Victor's son.

Dare stumbled backward as the denial socked in, landing against the sink as the man he'd believed that fateful day all those years ago calmly reached out and retrieved the robe he'd hooked beside the shower. The blue silk soaked up the excess water, clinging to the man's broad shoulders and powerful chest as he pulled the belt tight. His high cheeks and taut lips might still be flushed from the steam of his shower, but those dark green eyes were cold, as cold as Dare had ever seen them, as cold as they had been to him the night he'd begged the man for help and received an even colder fist in return.

"Took you long enough to figure that out."

It had. Thirteen years. But why, dammit? Had he still been so screwed up from his stay at Riker's that he'd been unable to read the truth?

"Well?"

"Why did you lie to me?" It sure as hell hadn't been to spare him pain, let alone to protect his mother—or had it? "Did Mom put you up to it? Threaten you with her will?" Only, that didn't make sense either. Miranda had left the bulk of it to him anyway. Victor hadn't even controlled the trust. Some lawyer upstate had. Nor had Victor cared. He'd made enough on his own by then anyway. "Did my mother—"

For the second time in as many minutes the shock slammed in. Only this time it struck with as much force as that cry in the night, ripping him not from his sleep but from his past. His childhood. His hopes and his dreams. His memories.

His very identity.

Mother in heaven. "Miranda never gave birth to me."

This time Victor stiffened—because there was only one way he could be as certain as he was. He'd felt it. It was ironic. His father finally believed him, believed he was an empath. Dare could see the fear in his eyes, feel it roiling up from within. He felt the plea that came with it, but it was too late. He could feel the confirmation within the man's heart even before he asked the questions. He knew why Victor had lied to him all those years ago. He hadn't done it to protect his wife. He'd done it to protect himself.

"The birth certificate—you signed it."

"So I was cuckolded, big deal."

"You forged it."

But there was more. For years growing up, Dare had believed he was incapable of reading the man he'd called Father. In a matter of minutes he'd discovered that not only could he see into the blackened depths of Victor Sabura's soul, he found more than he'd ever have believed possible. Victor might as well have been standing in front of the Supreme Court wearing little more than the briefs that were still dumped at the base of that rumpled bed, because he was trapped and he knew it. Convicted. Of more than mere forgery. His license to practice law revoked if Dare so much as breathed a word of the extent of his crime to the right people.

Dare took a moment to pull his own churning emotions into line, and then he clipped a nod toward the bedroom beyond. "Get dressed…Father. It seems I am going to be here long enough for you to fill me in on everything you know about my bloodline—as well as everything you know about the attempt on Stuart Van Heusen's life. And I do mean *everything*."

The moment Dare stepped through the Tristan's main glass doors he knew Abby was upset.

No—she was terrified.

And becoming more so by the moment.

Dare's own panic shot off the scale. He lunged across the lobby with barely a nod toward the doorman as Jerry tried to flag him down. An instantaneous read of the man's emotional aura as he raced past assured him that whatever Jerry wanted was important—but it wasn't urgent. Abby's terror was. Dare reached the elevators in record time, blessing the second lift's empty, waiting existence as he vaulted inside, every sensory receptor in his body tuned to the roiling fear emanating from above as he slammed his palm into the button for the eighteenth floor.

Abby's floor.

What in God's name had happened? Had that murdering bastard tracked her down already?

When he'd left that morning to arrange her and her brother's security, she'd still been asleep—scratch that, passed out. With Jerry serving as interim lookout and the remainder of the building's doors tied to an alarm system, he'd risked a visit stop at his father's town house in Gramercy Park. Damned near four hours later, he'd finally located the rutting bastard and had his entire world turned upside down—and that didn't even include the information he'd uncovered about his purported parents. At the moment, though, he couldn't help but wonder if the entire visit had been a mistake—because of the absolute fear he could still feel radiating down from above.

Unfortunately, the massive hit of adrenaline that had crashed into his bloodstream the second he'd felt Abby's fright was interfering with the connection.

Their connection.

Even as he prayed, he forced himself to breathe. To calm down.

*Concentrate.*

As the elevator crawled upward, Dare used every single biofeedback technique he'd studied over the years to try to slow his racing heart. To purge the numbing adrenaline from his blood. It was working, but not fast enough. It wasn't until the lift had reached the fifteenth floor that he was able to refine his assessment. Abby was deathly afraid, all right, but not of the faceless murderer she'd stumbled across outside Avery Fisher Hall last night. She was terrified of *him*.

By the seventeenth floor, he knew why.

*Damn.* Dare slammed the override button as the elevator approached the eighteenth floor and forced the lift to keep going. The second the doors opened onto the nineteenth floor, he shot outside, whipping around the corner and racing down the carpeted hall, barreling past the first empty apartment, then the second before turning down the final hall—

He was too late.

Abby was already at the end, standing in front of the door to the sole occupied apartment, her hunched side to him, the jacket he'd worn the night before over her arm, the replacement master key Jerry had slipped him already out of the jacket pocket and in her quaking hand. In the lock.

She pushed the door open and gasped. "Oh, my—"

"Who the hell are you and *what* do you think you're doing?"

Dare sprinted the final yards on desperation alone, reaching Abby's side and pulling her out of the way of an equally terrified and completely enraged Charlotte Dennison as well as the woman's gleaming and, at the moment, menacing cast-iron skillet. "I've got her, Charlotte. You did good—but you can back down now. This is Abby."

He tucked Abby's shaking body firmly against his, automatically absorbing the brunt of her shock along with the dregs of her hangover as he nodded to the battered woman and child cowering behind his assistant. Dare nodded to the Chinese émigré he'd spent all of ten minutes with the previous morning. Those ten minutes had been long enough to absorb the memory of ten years of sheer hell at her husband's fist. "It's okay, Mrs. Chang. Abby is no threat to you or your daughter. She doesn't know your husband. Even if she did, she wouldn't tell him anything. I give you my word."

The woman bobbed her head and turned, scooting her daughter deeper in the apartment until they were both out of sight. An equally relieved Charlotte smoothed the salt-and-pepper curls from her forehead as she lowered the skillet.

She smiled. "It's nice to meet you, Ms. Pembroke. I look forward to getting to know you better." Charlotte tacked on a faded-blue wink before he could stop her. "Later, of course."

The damage already done, Charlotte risked radiating one of those waves of amused motherly sympathy she cursed him with now and then before she, too, departed.

To be honest, the stunt wasn't entirely unexpected.

Unlike his father, Charlotte had managed to drag damned near the entire story out of him this morning. But then, he could actually share the details with her, couldn't he? Charlotte had believed him when he'd told her what had really happened during her sister's final moments all those years ago, as the police hadn't. She'd accepted the rest when he'd finally confessed it, too. Granted, she'd had the advantage of knowing her bastard of a brother-in-law as well as she'd known her sister. While his father, of course, had never even tried to get to know his own son. He'd always hoped eventually that would change.

This morning he'd learned it never would.

Dare pushed the disappointment aside. He stared down at the key still clutched in Abby's hand, determined to give her the time she needed to absorb what she'd seen, to sort out her own jumbled, changing emotions. Unfortunately, that key had opened more than a door to an apartment just now. It had cracked the door to the truth. As much as he could give her. Eventually he would have to give her the rest, before she figured it out on her own.

And she would.

Their connection was growing. Deepening. Whether he wanted it to or not. Just as it had with his mother—a mother he'd just learned was not his any more than his father was. Not biologically. To be honest, he wasn't surprised. Deep down, he'd known for years that he didn't belong in the Sabura home. He'd sensed there were others—that somewhere, he had siblings. Why else had he branded that mark on his chest? But he'd never sought them out. Not actively. He knew why. As difficult as accepting his mother's death had been, he hadn't dared risk searching for someone else like himself. Someone able to teach him to harness the curse he possessed and use it more than he was willing to.

Or worse.

What if he discovered that, yes, there was another man out there who possessed the right to call him son, but in the end cared nothing for him? What if he discovered his real family didn't want him any more than Victor or his mother had? Unwilling to relive the rejection, he'd sealed himself off. Unfortunately, that note he'd received suggested that at least one relation had found him first.

As had Abby.

She was nothing like him. She was normal. Wonderfully, perfectly *normal*. Better yet, their connection was nothing like the one he'd shared with his mother. It was stronger.

But was she?

"Abby?"

The query succeeded in burning away the bulk of her shock. She stepped away, far enough to break contact, but not so far as to cause panic in him, then turned. For a moment he saw her as Charlotte and his guests must have seen her: the rumpled clothes and snarled hair, her scraped and bruised temple from where she'd hit the street, the deathly pale skin and hollowed eyes left over from her own night of hell.

And then he looked deeper.

He could feel her already connecting the main pieces of the puzzle together…and giving him the benefit of the doubt, trusting that he'd fill in the rest when he could. The strength of her faith humbled him, as did her inner, truer beauty. He knew right then there was no escape.

God help him, the author of that anonymous note was correct. His heart was already snared.

She held out the replacement master key to the apartments, embarrassment washing through her as he took the key and slipped it into the pocket of his jeans. She kept his jacket, clutching it tightly as she apologized. "I'm sorry. I had no right to come here, much less open that door."

"Why did you?"

She turned to accompany him back down the deserted hall to the elevator. "The police sent another detective."

Despite her trust, he felt the chill.

"He told you about the murder, didn't he?"

She shook her head as they rounded the first corner. "Not really. Just enough to scare the bejesus out of me. But I'm beginning to think that was his plan all along. He was just out for information."

"About Van Heusen?"

She folded his jacket over her left arm and locked her right arm over it as they turned the final corner and reached the elevators. "About you."

It made sense. Not a lot, but enough. At the very least, it fit with that anonymous note. With what he'd been able to glean from his father this morning. He, Abby and Stuart Van Heusen were all connected. How, he didn't yet know. But he would find out. Dare punched the elevator button, waiting for her to precede him inside as the doors opened.

"What did the detective want to know?"

She captured his stare. "Mostly what you were doing with four apartments you didn't use."

The elevator doors closed.

Neither of them pushed any buttons.

"By the way, you were wrong. I do know who Mrs. Chang's husband is. He's a patron of the arts, ironically enough. Though the season before I left for Europe he rarely brought his wife to the symphony. We were told she'd taken ill, but anyone with a pair of eyes knew what was going on. She never looked like she does now, but there were times when her makeup didn't quite cover the bruises. Eventually

Chang started bringing his girl of the moment in her place. He had a number of moments, too. But I suspect that's par for Chang and his Chinese mafia pals." She dragged her breath in. "So how long have you and Charlotte been running your private underground, or rather high-rise, railroad for abused women?"

For far too long.

He sighed. "Since her sister died."

Her soft hazel gaze didn't waver. "Died...or was murdered?"

Despite his attempts to keep his voice steady, it came out in a whisper. "Murdered."

She nodded slowly. Carefully. "Can I ask what happened?"

"Yes." He reached around her shoulder and pushed the elevator pause button as the past crowded in.

The memories.

Janet Randall's innocent face. Battered. Bloodied.

Lifeless.

He stepped back from Abby and deliberately sealed his shoulders to the rear wall of the elevator, not so much for physical support, but so he wouldn't reach out for her. For the added emotional strength he'd not only discovered that touching Abby gave him, but that he now craved. "It started at Riker's. Janet Randall—Charlotte's younger sister—was married to my cell mate. You already know why I was there. Duane Randall was there to cool off."

"Cool off?"

Dare nodded. "Randall used to beat Janet regularly. The police had come out that Friday on yet another domestic dispute." He spat the term. An obscenely mild phrasing he'd detested for years. One that could never capture the utter violence it was used to represent. "As usual, Janet refused to press charges. She'd been beaten pretty badly that last time, however, suffered a broken arm and a concussion. The responding officer was new, eager to make a difference. He brought Ran-

dall in anyway and tossed him in a cell with me for the weekend. By the time we were released, I was convinced Randall
was headed home to finish the job. I was so certain, in fact, I
called the officer who'd arrested me." He paused as the memory of the cop's aura snapped in. The man's initial jaded attempt at patience—and then the outright disbelief.

"The officer who arrested you? Pike's mentor?"

Dare nodded. "Yes."

"What did he do?"

"Nothing."

It was a lie. Detective Moore had done something. He'd
asked him if Randall had actually confessed his intentions.
When he'd said no, Moore had dismissed him. Rudely. Unfortunately, spending the weekend in a cell with a man of
Duane Randall's intense rage had formed a similar connection to the one he'd shared with Brian last night, enhanced by
Randall's desire to use him as a replacement punching bag,
among other things.

The elevator walls closed in.

"Dare?"

He wrenched himself from the past, that cell, the vile beast
who had inhabited it with him, and focused on the gentle
beauty in front of him. She stepped closer. Even as he watched
Abby shift his jacket and reach out with her free hand, he
knew he should stop her. Touching would only strengthen the
connection. But he didn't. He couldn't. He needed it too
much. He needed her. Dare stared at the gentle hand on his
forearm, those soft, slender fingers, as he drew his air in
slowly, deliberately, drawing her in with it.

Her scent. Her essence. Her balm.

The ugliness faded.

He sighed. "I apologize. I didn't mean to frighten you. It's
just…not a memory I enjoy reliving." He forced a smile in an
attempt to reassure her. Unfortunately, it fell short.

She sucked in her breath. Sharply. "Please tell me you weren't—"

"No. I wasn't raped." Not physically. "But there are many ways to assault a person's soul."

"I don't understand."

For that he was eternally grateful. "Let's just say that after spending three days in the same cell as Duane Randall, I knew what he was really like and what his plans were upon his release. I didn't need to hear them. I *knew*."

As if on cue, the elevator lights dimmed.

Unlike that note he'd received, it wasn't some new psychic confirmation. Someone had simply requested a lift. He needed to hurry if they were going to finish this here.

Abby seemed to know it, too, because she drew her breath in again, this time slowly. "So when the cops wouldn't take you seriously, you tracked the man down yourself. You went to his house."

"Yes."

His breath bled out as she reached up and pressed her finger to his cheek, a millimeter from the start of his constant physical reminder of that day.

One of them.

Her soft brown gaze filled with tears as she drew her finger down, slowly tracing the scar's length. "The legend is wrong, isn't it? The one they printed in that magazine. The great Triple Dare didn't get this scar on his first climb, did he? He got it the night he tried to save Charlotte's sister. He got it from Duane Randall." Her finger reached the end of the scar at the base of his jaw.

There her tears slipped free.

"Yes."

"What happened?"

He swallowed hard. It didn't help. The memories continued to assault his brain. His body. His heart.

And her tears continued to flow.

"I dared to interfere with the disciplining of Randall's wife. We fought. I managed to knock him off me, but the knife was still in his hand. He fell on it. I called the police again." For all the good it had done. "Within minutes, he was dead. But so was Janet. I was...too late."

Abby nodded.

When she didn't pull her hand away to wipe her tears, he did it for her, reaching up to smooth them from her jaw, the corner of her quivering lips, up her cheeks. The errant one still clinging to her lashes. "I—I don't understand. You said no one believed you. But you were out of Riker's. That meant your father was home by then. Why didn't you go to him?"

"I did."

"Your father didn't believe you, either."

It was a statement, not a question. One he didn't bother denying. There was no point. They both knew it was true.

"There's more, isn't there? I can—" She broke off, flushed, drew her breath in deep before starting again. "I know this sounds really crazy, but—" She covered his right hand with hers and pulled it to her chest. The blood began roaring through his veins as she splayed it out above her left breast. He could feel her heart beating solidly beneath his palm, pulsing with the truth, even before she confessed it. "I swear I can feel it. You."

No! It was too soon, dammit. No matter how strong the connection.

But it wasn't and he knew it. Before long, *she* would know it. All of it. Whether he told her or not.

And then what?

Would she deny the truth for decades as his father had? Or would she bolt like his mother?

Or would she believe it? Accept it?

Accept *him*.

Much as he was beginning to pray for the latter, he couldn't risk it. Not now. He had more important worries on his mind than his heart.

Her life.

He was afraid of her.

No, not *of* her, exactly. More *for* her. Abby closed her eyes, tried to focus. But it was gone. She opened her eyes, suddenly feeling as foolish as she must have looked breaking in to that apartment. But she wasn't nearly as stunned.

Horrified, yes. But that had nothing to do with Dare.

She tightened her grip on his hand when he tried to move it, kept it sealed to her heart—and told him what was in it. "You're an amazing man, Darian Sabura."

He flushed. "Nonsense."

This time she didn't fight him when he tugged his hand away. She let it go. Him, too.

For now.

She held on to his coat as she turned, taking his place against the elevator wall as Dare stepped around her to restart the elevator. "So that night when you climbed in my window? You'd been on the job, so to speak."

He faced her as the lift lurched into motion.

Her stomach should have lurched with it, given there was nothing in it but ibuprofen and cognac fumes, but it didn't.

And he hadn't answered.

"Well?"

His dark brows arched.

"Don't give me that look. You know what I'm asking. Contrary to Detective Pike, you *do* have a job. I can't imagine creating new identities for desperate, battered women is easy. Or cheap. You're the money man, aren't you? The guy who looks great in a tux at all the right parties. Charlotte's the front. Though I suppose Jerry has a finger in things, too, at least when someone needs to stay here. What better place to hide a woman who doesn't want to be found?" All they had to do was wait until the dead of night, and none of the other residents would be the wiser. Especially since Dare owned the entire floor. "I'm guessing you round out your extra security with some of those unsavory associates Pike mentioned. Tell me, is that where you were this morning? Arranging a bit of invisible security for me? Possibly for my brother, too?"

She now knew it would be just like Dare to do that. She also knew he hadn't been home. Seconds after Hook had dropped his bombshell, Dare's cell phone had rung. Numbed, she'd actually answered it. The caller? Marlena. It seemed Abby had forgotten to sever the connection after Marlena had called the night before. Half an hour of busy signals had eaten at her friend. Hoping Dare had used his cell phone to call them after the stabbing the night before, Marlena had taken a chance and used her caller ID to phone Dare—and got her. Thankfully, Brian was okay. Physically.

But his memory was still missing.

It had been difficult, but Abby had forced herself to pretend she was still in Europe when she spoke to him. By the time she'd hung up and returned from the kitchen, Hook had left. But in reaching for Dare's jacket to return his phone, she'd remembered the key was still there. At first she'd tried to return his jacket. But when Dare hadn't answered the penthouse door, her burning curiosity—and, yes, the doubts—had driven her up to the nineteenth floor. The floor between theirs. The first two apartments had been furnished, but vacant. Sterile.

The third had not.

She held Dare's stare as the elevator stopped. "Well?"

He finally nodded. "Yes. I set up security. Yours should be arriving shortly. Brian's is already at the house. Don't worry, he'll never know. But you should probably tell Marlena and her husband. It may help them sleep easier. I hope I haven't presumed too much."

"You haven't." How could he? Hell, even Pike had been more interested in using her to take Dare down than protecting her from him. She nodded as they stepped out of the elevator and headed down the hall to her apartment. "I will tell Marlena, though. Thank you—from me and for Brian. And you *are* amazing. No matter how hard you work to conceal it."

Again, he didn't respond.

It didn't matter. She was right.

How many women and children had he and Charlotte helped over the years? Hundreds? A thousand?

Yet he'd never once taken credit.

Instead, he'd let the rumors and speculation about his playboy adrenaline-charged recreations make it into print, never once even hinting there was more. Certainly never defending himself to men like Pike. Because if he did, he'd endanger others. Greta Laurens was right. So was Abby's first impression that night in her apartment. There was a lot more to Darian Sabura than met the eye. Abby dropped her gaze to Dare's sinewy biceps as they reached her door. The parts of the man that met the eye were pretty damned good, too.

Including those scars. Especially those scars.

The night she'd first spotted them, she assumed the marks were little more than a painful testimony to the man's rugged lifestyle. She now knew they were more. He was more. And they were beautiful, because they were a direct reflection of the man within.

"Don't."

"Sorry. Too late." She started to slide her key in the lock when the door pushed open. Great, she'd been so consumed with another key's existence she'd forgotten to lock her own door. She dropped her keys on the foyer table, retaining Dare's jacket as he closed the door behind them. She glanced up as he caught up with her at the breakfast counter. "As for the rest—namely, what you were trying so damned hard to keep hidden in that lift—you'll tell me when you're ready."

Silence.

Unlike the series of pauses that had locked in earlier that morning with Hook, this one wasn't uncomfortable, not for her. But it was for him. "It's okay. I'm patient. Stubborn, too. Just ask my violin teachers." She laid his jacket over one of the high-back metal stools and entered the kitchen. Not a moment too soon, either.

Her stomach growled. Loudly.

She blushed.

But at least the noise served to lighten the mood.

He smiled. "Would you like me to make something while you shower? I'm not in the same league as Charlotte, but I can use a toaster and fry an egg."

For the first time since he'd grabbed her outside that apartment upstairs, her stomach rolled. She swallowed a groan. "Lord, no. And please don't even mention something that greasy again. But I am starving—obviously. So if you can handle the sight, I'd rather eat. It's been twenty-four hours since my last meal and, like it or not, I've got another pre-concert cutoff coming up soon. A cutoff I've learned to respect over the years." She tossed him a sheepish smile as she opened the cupboard to the right of his head and grabbed a can of soup. "Let's just say food and public performances don't mix, at least in me."

"Are you sure that's wise?"

She glanced at the can. "It's chicken and rice soup." Not overly filling and about as bland as you could get.

"I meant the concert." He shook his head. "Abby, you witnessed a murder last night. You have an…old friend in the hospital. Surely no one expects you to perform tonight."

She let the "old friend" euphemism go. But not the rest. "Sorry, but they do. *He* does."

"He?"

She reached past him again to snag a bowl. "Calvin Hollings, the Philharmonic's conductor. Otherwise known as 'The Show Must Go On.' I love the man to pieces, but—"

Dare closed his hand over hers, nudging the bowl down to the counter. "Abby, please. This isn't a joke." The sudden edge in his voice startled her because it was jagged. Raw.

He was truly afraid. For her.

Truth be told, so was she.

Unfortunately, she hadn't been kidding. "Believe me, the laughter's a front. However, I don't have a choice. Not only is this the last performance of the summer series, I have another solo tonight." Despite her best efforts, her voice quavered. "If Pike and that substitute for him they sent have their way, I might not be on stage next season."

Especially once they started raking through her finances.

Abby yanked open her drawer of utensils, desperately trying to keep her eyes from watering as she sifted through the nest. She gave up all pretense of searching for the opener and stood there as that night came into view. Katherine's haughty face. That damned cashier's check. She wished to God she'd followed her first instinct and told Stuart's mother where she could stick it. At the time she nearly had—until she'd realized how foolish rejecting it would be. Her dad might have been alive at the time, but he wasn't rich, nor was he ever going to be. When Katherine reminded her that someday she might need the money to care for her brother, she'd swallowed her pride and taken it. Cashed it.

Two months ago she'd finally spent it, too. Half of it anyway. On this place.

If Marlena hadn't stumbled across her bank statement after she'd returned from Europe and assumed she'd inherited a windfall from her father, the money would probably still be sitting in an account. Marlena was the one who'd approached

Greta Laurens about the apartment when she'd learned the woman was moving to Florida. Evidently, Greta was a closet fan, even owned Abby's debut solo CD. Greta had insisted on showing her the place, even though it had been far too expensive. The old woman insisted she was too old to care. Part of her estate was already earmarked for the arts. As far as Greta was concerned, the loss was a tax write-off for her, an investment for Abby.

Abby blinked back to the present as Dare reached into the utensil drawer. She sighed as he withdrew the can opener and closed the drawer for her. "It's ironic, you know."

Dare locked the opener to the can. "What is?"

"The money." She waved her hands about the kitchen. "This place is worth four times what I paid for it. Greta told me if something happened to Brian or me, I could always borrow against the equity she turned over to me. I still have half the money Katherine paid me. Yesterday morning I'd decided to do as Greta suggested. I was going to see a lawyer about borrowing back the rest against this place. I got a decent bump in salary for returning to the Philharmonic, so I'll be able to pay it off eventually. It'll be tight, but worth it to return the entire blessed amount to Katherine." She shook her head. "Something tells me Pike would never believe me if I told him, though."

"Don't."

She blinked up at Dare as he dragged her bowl forward and poured the soup in, crossing the kitchen to dump the can in the recycling bin.

He shook his head. "Don't take out the loan. Not yet. You may not have to."

"I don't understand."

To her surprise, he shrugged. "Neither do I. Not completely. But I wouldn't go screwing with your finances this soon. I uncovered several interesting facts this morning. Facts no one bothered to share with us last night. They involve Van Heusen and—"

"Drugs."

It was his turn to be surprised. "The detective told you?"

She nodded. But how had Dare found out? "You mean it's true? Stuart was really using them?"

"Possibly. But the abuse probably wasn't voluntary. At least, not in the beginning."

"In the *beginning?* He was doing them when we dated?"

"I don't think so." Dare put the soup in the microwave. "If you read that article in *Saucy,* then you know my father's a defense attorney, a good one—completely lacking in conscience, mind you, but damned good. Anyway, I stopped by his town house this morning. As I suspected, he was waiting for me. One of his contacts on the force had already called him."

"What did he have to say?"

"Did you follow the news surrounding Senator Gregory's death?"

"The one that was murdered a few weeks ago?"

Dare nodded as he turned back to the microwave. "Eight to be exact. As a matter of fact, Gregory was killed right here in the city the same day you first saw this apartment."

How had Dare known that?

She was about to ask him when she noticed something even odder. Dare was rubbing his chest absently, right over that tattoo he'd shifted out of her view the night she'd dropped off the tickets. He caught her stare and dropped his hand. She let the intriguing insight go as he opened the microwave. Now wasn't the time. Now was no longer the time for eating either, but he'd already set the bowl of soup on the counter in front of her along with a spoon.

"Eat while I finish."

She took the spoon.

"According to my father's source, Senator Gregory was

found dead in his hotel room. At the time there was no sign of forced entry or foul play."

"And now?"

"It seems the FBI has been able to link Gregory's death to a new, potentially lethal drug that delivers a unique and instantly addictive high. Somehow, a chemist has been able to isolate a person's DNA and then combine the necessary components of that unique genetic material with this new designer drug to produce a one-hit addiction that only works on their intended target. Think about it. If you could get someone hooked on a drug that only you can produce, you could blackmail anyone. Over anything. Unfortunately, they've had problems. Instead of hooking Gregory, they ended up killing him."

Good heavens— "Stuart!" She dropped the spoon. It clattered into the bowl, splashing drops of soup over the rim and onto the white counter.

Dare reached into an upper cupboard to withdraw a pair of the mugs Marlena had given her for her birthday the year before. He poured out the coffee she'd made after Detective Hook had woken her. Dare nudged one of the steaming mugs into her hand, probably hoping the smell would revive her. It did.

She licked her lips instead of risking a sip. With the turn this conversation had taken, she'd end up burning herself. "W-will Stuart recover?"

"No one knows. But I have to be honest, it doesn't look good. Pike neglected to tell us that an expended syringe was found near Van Heusen's body. The man wasn't stabbed, he was either given a fresh—or first—hit. They haven't yet been able to isolate the drug that induced Van Heusen's coma and compare it to the chemical makeup of the drug that did Senator Gregory in, but the fact that they can't—along with Van Heusen's career, political aspirations, as well as his social and political ties to Gregory—all suggests last night may have been another instant-addiction attempt gone awry."

"Then, other than the fact that Stuart was there to try to talk to me about the money I took from his mother, this has nothing to do with me. That man was lying in wait for him. His driver simply got caught in the cross fire."

"It would seem so."

She gave up all hope of regaining her appetite and set the coffee mug beside the bowl, then turned to slump back against the counter for support. "It makes sense. Detective Hook seemed obsessed with blackmail—Stuart's. I wonder what they wanted or had on him?"

Dare stilled.

Was it her imagination, or was that strange connection they'd shared in the elevator returning? She took a chance and just said it. "You know something, don't you? About Stuart. Why someone would blackmail him." She shook her head before Dare could open his mouth, already knowing he intended to deny it—and knowing he was trying to protect her. Again. "Don't. I think we've moved past the outright lies, don't you?"

This time Dare didn't deny anything. But he did cross the kitchen and stop at the breakfast counter beside his jacket. "I'd rather not say anything until I'm sure." In other words, he was afraid of hurting her. Though the odd connection she'd been experiencing around this man—with him—had faded with his retreat, she knew she was right. She could see it in those dark, emerald pools. The wariness.

Trust. He needed it. From her.

For the first time since they'd met, she gave it to him freely, completely. She nodded to his coat.

"You have to go, don't you?"

"Yes. I'm still trying to track down the FBI agent my father mentioned. He may be able to tell us what we need to know without having to go through Pike or this other detective you spoke to. But, Abby?"

"Yes?"

"Please, is there any way you can stay home tonight?"

"Not if I want to keep second chair." She wasn't scheduled to resume the position permanently until the fall season. But that wouldn't matter. Not with Hollings. He was still pissed she'd taken a year's hiatus to join the quartet and lick her wounds in Europe. She crossed the kitchen as well, stopping just shy of the counter. Of him. "Relax. As scary as all this drug stuff is, it means there's no kook trying to stalk me."

He stepped closer. So close, she could feel his desperation. "Abby, you *saw* the murder."

She knew that. Hell, she could still see it. Just when she thought she'd succeeded in banishing the memory, she'd close her eyes and see that slashing knife. Her brother being rammed into that car. His glasses lying in that poor man's blood. She shivered. "Yes, I did see it. But I didn't see the murderer."

"*He* doesn't know that."

"Dare, please." He had to stop looking at her like that. "I have to go. I'm sorry. Like you said, you've already arranged for someone to watch over me—*and* there's security at the theatre. Between them, I'll be fine. I doubt I'll be more nervous than usual." But she would, because the only person she felt completely safe with lately hadn't volunteered to accompany her. There was no use denying it.

It hurt. A lot.

Nor was there any use denying the rest. At least to herself. She was seriously attracted to this man. Falling for him faster than she should. How could she not? With most of the men she'd dated, Stuart in particular, what you saw was what you got. But with Dare, there were hidden depths, nuances to the man that continued to surprise her and draw her in when she least expected it. It had happened that first night when she'd spotted him scaling their building in his tuxedo. It had happened again last night and this morning as she'd listened to two driven detectives accuse Dare of a heinousness she now knew he was utterly incapable of. And it was happening now, as she stared at those strong, callused fingers, not even wondering, but somehow already knowing how gentle they could be, would be, on her flesh. That mouth. Those lips.

Soft, yet firm.

Physically marred, and yet perfect.

She reached up and traced the tip of her finger over the scar. A scar he'd yet to explain. A scar that like the one on his cheek, she also suspected hadn't been earned on some cliff. She teased it again and heard his swallow. Felt it. She nudged her gaze up and sank into that dark-emerald stare. His gaze was pleading with her. Dare was pleading. But part of him, the part she desperately wanted to obey, was also drawing her in. Deeper and deeper. She couldn't stop herself. It was as if she'd been seduced by the Pied Piper of Hamelin, only the music she couldn't resist was the silent melody in those eyes. The pull of Dare's song was too steady, too strong.

And absolutely hypnotic.

Before she'd realized what she'd done, she'd teased her fingers down his jaw, smoothing them over the solid, generous muscles of his chest. A moment later she was pressing in, holding on as she eased up onto her toes.

"Abby, don't. *Please.*"

She blinked. "Why not?"

They both knew he wanted it. He wanted her. It had been obvious that first night, right here in this kitchen, his inopportune arousal all but shouting it. He definitely wanted her. But he didn't *want* to want her.

She sank back onto her heels. "Okay. But remember what I said. I'm very patient."

That was what he was afraid of. Again, he didn't have to say it. But she had heard it. It was enough.

For now.

She slipped his jacket from the counter and held it out and

he took it, folding it over his arm as they rounded the break-fast counter. She was about to escort him to the door so she could shower and retrieve her spare violin from her trunk— she needed to get her fingers and her brain in tune for her solo that night— when she noticed the cell phone on the floor beside her chair. She must have dropped it earlier when she'd remembered the key.

"Just a second." She crossed the room and reached down— only to freeze as she realized that the phone wasn't all she'd missed. Suspicion and horror heaved into her stomach, instantly displacing her hunger in one nauseating surge.

A split second later, Dare shot across the room. "Abby, what is it? What's wrong?"

She shook her head as Dare helped her straighten, unable to tear her gaze from the lone bottle of cognac on the coffee table long enough to meet his. "The glasses. They're gone. Why?"

Even before Dare's dark curse filled the air, she knew.

DNA.

Someone wanted it. Badly enough to steal it. But whose genetic material had the thief been after? She shifted her gaze to search for the climbing magazine; it was also missing. Hers? Or Dare's?

And why?

# Chapter 8

Dare had missed her solo—again.

Abby didn't even care. Something was wrong. She could feel it. The second the music stopped, Abby shot to her feet, threading her way out of the string section while the applause still thundered. By the time she made it stage right, the other 105 members of the orchestra were just beginning to gather up their instruments and music—except Stephen. He met her at the exit, sans cello but brimming with the sympathy and concern every other musician she'd passed had wisely kept to themselves as he followed her backstage.

He patted her back as she stopped to tuck the Strad and her bow under her arm. "Abby, it happens. Don't let it get you down. Everyone blows an entrance at some point."

Everyone did. But not her. Not in fifteen years. And she hadn't just blown her entrance, she'd missed the entire first four bars of Brahms's Fourth Symphony.

Stephen tipped her chin, forcing her to meet his big-brotherly concern. "Are you okay?"

"I'm fine."

It was a lie. Part of it, anyway.

She wasn't as humiliated as he believed; she was terrified. Something was terribly wrong. "Stephen, I have to go. Thanks again for bringing the Strad. Tell Marlena I'll call Brian before he heads for bed, okay?" She left a gaping Stephen at the backstage door and fled out and down the hall as fast as her low heels and floor-length black skirt allowed.

Dare. She could still feel him. And something was definitely wrong. She no longer questioned how she knew.

She just did.

Had that monster who'd drugged Stuart and murdered his driver followed her and Dare out of the Tristan earlier? Or had he already been lying in wait here at Avery Fisher Hall, waiting to corner Dare after he'd departed her dressing room before she finished her last minute warm-up? Was Dare lying bleeding in some corner of the building? She'd caved in to the urge to scan the VIP section of the audience during the intermission. Dare wasn't there. He'd been missing—possibly in trouble—that long at least. After the way he'd insisted upon accompanying her tonight after they'd discovered the cognac glasses had been stolen, there was no way he'd have simply gotten bored and taken off.

So where the devil was he?

She forced herself to slow as she turned down the hall that led to her dressing room. Neither the FBI agent Dare's father had referred him to nor Detective Hook had had a chance to return his calls that afternoon. Maybe he'd left his cell phone on vibrate during the concert just in case. If either man had phoned, Dare could have retreated to her dressing room to take it. But if he had taken a call, the news wasn't good.

She just knew it.

She might be certifiable, but she swore she could feel it.

Abby wrenched open the door to her dressing room, disappointment searing in as she entered. Dare wasn't there. She didn't bother switching on the overhead light; the glow from the makeup table provided enough light for her to reach her violin case still lying open on the plush bench. But, as she stepped into the room, the leg of the spare chair caught her foot. She stumbled, cursing as the Strad and bow shot out of her hand, landing with a muffled thump on the carpet. She managed to right herself, then immediately reached down into the shadows to retrieve the violin—gasping as her fingers collided with something completely different.

Muscle.

Dare. She hadn't caught the chair's leg with her shoe, she'd caught *him*. She could make out his form, sprawled back into the chair as if he was sleeping or, worse, passed out. Neither scenario made sense. She left the Strad and bow lying on the carpet and reached for Dare instead.

"Are you okay? What hap—"

He groaned.

Her panic shot off the scale as she threaded her fingers into his hair. The strands were damp near his head. She pressed her fingers to his cheek, then his forehead and gasped. Twenty-four-hour bug her tush, the man was burning up again. Only this time his skin had nearly blistered her fingers. "Don't move. I'll be right back."

She needed a wet rag.

Unfortunately, the dressing room's bathroom was still out of order. Abby scooped up the Strad and bow and traded them for the extra cloth she kept inside her violin case. Then she tore out of the dressing room, straight into the communal bathroom at the end of the hall, nodding to two fellow musicians as she barreled inside. Her hands were shaking so violently, she dropped the rag in the sink.

"Abby?"

"I'm fine, Bess."

From the blond brow the flutist arched, Bess clearly didn't believe her. She didn't care. She didn't care if the entire symphony thought she was in the throes of a full-blown nervous breakdown. She had more important worries. Gut-wrenching suspicions. All of them centered around Dare. Why did his temperature keep skyrocketing at odd intervals? She knew enough to suspect that there was something wrong with Dare's immune system. Terribly wrong.

Sweet heaven, was it terminal?

Her stomach lurched as she squeezed out the rag and hurried out of the bathroom, plowing past the entire percussion section as she raced down the hall. She threw the door to the dressing room open and reached for the overhead switch only to realize light was already flooding the room. Dare was standing beside the chair, looking every inch the polished patron of the arts in his crisp snowy shirt, navy tie and matching tailored suit. His dusky features were still flushed and damp, but other than that he appeared—

"I'm fine. I'm sorry if I frightened you. I must have…eaten something that didn't agree with me."

She didn't believe it for a second. She knew sick when she saw it. He might be recovering before her very eyes, but she swore he'd been passed out when she'd knocked into him minutes before. Something was definitely wrong. She clenched the rag, ignoring the water dripping down her skirt. "Dare…are you ill? I mean, seriously?"

Was that why he didn't like to touch people? Was he contagious?

Half a dozen diseases snapped through her brain, each more frightening than the last. Dare crossed the room before she could voice a single one. She sucked in her breath as he reached up to cup her face, smoothing away the tears she hadn't even realized were stinging the corners of her eyes.

"Hey, it's okay. I swear, I'm fine. Something didn't agree with me tonight, that's all. Here." He lowered his right hand and snagged hers, pressing her palm to his cheek. "See? Temp's gone. The sweating, too." The scar on his bottom lip dipped in with his lopsided grin. "I'm beginning to think it's this place. Never did like crowds. They just don't agree with me. I've got a car waiting in the garage. What do you say? Can we leave?"

She licked her lips. Nodded. "Sure. Just let me wipe down the Strad and stow it properly."

But she didn't move. She couldn't.

Those enigmatic pools of green were playing havoc with her insides all over again, just as they had in her apartment that afternoon. He was hypnotizing her.

Seducing her.

And just as he had this afternoon, Dare knew it. Only this time, he *did* want to want it.

Her.

He released her hand to drag the tip of his thumb across her mouth, slowly but surely erasing the moisture her tongue had left behind, deliberately plucking at the strings of desire deep inside her belly until they began to thrum. His hand fell away as his entire body moved in close. Very close. Despite the heat radiating off him, she shivered again, because she could also feel his hunger. A growing masculine hunger that was all but crackling at its restraints.

His restraints.

She swore she could feel Dare strengthening those restraints, holding the pulsing desire at bay as he eased his head down slowly, deliberately dragging the moment out. The piercing anticipation. He took so long she nearly screamed with frustration—until his dark, smoky breath finally reached her flesh, bathing first her lashes, then her cheeks and then finally, mercifully, her lips.

But there he paused.

That was when she knew it was up to her. *This* was up to her. If she truly wanted more than this heady whisper of heat, this tantalizing taste of passion, she would have to reach for it.

She did.

A split second later their breaths mingled. Their lips fused. Their driving passions merged—

Until a crude chuckle filled the air.

"Well, well. Look at the cozy couple. Not bad for a pair of virtual strangers."

They tore apart.

Pike?

Her brain still fogged, she whirled toward the door. Sure enough, there was Pike, standing in yet another door she'd left open, his arms crossed, all but lounging against the jamb. How on earth had the man managed to remain there so long without her or Dare noticing his presence? A swift, rattled glance at Dare told her that he, too, wondered the same thing.

But Dare was also pissed. "What the hell do you want?"

The detective shrugged. "Me? You're the one who keeps calling the precinct."

Dare held Pike's stare. "Two calls. I left brief messages both times—for Detective Hook, not you."

To her amazement, Pike shrugged off the insult as he entered the room. "So I heard. Unfortunately, there's a problem. And knowing your track record with fairy tales, I figured I ought to stop by in person. See if you hadn't dreamed up the whole thing—or rather, the person."

Abby gasped. Was Pike implying what she thought he was?

The detective nodded. "Yep. Don't know who you're trying to reach because there isn't a cop by the name of Hook in my precinct—or any precinct in the five boroughs. I checked."

Abby clutched at the sleeve to Dare's black suit, driving her clipped nails deep into the iron muscles beneath. "That's impossible. Detective Hook questioned me himself this morning. In my apartment."

"That may be, Ms. Pembroke. But the man wasn't with us. You sure he had a gold detective's shield on him?"

"Yes." But she hadn't gotten a clear look at it, had she? She'd been a bit distracted by her hangover and Hook's sneezing fit. A fit she now realized had probably been staged. "Wait, the doorman." She tightened her grip on Dare's arm as she turned to him. "Jerry saw it. He told you."

Dare shook his head. "Like you, he just caught a flash of the thing. He was busy, remember?"

He was right. Dare had called her from the lobby after he'd left her apartment to talk to Jerry. It seemed there was a crisis in the building that morning. One of the residents had had a heart attack. Jerry had his hands full dealing with EMTs and a hysterical Mrs. Eernisse from 6B right about the time some cop had chosen to flash his badge and stride through the lobby. Faced with the choice of chasing after the man into the elevators or continuing to assist the EMTs, Jerry had opted for the latter. It wasn't until he'd seen Dare return that he realized he'd forgotten to follow up on the cop.

Dare frowned. "So we've got an impersonator on our hands."

"Wrong. *I've* got an impersonator on my hands. You, Sabura, have nothing more to do with this."

"The hell I don't. That bastard has our DNA."

Pike stiffened at that.

Dare smiled—grimly. "Yeah, we know all about Senator Gregory, the designer DNA drug and the blackmail attempts."

To Abby's surprise, Pike blew out a low, taunting whistle.

"Well, what do you know. Daddy may not like you, but it appears he's still covering your hide."

"The hell he is." Dare stepped away from her, barely restrained fury scorching off him as he entered the detective's personal space. "My old man didn't cover up squat then either and you know it. Just like you know there wasn't a shred of evidence in that house to tie me to Randall's death."

"Just that knife."

Dare glare narrowed, sharpened. "With *his* prints on it."

Pike responded with a thin, unexpectedly bitter smile. "Who knows, maybe someone used their X-ray vision to zap your prints off it. Don't suppose you know anyone capable of something like that?"

Dare's stare turned molten. "You never know."

What the devil was going on? Whatever this pissing contest concerned, it clearly was something that had happened between these two men—and that murder. Abby slipped in between them, determined to defuse the situation regardless. At least until she could get Dare alone. "If that's all you came for, Detective, you can leave. It's been a long evening on top of an extremely stressful couple of days. Quite honestly, I'm exhausted."

It was the truth.

One that must have made it into her voice because both men backed down. The atmosphere cooled twenty degrees in the moments that followed. Dare dropped his palm to her shoulder as they waited for Pike to leave.

He didn't. He swung his attention to her. "I'm afraid you're right, Ms. Pembroke. There is more."

"How much more?" Dare asked.

Pike looked at him. "From your statement earlier, I'm guessing you know the designer drug that killed Gregory had his DNA worked into the chemical makeup?"

Dare nodded. "In other words, you ran the trace amount of the drug left in that syringe against Van Heusen's DNA."

"That we did."

Was it her imagination or had Dare's fingers tensed? "And?" His voice sure had.

"And it didn't match. But it did match someone else's. Someone standing in this room." To her horror Pike dropped his gaze and stared directly at her. "Ms. Pembroke, I took the initiative and had the lab compare the DNA in the drug against the blood you left on Officer Ryder's handkerchief when he assisted you at the scene. That syringe was meant for you."

Dare braced his forearms against the ledge of the penthouse balcony, staring out into the New York night as he absorbed the harsh truth along with the combined emotional essence of over eight million people.

He needed help.

Desperately.

For the first time in his life he regretted sealing himself off from the city, slipping out into the streets and the overwhelming throng of society only when it was absolutely necessary—and even then, only at Charlotte's dogged insistence. It was ironic. He'd spent the past decade attempting to ease the heartache of others when he could, and yet, but for that one time, he'd never had the courage to offer up his own. Abby was wrong. He wasn't worthy of her admiration. He deserved her disgust.

Because he was a coward.

If he hadn't been so damned terrified of being ostracized yet again, he would have sought out others like him long ago. Others he could no longer pretend weren't there. His father might have no knowledge of their existence, but now that Dare had truly and completely opened his heart, he could *feel* them. Unfortunately, not one soul was close enough for his receptors to lock on to his or her core, to provide him with a directional beacon of sorts. The essence was simply too weak, the overwhelming crush of the city below, too strong. And worse, even though he now believed those others were searching for him as well—that they had been searching for him since the unearthly cry had woken him in the middle of the night all those weeks ago—Dare also knew it might well be too late.

For Abby.

That bombshell Pike had delivered in her dressing room earlier in the evening proved it. Dare pulled his right hand from the balcony railing and reached into his trouser pocket, withdrawing the plastic bag containing the odd pastoral postcard Abby had given him. It seemed Abby didn't trust Pike any more than he did. She'd waited until the detective had finished transcribing her description of the man who'd shown up at her apartment passing himself off as Detective Hook, then asked Pike to leave. Only then did she confide that someone had sent her flowers before her solo performance—along with a chilling note. Given her history with his mother, she'd assumed Van Heusen had sent it.

Dare flipped the plastic bag over and studied the other note, the one that had been mailed to him. He returned to study Abby's once more. Though both notes were anonymous, this note was handwritten. And more ominous in light of those DNA results: *I have more of what you need.*

There was a number scrawled beneath.

Unlike Abby, Dare had called it.

It was already out of service.

Even more ominous. Did whoever was behind the attempted druggings no longer need her? Better yet, why had she been targeted in the first place? Because of her artistic connections to the rich and powerful?

Or to get to him?

Dare flipped the bag over once more and studied the typed warning on his own missive: *He who seeks to destroy your heart, also seeks you.* He could no longer deny the underlying truth to the statement. Abby was his heart. But why seek them both, dammit? And why sketch that triquetra on the reverse?

To ensure his attention? To confirm that his instincts were correct—that there were at least two others like him? Perhaps even siblings long lost as he suspected?

Or, as he was also beginning to suspect, to warn him that those others had been targeted, as well?

If so, why not come out and say it?

Call him. Visit him. Hell, summon him to the far ends of the earth if need be. But give him more than questions.

He needed *answers.*

It was the only way he would be able to protect Abby. Instead, all he had at his disposal was Pike, a detective whose vendetta prevented him from being completely honest and forthright—though even Pike had admitted he now believed Dare wasn't involved in the assault on Van Heusen and his driver—and an FBI agent who'd yet to return his calls. Dare didn't care if the agent was currently working a critical case. If the agent didn't contact him soon, he would use every resource he possessed to hunt the man down himself.

Dare shoved the notes back into his pocket and stiffened. *Abby.*

He felt the sudden jolt of apprehension take hold of her. Within seconds, it had spread; grown to outright terror. By the time he felt the scream gathering at the base of her throat, he had already hooked his bare feet over the side of the balcony and scaled his way to the faux balustrade at the eighteenth floor. He was three rows of whitewashed bricks from her window when she stiffened.

Woke.

And he relaxed.

Still, he hung there, clinging to the weathered crevices between the bricks, waiting. He needed to make sure she was truly okay. Several more moments passed until he felt her stir. Rise. The connection between them had grown so strong these past few days, the intensity of her emotions running so high, he swore he could feel her swing her feet to the floor and pad barefoot across her bedroom and down the hall. He didn't need his sense to know where she was headed. Her music room. Another minute passed and he could feel Abby applying rosin to her bow, retrieving her violin and beginning to play. But the piece she chose was not the usual haunting fare of these past two weeks, nor was it even remotely harmonious. The refrain was jarring and disjointed, an outward reflection of the chaos and confusion roiling inside her. Overwhelming her.

*Damn.*

He should have followed his instincts and brought her upstairs for the night. He'd wanted to. But before he could offer, she'd told him she needed to call her brother and fill her friends in. And then she needed sleep.

He'd agreed. Only it was clear now that she hadn't gotten nearly enough. Nor was she likely to. Given the torment in her music, in her soul, neither would he.

He should go to her.

He would have to be careful, though. For not only was he a coward, he'd also discovered that around Abby he was unnervingly weak. Take that near kiss—their second in two days. If Pike hadn't interrupted this last one, he had no idea where it would have led. But he knew where he wanted it to lead. Like most men, he was no innocent. And like many men, he had made a habit out of seeking women who were interested in nothing more than sheer physical release—though for a different reason. Lately, he'd become consumed by the thought of what it would be like not just to have sex, but to truly make love to a woman. To Abby.

God help him, he knew she had begun thinking the same thing about him.

But even if she could get past his curse, how would he ever be able to reconcile his limits with her gift?

He'd deliberately scaled their building shortly before he'd headed downstairs to collect her for the concert in hopes the climb would buffer the worst of the roiling emotions within that hall, and it had. Unfortunately, the surcease hadn't lasted nearly long enough. He'd barely made it to intermission. From there, the concert was a blur. He must have made it to her dressing room, because that was where he was when her touch woke him. He wasn't sure what stunned him more—that he'd made it that far in his condition, or that one touch from Abby had been enough to bring him around.

When he felt her lower the violin and brush back the tears, he knew he desperately needed to restore her equilibrium. He had to go to her. Give her the comfort *she* now needed.

But would he be welcome?

He scaled the last of the bricks separating them and reached for her window. Her bedroom was dark.

But the window was unlocked.

Relief washed through him as he eased the pane up. He slipped inside her room, then closed the window as she began another more harmonious piece. He followed the music out of her room and down the hall, hoping she wouldn't see his presence as a violation as he stopped at the doorway to her darkened studio. She stood with her back to him, in front of the panoramic window, plying her violin against the velvet curtain of night, shimmering with the scattered jewels of the city's lights. She wore a simple dark blue T-shirt, cropped to her waist with a pair of subdued drawstring sleep pants that hung far too low against her hips for his peace of mind. Especially given the waterfall of unruly curls spilling down her back, offering a tantalizing glimpse of skin as she swayed in time with this new, soothing piece.

He'd never been much for outward features. He preferred to see a woman in the context of what lay within.

But here? Now?

With Abby?

He was becoming obsessed with the thought of what she would look like with nothing but those dark tresses splayed out beneath her smooth, ivory curves…and his coarser, darker body easing in. She must have read his thoughts.

At the very least, felt his presence.

The melody faded. She lowered her bow but didn't turn. Her husky murmur filled the room instead. "I thought you planted that ape outside my door so you could sleep."

He nodded. "I did."

"You're not sleeping."

"Neither are you."

"No." He felt her bittersweet smile, her sigh. "I'm not." She turned to the stool, scrubbing the tears from her cheeks with the back of her bow hand as he entered the room. She retrieved a cloth from the open case and methodically wiped the violin down, then tucked the instrument in its case. She wiped the bow next, then put it and the cloth to bed, as well.

That left them.

She turned, dropping her hands to her sides as she leaned back against the window. Her ragged sigh filled the shadows as she curled her fingers beneath the sill. "I should have taken it." She couldn't be referring to the money Katherine had given her, because she still regretted that.

"It?"

She shrugged. "Marlena offered us a ride. Right before we left the theatre. I should have taken it."

Even from here, the emotions flowed in. The doubt and the regret. The guilt. The latter belonging to him more than her.

"What happened to your brother is not your fault. You have to know that. Because it's true."

She shook her head. "You don't understand. I knew something was wrong, even before I saw that knife. I know it sounds crazy, but I *felt* it."

He stepped forward, drawn in by the ache in her heart. Her confusion. How did he say this? "Abby, it isn't crazy. Most people get those feelings—and most people ignore them." He ought to know. He hadn't felt the malevolence in that man; he'd been reacting to her instincts at the time.

"So why didn't I listen?"

He risked another step. "Because you're normal. Innately hopeful." Amazingly, beautifully so.

She wiped the fresh tears that began to trickle down her cheeks. "Really? So why do I have the feeling that you would have listened?"

"Abby—"

"Wouldn't you?"

He couldn't lie. Lord knew, there were too many falsehoods between them as it was. He sighed. "Yes. I would have listened."

He had.

That was what had saved her—from that thug and that van. But he couldn't have done it on his own. He'd been too screwed up that night as he'd staggered out of the concert hall.

She scrubbed her cheeks again. "I wish I was more like you. Maybe then I wouldn't be in this mess. My brother wouldn't be in this mess."

"It will get better, I promise. Brian will get better."

"Really?" His heart tore as she took yet another futile swipe at the tears. "And what am I supposed to do until then? Dammit, I don't even know why someone is after me." She stabbed a finger toward the open case. "I play the violin for crying out loud. I'm not designing some top-secret military system. What if whoever tried to drug me does it again—and succeeds? What happens to Brian then? Hell, even if we do figure this out, how long can I isolate him from the world? And what happens when Brian does remember? Will the shock send him over the edge? Even if it doesn't, will he understand why I lied to him? Will he forgive me? And what if—" His heart nearly split in two as she paused to drag her air in deep, along with the full measure of her terror. "What if, despite your guards, that monster gets to him first?"

Dare could not just stand there and do nothing. He stepped all the way in, reached out and smoothed his fingers down her face, erasing the tears she'd missed. Absorbing the panic, but leaving the rest. A moment passed, then two as she calmed down. And then her soft sigh washed into the shadows.

"How do you do that?"

He jerked his hand away—but she grabbed it. She brought his fingers back to her cheek, threaded hers among them. "It's okay. It's just that you touch me and it's like…I still feel it, but it's not as scary anymore. It's you, isn't it?"

Yes. But it was also them.

He knew the difference. He could feel the difference.

He could feel her.

As much as he was willing to accept from others, they never absorbed anything of him in return. She did. Somehow she was able to diffuse the darkness and the demons that simmered within, plaguing him. As if he found balance in her light. Especially here in the heady shadows.

"Dare?"

"Hmm?"

"Do you think I should have given the note to Pike?"

"No…and yes."

He felt rather than saw her lips quirk. "Now, there's a definitive answer if I ever heard one."

She was right.

He chuckled. "I apologize. I'm afraid I know the good detective too well to offer a more solid opinion, especially an unbiased one."

Silence crowded between them. Thickening the shadows.

But she didn't ask. She was right about one thing. She was patient. Dangerously so.

He sighed. "I left another message with the FBI agent. According to his voice mail, he's tied up on another case. We'll give him until tomorrow afternoon. If he calls, we'll offer the note to him first." His note, as well. Though he wouldn't offer an explanation regarding the triquetra beyond the fact that he had one tattooed on his chest.

"What if he doesn't call?"

Dare shrugged. "Then I'll have to stop by my father's again. See if he can't recommend another agent."

Not his preferred choice of action.

But she nodded. "Okay." She released his hand, then used her fingers to push the bulk of her hair past her shoulders.

He wished she hadn't.

Standing in the dark as they were, with the city lights glowing behind her, he could make out the enchanting curves of her breasts clearly. For once his reaction was based solidly in the physical—and it didn't help his concentration.

She dropped her hands to the sill and sighed. "Who knows? Maybe something good will come from all this."

He blinked.

"You and your dad. You guys are talking again."

Dare couldn't help it, he laughed. "I doubt that. No one talks to Victor Sabura. Victor talks. Everyone else listens. And I stopped doing that a long time ago."

"Why?"

He turned then and stepped up to the stool she'd placed near the window. One of his sleeves loosened as he reached out to trail his finger down the violin's satin finish.

"Dare?"

He kept his stare on the violin as he rerolled his sleeves, stopping below his elbows. He should probably button the shirt and tuck the tail in, but he was comfortable and she didn't seem to mind. Nothing left to do to stall, he turned and faced her, grateful for the dark. "Victor isn't my father. Not really." Not in the ways that counted.

"Then…the rumors in that magazine are true?"

"Which one would that be?" He didn't know why he pushed it. He didn't need to hear her voice it. He'd lived it long enough to understand her hesitation. Like most societies, the majority of New York's upper crust was sanctimonious as hell. But Abby wasn't. "I take it you're referring to the one that concerns my mother. The speculation that she'd had an affair around thirty years ago, an affair I'm reputed to be the untimely offspring off."

"Are you?"

He shrugged. "I have no idea. But it doesn't matter. The irony of it is that Miranda wasn't my mother either. I discovered that yesterday, too."

Once again, silence settled into the shadows.

He felt her form the words half a dozen times before she finally forced them out. "Then you're adopted."

"Hmm. In a way."

"In a way?" She straightened against the window. "I'm afraid I don't understand."

"Neither do I. Victor was a bit sketchy on the details, evidently because my mother had been sketchy decades before. He did tell me they were having problems in their marriage. Some of those problems involved fertility. Miranda reacted the way a woman of her unlimited means and inclination could."

"And how was that?"

"Some women purchase puppies. She purchased a son."

Abby gasped.

He shrugged. "In her defense, she did it to try and save her marriage. But the marriage was doomed anyway. Miranda only married Victor because her father forbade it. She soon learned firsthand why."

He didn't need to see Abby stiffen against the window to feel her shock. Suspicion followed. Given what she'd learned about how he and Charlotte filled their days, he supposed it wasn't out of order either. "Dare, your father didn't abuse your mother, did he?"

"No. Not physically. He had his unique brand of abuse, centering around the Expectations of Victor."

"And if you didn't live up to those expectations?"

"You heard about it. Day in and day out. Week after week until he wore you down or you got out."

"So you got out. That's why you went to boarding school." He nodded.

"But your mother couldn't leave...or wouldn't."

"Correct."

"That must have been hard for you, growing up like that. I mean, in my house things were pretty tight financially, especially after my mom was diagnosed with breast cancer. After that the bank owned more of my dad's store than he did. But I was encouraged to follow my dreams. So was Brian. Sure, we stumbled a bit. Made a lot of mistakes, too—especially me. But there was always plenty of love and forgiveness to go around. And there was always Brian. You haven't exactly seen my brother at his best so you'll have to take my word for it, but Brian can make anyone smile."

He felt her own smile blossom from within.

He cherished the gift more than he normally would have because until that moment, he hadn't realized he'd never actually seen his mother smile. Not a real smile.

Nor did he remember feeling it.

Just that polite mask. That stark void beneath.

A void she'd desperately tried to flood with alcohol.

He heard Abby's approach as the inevitable melancholy leached in. Felt her essence grow stronger, closer. But it wasn't until she reached out to cover his hand that he also realized he'd been absently rubbing his tattoo.

"You're upset."

He shook his head. "Not really." More regretful and resigned. "Let's just say it explains a lot."

When he didn't add more, she released his hand and turned to the stool. She smoothed the cloth over the violin again and closed the case, returning it to the trunk he'd noticed several feet away. She locked the trunk and returned to his side. "You're going to look for your birth mother, aren't you? Find out if you have any brothers or sisters."

Though he'd only made the decision minutes before he'd climbed down his balcony to come here, he didn't mind sharing it with her. "Yes."

"Good. I think you should."

"I'm glad you approve. Unfortunately, there's a good chance I won't be successful."

"Surely with your money and connections—"

"*Miranda's* money. My trust came from her, with a mere stipend diverted to Victor. The same money she used to ensure that no records survived."

"You can do it."

Again that heady faith. It was more addictive than the adrenaline he'd used to buffer himself from the world. But a few moments later, her faith gave way to curiosity and apprehension and he asked, "You want to know about the other rumor, don't you?" The more lurid one.

She shook her head. "No. It's—"

He took her hand, welcoming the essence that came with

it. "It's okay. I've read the magazine. I know what the article says. Part of it's true."

"Which part?"

He lowered himself to the stool, drawing her hand with him and settling it on his thigh so she would know her touch was welcome. "Yes, my mother was struck by a subway train and killed instantly. As to the rest—namely, was there alcohol in her system? Yes, to that, too. But was it because she was a drunk, as my father claimed, or had she simply swallowed the necessary courage? An interesting question." One that had haunted him for years.

As had the setting and the timing.

His mother had headed down into that subway station three days after Janet's murder, two days after he'd discovered his roiling emotions had spilled over into Miranda that fateful night. His mother had sensed his terror and his horror. Only, she hadn't wanted to accept it. Not the emotions, or the knowledge of Dare's power; he could feel from anyone and everyone if he tried.

Why was a woman who never went anywhere without her driver suddenly alone on a crowded, rush-hour subway platform? Or was his mother really there hoping to use those people and their emotions to obscure the connection she'd learned she shared with him? A connection she didn't want.

Dare swallowed the doubts.

It didn't help.

He still choked on the guilt. And his voice still came out raw, hoarse. "After Randall murdered his wife, I went to see my mother. I asked her to stop drinking. I begged her. I even told her in no uncertain terms what her pain had done—was still doing—to me. That was the last time we spoke. The next day she was dead. Did she slip or did she jump? I just don't know." He never would.

He felt Abby's warm, gentle fingers on his cheek. On the

scar that had started it all. "What happened with your mom…is that why you've shut yourself off from everyone except for Charlotte and those who help you both?"

"That's part of it."

A large part.

She threaded her fingers into his hair. "And what about me? Is it why you're so afraid of me? Us?"

He sucked in his breath, gripped it tight.

Gripped the truth even tighter.

Her fingers slipped over his jaw and trailed down his chest. She tucked them beneath the open edges of his shirt and traced his tattoo. "It's okay. You don't have to answer. You will when you're ready." She turned in his arms and leaned back into him, settling her head over his heart.

He knew it was for the best.

But the urge to unburden the worst was still there.

He strangled it for now, gently combing his fingers through Abby's hair instead, using the slow, soothing motion along with their physical contact to help draw her into the restful sleep she would need to face the following day. He already knew where he planned on taking her. Somewhere where whoever was after them would be forced to stand out—whether the bastard wanted to or not.

It was the only way.

He had to end this. To keep her safe, yes. But also because he was finally ready to tell her the rest. He had to risk it. He had to see if they could make this—them—work.

He watched Abby's eyelashes sink lower and lower as he continued to comb her curls with his fingers, felt her slip deep into sleep as her slender weight eased into his. When he was sure she wouldn't wake, he bent down and lifted her in his arms, carrying her out of the music room, down the hall and into her bedroom before he changed his mind. Fortunately, her bedcovers were already pushed to the side. He settled her head on her pillow and smoothed the ivory comforter up to her chin, then pressed a light, selfish kiss to her lips.

Then he turned to leave the way he'd come.

But as he slipped out into the night and raised the window, he caught her soft, heartfelt whisper.

"Please, don't fall."

Unfortunately, it was too late. He already had. He was utterly and completely in love with her.

## Chapter 9

Abby forced the butterflies in her belly to still as she craned her neck to take in the massive slab of quartzite stretching up into the midmorning sky. Though Dare had sworn the cliff was barely sixty feet high, it might as well be six hundred—at least to her. Because as soon as Dare finished anchoring the woefully slender rope attached to her waist to the makeshift pulley he was currently rigging between two trees at the top of that cliff, *she'd* be scaling it. The fact that she was still standing here, waiting, meant she was either insane or she'd fallen head over heels for this guy.

While the latter thought didn't give Abby pause, she did pray it was the only falling she'd be doing today.

When Dare had shown up at her apartment this morning at the ungodly hour of six, wanting to know if she was interested in accompanying him on a trip a half hour north of the city to visit the Shawangunk Mountains and check out a potential first top-roping site for a fellow climber's kid, she'd jumped at the chance—but only if Dare would agree to give *her* a first lesson in climbing while they were at it.

Dare had been stunned. Heck, with her aversion to heights, she'd been stunned, too. Despite the butterflies still crowding into her belly, she did want to do this. She needed to. More than anything, she wanted to know what it was about scaling a thousand feet of sheer rock that made Dare come back to do it again and again—without the benefit of the very length of nylon he'd insisted she use.

Was it really just for the adrenaline?

Or was it more?

As much as she'd learned about this man over the past few days, Abby suspected it was the latter. She was also pretty sure it had something to do with the fact that there was no one around for miles. At least, no one they could see. Just winding trails, stark cliffs and lush trees filled with the soothing symphony of chirping birds. The scenic drive into the Gunks had done them both good. She hadn't had a flashback to that horrible knifing since they'd left the city.

Even more amazing, Atlas had lost his globe.

She wasn't exactly sure when it had happened, but she definitely remembered the moment she'd looked across the front seat of Dare's SUV and realized that for the first time since they'd met, Dare was completely relaxed...until he'd caught her eye, reached across the armrests and taken her hand. Within seconds his contentment had faded, and her pulse had quickened as she felt another emotion sear into its place.

Desire.

She'd known then that not only did Dare want her, he also wanted a *them*. Everything about this trip confirmed it. That he was willing to bring her here, to let her inside his private world, inside the real him, meant more to her than any amount of money Katherine or anyone else could shower on her. Startlingly, it even meant more than soloing with the New York

Philharmonic at the ripe old age of fifteen...and at twenty-four. Yeah, she'd definitely fallen for the guy—right there in her music room, no less. How could she not, knowing the horror he'd gone through as a boy—and knowing the man he'd managed to become despite that horror? After Dare's kiss had roused her the night before, she'd lain in bed awake for some time thinking about it. Thinking about him. Wondering and worrying.

Not that Dare would fall off their building and injure himself. Despite his nickname, he was much too cautious. She'd seen evidence of that all morning. No, she was more concerned with the other, more painful blows Dare had suffered, those inner scars she'd sensed from the beginning. Not so much from Randall's vile deeds, as from his parents' rejection. Dare hadn't needed to repeat the details for her to recognize the depth of his pain. She'd seen it in the shadows of his eyes.

Worse, she felt it in the desperate, desolate shadows still cloaking his heart.

It was a testimony to Dare's strength that he'd survived at all. But he *had* survived. He'd also gone on to devote his time and resources to those who truly needed it. Pike was wrong. She might not have known Dare long, but she did know him better than any other man she'd ever met. The best part was, she liked what she knew. She only wished she could introduce him to Brian. She'd give anything for them to get to know each other. And if she was lucky—

What the—

Panic surged as Abby swung around, only to flee just as rapidly as several small rocks—not Dare—skittered down the side of the cliff. Unfortunately, the panic snapped back, this time with a vengeance, as she spotted Dare standing precariously close to the leading edge of the cliff, loosely coiling the second half of the rope already attached to the safety harness he'd purchased for her on the way here.

"Heads up, Abby!"

She stepped away from the base of the cliff as Dare tossed the rope over the side. The rope played out down the quartzite slab, a healthy excess pooling near her feet. She craned her neck as Dare turned to double-check the makeshift pulley. Despite the distance separating them, she could make out his breathtaking shoulders and broad, tapered back. She savored the sight.

When Dare had removed his shirt earlier, she'd been surprised, especially given that he still hadn't discussed his tattoo. Her curiosity had quickly evaporated beneath a healthy dose of lust as Dare shouldered her rope and scaled the cliff. That same lust returned now as he made his way back down the wall of rock in a mesmerizing ballet of confident hand-and footholds and religiously honed muscle.

By the time Dare made it to the halfway point, a sheen of sweat glistened along his dusky skin, causing a warm ache to spread through Abby's core. Mercy, he was gorgeous. Dare reached the base and turned. The moment his gaze engulfed her, she knew he knew what she'd been thinking.

His lopsided smile quirked and spread.

Her breath hitched.

"You ready?"

Was she ever!

He held out his hand, and her lust fled as the apprehension snapped back in. She'd made the mistake of looking beyond those strong, callused fingers to that imposing wall of rock. Suddenly, the enormity of what she was about to do bit in.

"Abby?"

She located her best stage smile and stitched it on as she marched forward. "I'm ready."

Liar.

He knew it, too. Dare reached out and tucked a stray wisp into her braid as she reached his side. He tipped her chin, her breath catching once more as he soothed his thumb along her bottom lip. "You don't have to do this."

"I know. I want to. It's just—"

How did she say this?

He dropped his hand to her shoulder and squeezed gently. "Abby, if you're worried about embarrassing yourself, don't. You can't. Not in front of me."

"Oh, yeah? You're the great Triple Dare. You climb buildings and cliffs at the drop of a hat. I bet you lift weights, too. Me, I wield a bow."

He tapped her nose as he smiled. "And a mean bow it is. But it won't matter. You'll be able to handle this one, I promise. It's a five-point-five at best." Her confusion must have shown because his smile deepened. "Barely a bunny slope, just uphill."

"Nice analogy, but, um, I don't ski so well either. Lousy stamina, questionable balance." Zero nerve.

He shook his head. "With legs like yours, I don't believe it." She shivered as he dropped his hand to hem of her shorts, trailing his fingers down her thighs to underscore his point. The ache in her belly simmered anew.

Disappointment replaced it as his hand fell away.

He cleared his throat. "Perhaps we should get started."

*Pity.* She'd rather stand right here. Like this. It was safer in all the right ways.

And deliciously dangerous.

Unfortunately, he was still holding back. Ironically, today's reluctance was from an entirely different source than last night's. Dare might be more relaxed than she'd ever seen him, but he was also on the alert. He had been since the moment they'd left his Blazer in the parking lot. The man was doing his darnedest to pretend this was all some lighthearted excursion, a "let's-get-to-know-each-other-better" date.

As late as yesterday, she might have bought it. Today, she knew better. She'd gotten to know *him* better.

Though she'd yet to figure out what was behind the darkest of his moods, she could already read the majority of them. While she doubted anyone could have followed them all the way here, she had no intention of adding to Dare's worries. She stared up the cliff, automatically searching for the various hand- and footholds Dare had discussed during the down-and-dirty lesson she'd received upon their arrival, pleased she could actually plot out her initial moves. She'd just have to trust the other holds would be there when *she* got there.

She stepped up to the base of the cliff. "Well, are we going to do this, or what?"

He nodded. "Would you like a boost?"

"Definitely."

She waited patiently as Dare checked her climbing harness one last time, before retrieving his end of the belaying rope he'd rigged in case she lost her grip. She shoved the terrifying thought aside. If Dare was a climber, then she needed to share his interests, or at least understand them. By the time he tucked the top rope beneath his arm, then bent down in front of her, her resolve had solidified. She placed the right sole of her new climbing shoes into his hands, using his strength to propel her up the face of the cliff and to her first handful of rock. The quartzite was warmer than she'd expected, no doubt from the sun already beginning to bake the late-morning air.

"Got it?"

"Uh-huh." She instinctively fitted her left foot into a crevice, then her right, pleased when Dare's hands fell away from her legs—and she didn't fall from the rock. The next several moves went as smoothly as her first, though she had to pause to push the belaying rope out of her way twice. The moment she did, Dare returned the light tension he'd been maintaining for her peace of mind. He was right. The constant tug did help her confidence and hence, her concentration.

"That's it. You're doing great! Keep going, Abby."

She reached and strained in unison with the encouragement Dare continued to offer from below. Before she knew it, she'd covered a good ten feet of the cliff and was enjoying every moment of it. It was hard work, sure. And she was well into a decent sweat, but there was an incredible satisfaction in reaching and achieving each successive hold. Another five minutes and she'd gotten so far into it, she made the mistake of looking down.

Her stomach clenched.

As if on cue, Dare increased the tension on the belaying line. "You're okay. Take a deep breath. It'll pass."

The terror didn't exactly leave, but she did screw up enough courage to jerk her head back up so she could search for her next handhold. She found it—and reached for it. Then another and another. Though fear had forced her to shorten her reach, she was still making progress and gradually settling into a decent rhythm as Dare continued to encourage her from below. Another minute and she reached a narrow protrusion of quartzite that allowed her to take a breather. She gathered her strength and forced herself to continue.

Another minute and another reach and she decided she should have hung out at the micro ledge a bit longer because she was definitely feeling the burn. Her arms had begun to ache, her thighs and calves as well. Her fingers and toes had gotten in on the act as well. Darn near every muscle in her body hurt. By the time she finished her next reach, she wasn't sure she'd be able to manage another.

"Don't stop, now, Abby. You're almost there."

She glanced up. She was. She could make out the top of the cliff, roughly ten, twelve feet up. She spotted her next handhold and reached for it. Made it. Owned it. Energized by the coming victory, she shoved her toes into the next foothold with more force than she should have—and cursed.

Her foot was stuck.

She gave it another tug, then tried slowly twisting her foot. Again, it refused to budge.

"What's wrong?"

She risked a quick glance down. Another lousy move.

The remains of the breakfast they'd stopped for after Dare had purchased her climbing gear turned over.

"Abby?"

"My foot's stuck!"

"Try twisting it—but gently."

"I did!"

"Okay. Hold on, I'm coming up."

He was *what?*

No! If he climbed up, who would be holding the other end of her rope? She glanced down, forcing herself to ignore the renewed sloshing in her stomach as she frantically searched her field of view for Dare. She couldn't see him. But she could hear him. He continued to call up encouragement as she turned her face into the cliff and dug her fingers into the narrow crevices beneath, clinging for dear life.

A minute passed.

Somewhere into the next, the burning in her arms edged from painful into excruciating. Her arms began to shake. Even with Dare's constantly soothing and steadily closing voice, it was everything she could do to hold on. She closed her eyes, blocking out every other sense other than touch—hearing included—as she dug her sweaty fingers into the crevices as far as they would go. *Please, God, don't let me fall.* She had friends. Responsibilities. A brother.

If she was really lucky, Dare.

Moments later, he reached her side.

She swore she could feel the comforting heat from his body seeping into hers. She even swore she could feel him trying to calm her down on some strange subliminal level, but she refused to listen. She was too scared. Petrified.

Hell, she couldn't even open her eyes. Her lids wouldn't cooperate.

"It's okay, Abby. I'm here. You can let go now."

"No." Sure he'd tucked her in bed twice. But they were on the side of a cliff for crying out loud.

"Honey—"

"No!" She forced her lids to cooperate. Dare's face snapped into view. He was just out of arms' reach, gripping the only other protrusions of rock nearby. As usual, he had no rope. And they were roughly fifty feet up. "Please, I'll get it loose myself. Go down before you fall. Or up. Just *go*."

That dark-emerald stare captured hers across the cliff. His low, steady voice filled her. "Abby, listen to me. I won't fall. Nor will you. But you have to let me help you."

"But the rope—"

"It's secure. I tied it to a tree."

But she could still feel the slack in the line. Couldn't she? Suddenly she wasn't sure. It looked snug, but she was too terrified to loosen her grip to check.

"Sweetheart, you trust me, don't you?"

She jerked a nod.

"Then you have to listen to me. All you have to do is let go of the rock. You'll fall back a few inches, perhaps a foot or two, but that's it. Taking the pressure off your leg might be enough to release your foot. If not, we'll go from there. Either way, you *won't* fall. I promise."

She clipped another nod.

"You ready?"

*No.*

"Yes." She dragged her air in deep and let go. A split second later, she jerked to a stop. But the force of the motion swung her toward Dare. Oh, God, she was going to knock him off the cliff. She pushed against the wall of rock, frantically trying to stop herself. Unfortunately, her efforts sent her colliding directly into the solid muscles of his chest. Dare's arm immediately banded about her.

His husky reassurance washed her ear. "Easy, honey. I've got you." He did. While she'd been busy panicking, Dare had been reaching. He'd caught the belaying rope with one hand, her body with his other. His climbing shoes were firmly hooked to the narrow protrusion of rock she'd rested at several moves earlier. He was in no danger of falling anytime soon.

Thank God.

"How's your foot?"

"It's fine."

He'd guessed correctly. Taking the weight off her leg had done the trick. She was free. Well, not exactly free. Instead of being trapped by rock, she was now trapped by solid muscle. Dare's muscle. Not that she was complaining, mind you. Especially since the remainder of her terror had bled off. Frankly, she couldn't have planned it better if she tried.

Then it hit her. He didn't think she *had* tried, did he?

"Abby?" Her name rumbled between them, low and intimate. Given the fire licking her cheeks, he had to know the answer. She spelled it out anyway.

"I'm fine. I'm just feeling really foolish. I swear I didn't…" The fire increased as she glanced at her dangling feet, then back at them. "You know."

He nodded. "I know."

Relief seeped in. She pulled in her breath along with it and got a lungful of Dare. His scent. His heat. Heavens, did the man smell good! As it had that first night in her apartment, the slight sheen of perspiration that covered his skin enhanced his natural male fragrance. And as she had that first night, she was reacting the same way to it. To him.

She shouldn't be. Not forty feet up.

She blew out her air, attempting to quell the desire. It didn't work. She still wanted him. Here. Now.

Any way he wanted.

She forced a smile of her own, praying he hadn't noticed her body's errant reaction to his. "I probably should have mentioned this earlier. But, um, I'm actually nervous of heights. And when I looked down—"

"You panicked." He shrugged. "Don't worry about it. Happens the first time to almost everyone. Me included."

That broke the spell.

She laughed. "Somehow I doubt you ever shook in your boots." Even now, with one massive hand still clamped about her rope, the other hooked to sheer rock, he looked completely at ease—and it had nothing to do with the added security of that micro ledge.

Dare was simply and completely in his element.

But he shook his head. "What you see is the result of years of practice. You should have seen me my first time. It wasn't pretty. Hell, neither was I." He stopped, appeared to wrestle with something. "Abby, there are a couple of details about my early climbing days that article got wrong. For one, I didn't head out to the Gunks with friends on some wild trip. At least, they weren't friends when we first hooked up."

"I don't understand."

He sighed. "I took off after my mom died. Only I was too messed up to think. I didn't take enough cash. I ended up not far from here. A couple of climbers found me. They fed me and let me hang out at their camp while my face healed. When I was up to it, they also gave me my first taste of bouldering. I was barely twelve feet off the ground and almost there when I looked down. Suddenly, I was so damned scared I couldn't finish. But I couldn't head down either. And they knew better than to endanger themselves with a panicked cherry. Nothing else worked so they started teasing me. Mercilessly. Hell, even then it still took three rounds of downright ribald taunts and dares before I budged."

She blinked. Three? Triple Dare?

He flashed a sheepish grin. "Not exactly the glamour story you expected, eh? Anyway, point is, I was terrified of heights. Deep down, I still am." His smile faded completely. "I guess that's what gives it the extra punch I usually need to…" He trailed off. Once again, she could feel the battle within him to give her the rest.

The truth.

She risked prompting, "What do you need?" For an instant, she swore that damned globe had returned to his shoulders. She could almost feel him bowing beneath the weight, just before he heaved it off.

"The rush. It…helps me forget."

Forget what? His past?

That didn't make sense. Not really. While his childhood held some pretty horrific moments, he'd moved beyond them. She took another chance. "What exactly do you need to forget?"

This time the silence locked in so firmly, she could hear the birds in the distance for the first time since she'd started up the cliff. It lasted so long, she made out the pings of several tiny rocks as they skittered down the side of the cliff as Dare adjusted his foothold on the narrow ledge. He shifted his stare to the wall of quartzite behind her.

"Dare?"

"Everyone."

Of all the answers she'd expected, that hadn't been one of them. Not to mention it made even less sense than his previous confession. But it rang with truth. Abby lowered her own voice to a whisper. She was afraid. More than she'd been when she couldn't dislodge her foot. More than she'd been when she'd seen that monster out beside Stuart's limo.

"Does that—" It wouldn't come out. She opened her mouth again, forcing the question past the knot in her throat. The one in her heart. "Does that include me?"

Dare wrenched his stare from the cliff and fused it to hers. "God, no. Definitely not you. If anything, I—"

He stopped.

She waited. Prayed.

Nothing.

That was when she knew. It *was* her. Somehow, whatever was eating at this man, came down to just her. And no matter how hard Dare tried, he couldn't get past it. Whatever was eating at him hurt like the devil. She was hurting him.

That she couldn't do.

Abby peeled her left hand from the rope and threaded her fingers through the inky waves of his hair, smoothing them from the scar that ran down the side of his face. Tears stung at her eyes as she traced the scar on his bottom lip. But the tears weren't for her. Not even for them. They were for him. "It's okay. I shouldn't have pushed. In addition to being patient, I'm pretty stubborn. Sometimes that's not a good thing, though. Not when it hurts someone I've come to care—"

He jerked his head down before she could finish and covered her mouth with his. She gasped at the shock. And then, she gasped again. This time at the dark, sultry heat that followed. He swallowed both—and came back for more.

He came back for her.

Before her heart could finish pounding out its next beat, the arm about her shoulders banded tighter. He tugged her close, anchoring her against his chest. For a moment she was terrified he'd lose his grip on the rope and the ledge and fall. And then, she couldn't think anymore.

All she could do was feel. Him. His pent-up passion.

It ripped free as he claimed her mouth in a savage, breathtaking assault. He plundered long and hard. Deep. His teeth scraped into hers as he angled his head to take their kiss even deeper. Within seconds he'd delved farther than any man ever had, taken more from her than any man ever would—and still he demanded more. She gave it to him freely, gave herself, reveling in the fiery need in his kiss, the heady danger of having his mouth covering hers while she was fifty feet off the ground and headed straight into the most blissful free fall of all—with him. Just when she thought it couldn't get any better, Dare dragged his mouth from hers, ratcheting up their combined passions as he razed his lips down the column of her neck, stopping at the base to nip, suck and nuzzle the tender hollow he found.

But then he slowed.

She arched her neck in protest, silently begging for more.

She didn't get it.

His ragged breath bathed her throat as he dragged his mouth to her ear, filling her with his voice instead of him. "Abby, I—" She felt him swallow, pull his air in deep. Then he started again. "This isn't a good idea."

Wrong. This was a great idea. The best he'd had all morning. Instead of arguing, she turned her head and answered the need still burning within her. His entire body quaked as she brought her mouth back to his, deliberately trailing the tip of her tongue along the scar on his bottom lip—slowly, sensuously. Soothing, tasting.

He caved in to her brazen invitation with a groan and captured her mouth once more. Three glorious, molten moments followed, and then he tore away. This time he dug his fingers into her shoulder, using the leverage in his arm to wrench her firmly several inches away from him. He held her there as he sealed his mouth to her ear, his ragged breath searing in along with his plea, "Honey, we have to stop. It's too dangerous."

He was right.

She struggled to find her own breath as she nodded. "Okay. Let's get down from here so we can finish."

He shook his head. "That's not what I meant." His breathing slowed, began to even out as he shifted against the rope, the narrow ledge. He pressed his forehead to hers. "We shouldn't be doing this at all. Not out here. It's not safe. I—" He broke off. "Damn. I did not want to do this today. Let alone here." He broke off again, but this time to draw in a deep, steadying breath. "Honey, I know you don't understand, but you will. Soon. It's just…I can't think when we're this close. I can't feel. Not anyone else. Just you and me. Us."

But that was a good thing, right?

Before she could question him, he stiffened. Cursed. Before she realized what had happened, Dare had shoved her into the side of the cliff, covering her body with his. She groaned as her forehead accidentally connected with rock. To her shock, his hand snapped to her mouth, sealed it. Panic blistered in. She was about to jerk away when she heard it.

Saw it.

A mother of a boulder. It was ricocheting down the cliff— straight for them.

Before she could loose her scream, Dare clamped his hand tighter and pushed them both out of the way—straight out from the side of the cliff. Nausea surged as they swung back. But before she smacked into the rock, Dare twisted his entire body, taking the brunt of the impact along his left side as the boulder bounded safely past them. Though she barely heard his terse grunt, she knew the blow had to have hurt like hell, because his arms were trembling.

And his feet were no longer hooked to that narrow protrusion of rock.

She ignored the taut, groaning rope. "Are you—"

"Shh." His harsh whisper slashed through her. "The bastard's still up there."

Bastard? What? Who—

*Good God, no!*

Dare nodded as he released her mouth. She craned her neck instinctively. She could see the upper ledge of the cliff, but that was it. She couldn't hear anything either, not even the birds. Was that it? Was the eerie silence telling him something? That she could understand. But how could he possibly know someone was up there? The boulder could have been knocked loose from a higher level up the stepped side of the quartzite wall. And then she heard them.

Footfalls.

Terror grabbed her as the rhythmic thumps drew closer, breaking just above the distant rustle of leaves. Memories of the other night crashed in. Her brother getting smashed into the limo's window. That gleaming knife. The scarlet puddle Officer Ryder had escorted her past. That poor driver's glassy stare. She shuddered even as Dare finally relaxed.

"It's okay. He's gone. He must have wanted it to look like an accident."

*Because he didn't cut the rope.*

Dare didn't say it. He didn't have to.

The knife slashed into her brain once more and this time it refused to leave. What if Dare was wrong? What if that monster hadn't left? What if he was lying in wait, just as he had with Stuart, lulling them into a false sense of security so they'd come up? By the time Dare cleared the ledge that knife would be slicing in.

"Honey? Did you hear me? You can relax. I need you to let go of me so I can climb up—"

"No!" She grabbed Dare's arm, digging her fingers into his bicep as she buried her face into his chest. "Don't."

That bastard had already killed one man because of her, and Stuart, she knew because Dare had called the hospital before they left, was still hanging by a thread. She couldn't let anything happen to Dare. She wouldn't. Even if that monster didn't have a knife, he could have another boulder handy. What if Dare let go of her and the rope and it came crashing down?

"Please, don't go."

"Hey, now. It's okay, I promise. He's gone."

She swore she could feel Dare pleading with her silently as well, trying to soothe her. She ignored it. She ignored him.

She had to.

"Sweetheart, please. You have to let me go. I'll climb up, then pull you up. It'll be quicker."

She shook her head and clung harder.

"Abby, look at me." His tone brooked no argument.

She obeyed.

"The man is gone."

She shook her head. "You can't know that—"

"Yes, I can. I do. You have to trust me."

She wanted to. But how could she?

To her horror, Dare tightened his grip on the rope with one hand, then reached behind his back with his other to peel her arm from his torso. But instead of letting go, he tugged her palm to his chest and sealed it directly over his tattoo.

His heart.

"Honey, I'm certain he's gone…because I can't feel him anymore."

Zeno eased up on the gas of his rent-a-wreck Jeep, allowing the Blazer to ease completely out of sight. There was no need to speed up. He'd only risk exposing himself, especially since he knew exactly where his mark was headed.

Sending a boulder down the cliff had been a lousy idea.

Thankfully, it hadn't been his.

But this new plan? Hell, he'd even called the boss and run it past him, just in case. The boss had agreed. It was perfect. Guaranteed to split up the lovebirds. Then he'd get to drag out ol' Sally and go to town on one he'd been given permission to kill. And leave the other for the boss.

# Chapter 10

He should have told her when he had the chance.

Dare braced his forearms against the balustrade of his balcony and stared down at the city through the lengthening shadows of late afternoon. He didn't need to turn around to know Abby still lay on his bed in too deep a sleep to turn from the position he'd placed her in four hours ago.

He was still kicking himself over that sin, too.

It had started out innocently enough. After all, the time might have come for him to bare his soul, but the Gunks sure as heck weren't the place. Not given the situation they'd been in at the time. Even after he'd managed to extricate himself from Abby's terrified arms so he could scale the cliff and pull her up, he still had other priorities. Namely, her safety. While he hadn't sensed the bastard, he was also reluctant to stake Abby's life on his suddenly intermittent curse. It had failed him too many times around her for him to risk it.

So he'd lied.

A lie by omission, true. But a lie just the same.

Namely, he hadn't corrected Abby when she'd assumed he was relying on some highly honed outdoorsman's sense. And then he'd deliberately held her hand all the way to the car. Yes, he'd done it to steady her shaking footing as well as to ease her fears. But he'd also taken advantage of the contact to suggest to her over and over that she shouldn't fight the natural exhaustion that followed a massive flood of adrenaline. By the time they'd reached the interstate, she was all but snoring softly against his side in the front seat of his Blazer. A quick call to Jerry as they reached the city and he hadn't needed to wake her to bring her inside the Tristan. The doorman had left the service elevator unlocked enough times in the past for him and Charlotte. No one had seen him carry Abby into the lift at the rear of the parking garage. From there, it had been a straight shot into his apartment.

He'd never even considered leaving Abby at hers.

After that boulder incident, he had no intention of leaving her alone again. Not even if she walked out on him. He might not be sure how he'd manage that, but he would. Either way, he sure as hell wouldn't be kissing her again until this was over.

That kiss.

He was still trying to absorb it. Kissing Abby had been all he'd known it would be and more. It was the *more* that scared the hell out of him. He'd known that by climbing even that short a cliff, his sense would be dulled, but since there were no throngs of city-goers around to further mask an intruder's presence, he hadn't been worried. He should have been—but for a completely different reason. That kiss. For a moment there, his essence had merged with hers so completely, he'd forgotten where they were. What they'd been doing. Worst of all, he'd forgotten about the looming threat. He could have easily gotten Abby killed for the sake of one passionate encounter, however mind-blowing that encounter had been.

There would be others, dammit. He had to believe that. But only if he kept his distance long enough. Only then could he keep her safe.

He had to tell her. There was no other way.

Abby had to know who he really was. *What* he was. Most of all, she had to understand what she was capable of doing to him. Perhaps then she'd understand that he didn't want to distance himself from her, he had to.

Just do it. Wake her. Tell her. It was the only way.

His resolve strengthened, Dare pushed off the balcony and turned his back on the city, taking in Abby's slender form as he reached the French doors leading to his bedroom. He nudged the doors open, drawing her essence in freely as he entered the room. She lay on her side, curled into his dark gray pillow, the silken rope of her hair tangled in her hands. He stopped beside her shoulders to extricate the braid and tuck it behind her back, taken as always by her serene beauty as she slept. Unable to stop himself, he drew his gaze to the bow of her lips, mesmerized by the sound of her breath washing in and out. In many ways the gentle rhythm mimicked the cleansing effect she had over his soul whenever she was this near.

And when he touched her?

Dare clenched his fingers against memory, lest he cave in to the urge to renew that sweetest of sensations again. Here. Now. He slipped his gaze down the lithe curves of her body, struck with how fragile she truly was. It was easy to overlook, given the steady strength of her spirit. He could only hope that spirit was as forgiving and accepting as he prayed. Dare opened his mouth to rouse her and find out—and froze.

Someone was near.

A man. One whose essence he'd never met before. He couldn't be sure of much more, due to the distance as well as to the oversized pictures he'd hung along the walls of his living room—specifically for the glass that covered them. Whoever the man was, he was still in the main elevator, approaching Abby's floor. Why hadn't Jerry buzzed up a warning? Unfortunately, there was no time to find out. Dare turned away from the bed, heading down the hall and out into the living room as the lift violated the buffer he'd established on the nineteenth floor. By the time the elevator reached the penthouse level, Dare had reached his apartment door. He still had no idea who was on the other side, but he did know the man wasn't seeking Abby.

His uninvited and unannounced guest was seeking *him.*

Dare opened the door a split second before the bell chimed. Feigned surprise filled his guest's dark-brown gaze—but not his aura as the man pulled his oversized paw from the buzzer. Dare sketched a smile he didn't feel as he stared up into a set of dark, clipped features that were a dead-on match for the description Abby had given Pike the day before.

"Detective Hook, I presume…or not."

The guy flushed. An intriguing sight, given the man had a good two inches on him. He nodded. "Good evening, Mr. Sabura. I apologize if I've caught you at an inconvenient time. By the way, don't bother firing your doorman. I badged my way up." The man withdrew a black bifold wallet from the inner pocket of his suit jacket and passed it over.

Dare swallowed a curse as he studied the credentials within. It appeared the one man he'd been trying to reach on the phone these past two days had deigned to pay him a visit…*after* scaring the hell out of Abby. He tossed the badge back. "Special Agent Brooks, I'm sure you're aware there's penalty for impersonating a New York City detective, even for a member of the FBI. And then there's that pesky offense called theft." The cognac glasses, the magazine. The flicker of guilt Dare felt proved Brooks had taken them—without a warrant.

The agent returned his nod with a cool clip of his own. "I'm aware of the penalties. Just as I'm sure you're aware that, while what you do for a living isn't technically illegal, some of the ways you and your associate accomplish your goals are…questionable at best."

Touché.

"So, where do we go from here, Agent Brooks?"

"Your living room?"

Not his preferred option.

The man might not be after Abby, but she was still asleep in his bedroom. She'd suffered another serious shock this morning. He didn't need her waking and finding this gorilla in his home, especially when he'd yet to get a decent read on the agent's intent. On the other hand, according to his father's sources with the New York police, Brooks was reputed to be the one man who might be able to provide him with information concerning that designer drug as well as the thug who'd attempted to inject it into Abby. The need to protect her drove Dare into his own apartment. He swept his hand toward his dark-brown leather couch set and glass coffee table.

"Have a seat."

"Thanks. I'll stand." But Brooks did enter.

He took his time, however, openly casing the entranceway and beyond as he walked the perimeter of the sparsely decorated living room in a subdued stroll more suited to a Sunday in the park—or a deserted museum. Brooks paused to study the five-foot-tall-by-three-foot-wide, black-and-white blow-up of the photo Dare had taken of the Limestone Pinnacles outside Guilin, China, three years ago, then moved on to an equally oversized shot of the haunting cliffs that framed the entrance to Norway's Sognafjorden. The man passed a five-by-five-foot landscape of Victoria Falls taken from a Zambian vantage, before coming to a complete halt in front of the panoramic shot resting at the edge of the cream carpet, propped up against the wall. Figures. Dare had decided to rotate that particular photo back into his collection three days before, but hadn't yet gotten around to hanging it.

Dare waited none too patiently as Brooks hefted the over-sized frame, appearing to admire the snowy peak command-ing center view as the guy turned to face him. That dark, razor stare sliced up, straight through him.

"Mount Everest, right?"

"Yup."

"You climbed it when you were what? Sixteen?"

"Seventeen." And again at twenty-nine. Shortly after 9-11.

He'd have scaled a cliff to the moon that year if one had been available. Everest had been the best he could do.

Brooks tipped his head back toward the final black-and-white hanging on the wall. "That last one. That's Mount Ki-lauea, isn't it?" The man waited, Everest frame still in hand. That damned obscuring slice of glass covering it, between them.

Why?

Surely he didn't know...did he?

Impossible. Yes, the man was FBI. And, yes, based on the agent's visit with Abby, Brooks had probably read that police report along with his juvenile record, even though the damned thing was supposed to be sealed. But the glass wasn't in there. He might have been stupid enough to confide his curse to Pike's partner all those years ago, but he'd been smart enough not to reveal the existence of his surcease, as well as his Achil-les' heel, much less its source.

"Well?"

Dare frowned into the man's stare. "Mauna Loa. Kilauea spews her lava on the southeastern slope. Speaking of which, I presume you're ready to spew whatever it is you came here to say—or are you waiting for me to serve up a couple of aperitifs along with the current copy of *National Geographic?* If so, let me save you the trouble. I rarely drink and never with strangers."

That stare remained steady, piercing. "Yeah, I heard that about you."

*That* gave Dare pause. Hell, even Pike hadn't burrowed that deeply into his background this quickly. Perhaps Brooks did know. Either that, or the agent was hellishly lucky. Because that blasted glass-encased photo was still in hand, firmly centered between them, shielding the bulk of Brooks's emotions from him. While Dare's receptors were picking up the faint whisper of feeling seeping about the edges of the glass, the result was more frustrating than revealing, taunting his inner sense with a ghostly impression he couldn't quite focus on.

"What do you want, Agent?"

"Answers."

"Then start posing the damned questions."

Before Abby woke—

Too late. She'd begun to stir. Great. If Brooks kept this waltz up much longer—

"What do you know about genetics, Mr. Sabura?"

Genetics? This was about the drugs, then?

Dare relaxed, though not by much. "I know about the DNA narcotic and its instant addictive quality, if that's what you're referring to. I also know the drug in the syringe used to inject Van Heusen was originally intended for my neighbor, Abigail Pembroke. Detective Pike stopped by the symphony last night and filled the two of us in. It appears, however, that *you* and Pike are not on speaking terms, since Pike had no idea you'd already shown up at Abby's apartment and interrogated her."

Brooks didn't bother feigning embarrassment over his less-than-by-the-book procedures. Dare caught the man's shrug over the top of the Everest frame. "To be honest, my sources in the NYPD informed me that Pike was slightly biased when it came to you. I needed objectivity. However, I've since informed Pike that I was by here yesterday. He won't be bothering Ms. Pembroke again regarding the phantom Detective Hook."

"Then why did you lie to her in the first place?"

Another shrug. "As I said, I needed objectivity. Let's just say that given your involvement with the woman, I wasn't certain I'd get it. I didn't set out to deceive Ms. Pembroke, however. But when she misheard—"

"You took advantage of the situation. Of her."

The former Dare could understand, though barely. The latter, however, pissed him off. Completely. Nevertheless, now was not the time to take this man to task over either, because the lady in question had stirred a second time and this time she was beginning to wake. Unfortunately, the same horizontal buffer of photos that helped him sleep at night by dulling the latent emotions of the surrounding high-rise dwellers prevented him from knowing just how awake Abby was now. Was she lying on his bed, acclimating herself as she was wont to do most mornings? Or was she heading for his bathroom to splash off the effects of her deep sleep and the morning's exertions before heading out here?

Relief flooded Dare as he caught the sound of his shower starting. He'd earned a five- or ten-minute reprieve at least. "All right, Agent Brooks. You're here now—as yourself. What the hell, we both need answers. I go first. I'd like you to identify a few of the other players." Starting with that knife-wielding bastard. "Who stabbed Van Heusen's driver?"

Brooks shook his head. "I don't know."

"Then what do you know?"

The man's lips thinned. "A hell of a lot less than I'd like."

"Then why waste time stopping by? You could have just punched in the number I left on your voice mail and played twenty questions over the phone."

Dare stiffened as something flickered in the man's stare, as well as in the portion of his aura bleeding around the frame. Brooks might not know as much as he'd like, but he knew something. Something he wasn't anxious to reveal because he wasn't sure the information would be welcome.

*He who seeks to destroy your heart also seeks you.*

Dare stiffened as the rest locked in. The glasses they'd used to consume the cognac. Two glasses. Glasses Brooks had taken. Unlike the NYPD, the FBI now had access to both Abby's DNA and his, as well as to top-notch genetics labs. And genetics was a topic Brooks himself had initially broached. That had to be significant. Like Pike, Dare had assumed that thug had been lying in wait for Abby outside Avery Fisher Hall.

But what if the bastard hadn't been after her?

What if that thug had followed *him* to the concert?

"The DNA in that syringe—was Pike wrong?"

Hell, for all he knew, Pike had lied to make his case. It wouldn't have been the first time.

Brooks shifted his grip on the Everest frame, resting his hands atop it, drumming his fingers along the brass edge almost as an afterthought—or was it? Either way, the glass cover was still positioned directly between them, still obscuring the majority of the agent's aura. "No, the DNA in that syringe matches the blood she left on that cop's handkerchief. I also ran samples off both those glasses against the syringe. Hers matched, yours didn't."

The whisper of aura bleeding over the top of the frame confirmed it. But it still didn't make sense. Why would anyone want to blackmail Abby? Dare spun around and stalked the length of his living room to stare out of the French doors that connected this side of the penthouse with the wraparound balcony. He spun back around as Brooks turned. The man appeared to be absently shifting the oversized frame along with his body in an effort to maintain eye contact. But for a split second, the man was completely exposed.

The truth punched in.

Dare cursed. "You know why they want her."

By the time the agent's dark brow shot up, the frame was firmly in place—and the impression was gone.

"Now how could you possibly—"

"Cut the crap, Brooks. I know you've got an ulterior motive for showing up here. One that has nothing to do with your case. You want proof, want to check out your entourage—or lack thereof. We both know that if you were here in an official capacity, you'd have some NYPD dick in tow, just to make sure you weren't stepping on anyone's jurisdictional toes. You don't. Ten to one your Feebee boss has no idea you're in my home, either." A home that due to his own recent pacing—and the new, relative position of those glass-covered pictures—Dare could no longer clearly pinpoint Abby within. But he could still hear the shower. Dare kept going. "As I see it you have a choice. You have exactly two seconds to explain why you're here or—armed or not—I'll drag you through those doors by your ankles, hang you over the side of my balcony and shake it out of you."

The razor edge returned to the man's stare. "You really think you could take me?"

"Are you willing to take the chance?"

The most unexpected of emotions simmered around the edges of the Everest frame as Dare waited.

Amusement.

A moment later it faded. Seriousness returned as Brooks nodded. "I'm pretty sure they want Ms. Pembroke, if only to eliminate a potential witness. But initially I think they only wanted her because they needed her to get to you."

His shock must have shown.

Either that or Brooks was as skilled at reading emotion as he usually was, because the agent offered up a wry smile. "It's not as hard a leap as you think, Sabura. She's got nothing the man I'm after wants. You, on the other hand, are a different story. Unfortunately, you're also a near-total recluse. One who guards his personal space so zealously that even your own doorman doesn't remember ever shaking your hand. On those rare occasions when you do appear in public, you show up late and leave early, to the point of rudeness. You live alone, you dine alone. Hell, you even climb alone. You have no friends to speak of. Your adoptive mother died when you were a teenager. Despite your recent visit to your adoptive father's town house, you're completely estranged from him, too. You don't even socialize with your associate, Charlotte Dennison. In fact in the forty-eight hours I've been investigating you—which is usually enough for me to uncover a man's entire life, mind you—I've been able to identify a grand total of one person on this earth you've let inside your world."

"Abby."

Brooks nodded. "Abby."

It was true then, because of him, the woman he loved had nearly been killed. Twice. "Who's after me? What the hell does he want?" More important, if he gave it, would that knife-wielding thug leave Abby alone? Unfortunately, Dare already knew the answer. He didn't need to attend the FBI academy to know Abby was now firmly in that bastard's crosshairs. He'd told her so himself just last night.

Dare cursed—darkly.

Brooks nodded. "It's worse than you think. The guy behind the designer drug is a major black-market player. His home base is in Europe. Recently, however, he began a stateside expansion in the regular illegal drug markets, presumably to finance the research on his designer, one-shot, one-hook narcotic. He goes by the name Titan. Ever heard of him?"

"No." But Dare wished he had.

Brooks shifted his grip on the Everest photo, withdrawing a square of paper from his suit pocket with his free hand. He passed it over the top of the frame. Dare accepted the paper and opened it. Someone had drawn a charcoal sketch of a guy in his mid-fifties on the sheet. His face was slender, though not overly so. Definitely refined. Genteel. The man's close-cropped hair was sleek, though it had heavy silvering, as did his goatee. His eyes, cheeks and mouth were the most intriguing elements, though, because they were faintly Italian. Unfortunately, none struck a chord.

Dare memorized the man's face, then passed the sketch back. "Sorry, I haven't seen him."

He didn't need his intermittent sense to feel Brooks's disappointment. The man's deep frown revealed it for him. The agent sighed as he drummed his fingers atop the frame. "Can't say I'm surprised. If I've learned one thing in the three years I've been tracking the bastard, it's that Titan doesn't like to reveal himself until it's too late."

Dare stepped forward. "That's it? You've been tracking the man for three years and all you have is a half-assed sketch and a one-word moniker?" Bull. He knew the agent was withholding something. If he had to drive the man into the wall to get it out of him, he would.

A split second later Brooks released it. It came in the form of a wave of pure unadulterated rage, searing around the edges of the glass—but the agent's fury wasn't directed at Dare. Before Dare could gain so much as an impression of who it might be focused on, the rage was gone.

No, make that contained. Completely.

The thin twist of lips Brooks offered was constructed of the same steel as the lid he'd slammed over the top. "No, I don't have more on the bastard. I wish to God I did. I do know Titan doesn't want money. Not from you. What he wants *is* you."

Dread punched into Dare's gut as the agent dropped his gaze—slowly, deliberately. By the time the man's pointed stare settled on the sheet of glass still forging the emotional buffer between them, Dare's heart had kicked into overdrive, sending a torrent of blood pounding through his veins.

Adrenaline came with it. A dull roar filled his ears as the certainty pounded in. The placing of that frame was no absentminded accident. Brooks knew what glass did to him.

But did that mean the man believed? Pike hadn't. The detective still didn't. Not really. But that didn't mean Pike wasn't careful to keep his distance. Dare knew why. Years ago, when he'd been begging the cops to prevent Janet's murder, he'd spilled the extent of his curse to the guy's mentor. In his adolescent desperation, he'd even confessed that sometimes, if the connection was strong enough and the other person was subconsciously accepting enough, he could suggest things, much as he'd done earlier with Abby. His futile hope had been that if the cops got him there in time, he could convince Randall—

Abby!

Good God, he'd been so consumed with Brooks, he'd forgotten she was in the other room. Was she still in the shower? Was that why he couldn't get a fix on her essence? Or had she finished bathing, noticed he had a guest and decided to wait on the balcony? Maybe it was the jolt of adrenaline surging through his veins, affecting him more than he'd hoped.

Dare forced his heart rate to slow long enough to ease the roar of blood in his ears. Relief swamped him as he caught the faint sound of running water, until he glanced at his watch. Surely Abby had finished by now—

"Well?"

He snapped his stare to Brooks. The man was still waiting. Watching. And to Dare's utter shock, there was another impression swirling around the edges of that frame.

Brooks *believed*.

"You are an empath, aren't you? You can sense the emotions of those around you."

The shock still rocketing through him, Dare nodded.

"Do you have limits? Other than the glass, I mean?"

Again he nodded, this time numbly. "Distance lessens the effect. Though in a city like this, there's always a latent crush. Touch strengthens it. But as you read in that report, it depends on the person I'm touching."

This time Brooks nodded.

Still, how had the man known about the glass in the first place? Was Brooks an empath, too? That would explain how—

"No," Brooks replied to the unspoken question. "I'm just good at my job. As for what you're feeling now, it's all over your face, Sabura. If you know how to find it. Changes in pupil size, subtle but visible pulse points, skin tone. As for the distance limits, I figured that out on my own once I realized you really weren't doing a thing with the empty apartments below but for the occasional emergency guest, so to speak."

Dare swallowed his comeback on that one. It was enough that Brooks had chosen to overlook his career. The agent was right. Some of the means he used to accomplish his goals were questionable. "What about the glass?"

Brooks nodded. "Hmm. The glass. That one did take a bit of digging. It's all there, though. Starting with the contractor's receipts. The remodeling specs are still on file with the city from when you applied for your permit. You have to admit that eight-foot-wide hexagonal shower of yours was a hell of an expenditure, even for a man of your means. More telling, though, is that it's a damned luxurious item for a man who's clearly not into—" Brooks lifted his right hand and swept it about the spartan room "—creature comforts. Let's just say the suspicion was planted at the building inspector's office. Then I show up here and find all these pretty pictures. Or are they just an excuse for more glass?"

It was all true.

Brilliant deductive work, too.

Unfortunately, Dare wasn't the only one who'd heard the blow-by-blow account. The adrenaline surging through his veins had finally cleared enough for him to get not only a decent read on Abby, but a crystal-clear one. Dare turned his back on Brooks as Abby stepped all the way into the living room. She was still dressed in the blue tank-top and short set she'd worn that morning, and though her curls were loose and flowing down her back, they were still bone-dry, even around her temples. Her cheeks were still smeared with the dry sweat and dirt of her climb. She must have been standing directly behind one of those pictures. From the look in her eyes—the shock, confusion and horror reverberating through her heart—she'd been there the entire time.

He reached for her. "Abby—"

She flinched. "Don't. Please. Don't touch me." Anger crowded into her eyes and into her soul as she stared up at him. "These past two weeks, that whisper I've been hearing in my head, the feelings and persuasion that weren't really mine, the ones I was afraid meant I was going nuts…that was you, wasn't it? Somehow. *Inside* me."

"Yes."

Betrayal joined the mix, quickly overtaking her fury. "You made me feel things I didn't want to feel?"

He shook his head. "No. I swear. Abby, I can't make you feel what's not already there. I can only bring out the emotions that are—"

"Stop! You're doing it now, aren't you?"

*Damn.* He was.

Though not the way she thought.

It took more effort than he'd cared to admit, but he managed to pull his essence back into himself. To not share it, much less commingle it with hers as he'd begun to do without thinking. Maybe that was part of the mating ritual for men like him. He didn't know. He'd never mated before. Not really. Not with his heart. Whatever the reason, Abby clearly didn't want him inside her. That he could still feel from the outside.

"Abby, I'm sorry. I didn't mean to offend you. And I certainly never meant to hurt you. All I wanted to do was help ease your fears. Your pain. But it—I—went too far."

He'd also said too much.

At least in front of their now-rapt audience. Or perhaps she was simply too smart, because she figured out the rest.

"What about my brother? Did you help Brian, too? Is that why he can't even remember me?"

"Yes. I did help him that night. But I screwed up. Brian was too traumatized by the attack. He wanted to forget too much." Her soft gasp sharpened his perception of her pain.

His own, too.

"Are you saying Brian doesn't *want* to remember m-me?"

"No. The memory loss is connected to the attack, but it's connected to your father's death, as well. He's still not ready to accept either. You just got lost in his needs."

She nodded slowly, as if she was desperately trying to hold herself together. Which she was. "And when will my brother be ready to remember? When will he remember me?"

"Honey, I don't know. I wish I did."

"But you at least know he *will*."

He didn't answer. He couldn't.

It didn't matter. She'd read his heart this time. She drew her air in again, slower this time. "I see." The ache within his chest cut even deeper as she murmured something about heading back into his bathroom to turn off his shower. Then she needed to leave. It was time for her to head to her apartment and call her brother…from Europe.

No, don't bother accompanying her. He had a guest. Besides, she wanted to be alone.

Completely alone.

But as she turned and headed into his bedroom, around that damned row of makeshift glass, he was the one who was alone. Again. At that moment he'd have given everything he had to rid himself of the curse. To be the man she wanted. The man she needed. But he couldn't.

God knew he'd tried.

Dare turned back to Brooks as the shower ceased, felt the compassion bleeding out around that damned frame. Normal human compassion. There was no way Brooks was an empath, because his own pain didn't lessen. Not even a bit. But at least he'd finally figured out why Brooks had been shielding himself. Like Abby, the man was deathly afraid he would alter his perceptions before he had a chance to decide if they were his own. It seemed that neither of them were willing to believe that he couldn't bend someone against his will.

It was ironic.

They were both willing to accept that he was a freak of nature, but neither wanted to accept that he wasn't a magician.

At least he could give Brooks what he needed. It had to be what the agent had been waiting for. Why not? One of them deserved to be content. Dare crossed his living room, stopping within inches of the rear of that oversized frame, giving Brooks an up-close, unobstructed view of his pupils and whatever else the man needed to evaluate his heart. Only then did he voice what every cop—federal or not—needed to hear and judge for himself. "I did not kill Janet Randall."

Brooks studied him for what seemed like an eternity. And then he nodded.

Accepted.

Once again, Brooks turned with that damned picture in hand, but this time he set it on the floor against the wall. He turned back and extended his hand. "Liam Brooks. It's nice to meet you finally, Dare, to be able to expose myself in more ways than one, so to speak." The man cracked a genuine for the first time since he'd stepped into the apartm

Dare took the man's hand—and accepted the
and increase his reading. He flinched, not h

lief still searing into Liam Brooks, but because of the intensity of it.

The reason for it.

Dare was dimly aware of Liam releasing his hand. It didn't matter—he was still feeling it. All of it. He knew why Liam had wanted that DNA—*his* DNA. Not because Agent Brooks suspected him of murder, but because Liam Brooks shared a connection—the most intimate of connections—with a woman who had also shared the same womb as Dare. So much made sense now. The gnawing void he'd felt his entire life. The inexplicable knowledge that it wasn't supposed to be. That he wasn't supposed to be alone. That cry in the night months before.

His tattoo most of all.

"I have a sister."

Liam nodded. "Danielle Caldwell, now Brooks. We were recently married. I'm sorry you couldn't be there. And I'm sorry I was such a hard-ass. Now that you know, I think you'll understand why I needed to be certain what kind of a man you were before I told you about Dani. We'll have to get you two together once it's safe."

*Safe.*

Son of a bitch. "Titan." That cry. Something else he'd felt inside Liam made sense. "Dani has a son. A son who was taken from her. I heard the cry in my sleep, woke up in a cold sweat, but the impression was gone by then. The boy, he's okay now, right?" He had to be. His initial reading of Liam Brooks might have been short-lived, but it had been thorough. Brooks was not the sort of man to shun the child of the woman he loved, even if that child was not of his own blood. Nor was he the sort of man who could be this content with his home life if that child was still missing. Liam's nod confirmed it.

. name is Alex. And yes, Titan kidnapped him. Dani,

too. But they're both safe now. Titan's moved on. He's had to. It's you I'm worried about now."

"What about the other triplet?"

Dare felt Liam's shock even before it snapped up the man's spine, stiffening it. "Triplet?"

"Of course. Isn't that how you knew to look for me?"

Liam shook his head. "No. I found you because I was following Titan's trail. I wouldn't even be in New York if it wasn't for Van Heusen and that drug. When I showed up to talk to Pike, he had your juvie record out on his desk. The man's convinced you're up to no good, by the way. Hate to defend the ass, but you can't really blame him."

"I know." He didn't.

How many times had he passed a detective on the street consumed by the perp that got away? A detective who'd labored for years over a cold case, sometimes even knowing the rapist or murderer, but unable to touch the bastard due to lack of evidence, or worse, a perp who got off on a technicality? No, he didn't blame Pike. Pike might be a bastard and a half, but he was also a decent cop with scars of his own. It was the only reason Dare had never pushed it. "So that's how you found me? He showed you my picture and it reminded you of Dani?"

Brooks nodded. "Alex especially. You were older in the picture than the boy, but you're a ringer for him. The DNA I took from that glass confirmed it. Dani is your sister and she is a triplet. But Dare, she has another brother and a sister, as well. They're all older than you by three years."

Good Lord. Dare swallowed his shock. The budding hope. "Just how many siblings do I have?"

"I don't know. Until I saw your mug shot, I thought Dani had just the two. What about you? Dani mentioned once that she heard an infant cry when she was young, but the memory's fuzzy. She has no idea exactly what she heard, n who it was. Are you sure you're a triplet? Did your parents tell you? Someone who knew you before you were adopted?"

"No." Far from it. "I told myself. When I was seventeen, I visited a tattoo parlor to commemorate climbing that mountain you had in your hands. I ended up with this." Dare peeled his T-shirt off so the agent could get a better look. From the confusion on the man's face, Dare could tell Liam didn't know any more about the trinity symbol than Dare had when he'd first seen it—despite the driving need to brand it into his chest, directly over his heart.

"What is it?"

"A triquetra. It means trinity. Three-in-one. Deep down, I always suspected I was a triplet. But if Dani's my sister and she's a triplet, perhaps it's meant to represent them."

Liam nodded. "Perhaps."

But they were thinking the same thing. What if it wasn't? What if there was another set of triplets? Where did it end?

"How about your folks? Have they ever shed any light on your adoption?"

Dare shook his head. "No. And they won't. My father knows nothing. He never wanted to, much less wanted me. He still doesn't. As for my mother, all I know is that she purchased me. I have no idea from whom or even where. She must have paid the seller well because there's no trail. Whatever she knew, she took to her grave."

"I'm sorry."

Dare shrugged. There were only two people capable of easing that particular pain, and one was dead. The other might have decided not to flee the penthouse after all, but she was only marking time inside his bedroom, trying to absorb the shock and the violation as she waited for Liam to leave so she could question him more about her brother, about what he'd done to Brian and how she might be able to reverse it. After that, Abby had every intention of leaving, too.

He couldn't blame her.

He had violated her. Over and over. Without her knowledge, let alone her permission. He could feel her questioning her feelings for him even now. Wondering if they truly were *her* feelings. They were. But damned if he knew how to prove it.

Brooks cleared his throat. "I, uh, apologize for that, too. Didn't mean to catch you by the short hairs in front of your, uh, neighbor."

Dare didn't correct the term. This morning he would have. This evening he didn't know what he and Abby were anymore. Or if they had a chance of getting back to where they'd been. But the blame wasn't Liam's. "It's not your fault. I should have told her. I intended to. But I didn't know how to say it."

The man nodded sagely. "It's a conversation stopper, I'll give you that."

"Then Dani's an empath, too?"

"No. She has the gift of intuition. Her sister, Elizabeth, is telekinetic. According to Dani, their brother, Anthony, can manipulate electrical energy. As far as I know, your gift is unique."

"Gift." Dare shook his head. "Try curse."

Liam fell silent. Dare didn't even bother trying to convince him otherwise. How could he? Liam had read that police report. How could knowing something like that was about to happen and not being able to prevent it ever be anything but a curse?

"Liam, I—" Dare cut himself off as the man's cell phone shrilled. He waited as the guy reached beneath his suit jacket and withdrew the phone from his waist.

Liam frowned as he noted the number, then returned the phone to his belt unanswered. "It's Pike. I'm late for a meeting with the guy."

"You need to go."

"Yeah. It's probably a good thing, though. I imagine you've got some explaining to do."

That he did.

"For what it's worth, good luck. I hope it works out." Liam turned to head for the door.

"Wait."

Dare pulled his T-shirt back on, then reached up to unhook the picture of Mauna Loa from the wall, turning the frame and placing the picture on the floor before he set about retrieving the two plastic bags he'd secreted beneath a razor slit in the picture's backing. He met Liam at the door and held out the bag containing a card. "This may have come from the guy you're after. It was sent to the symphony the evening of the attack along with a bunch of calla lilies from Flowers by Delilah. Unfortunately, the lilies were ordered over the phone. Cash and the note were delivered by a kid. I've got a streetwise associate on it, but he hasn't had any luck tracking the kid down. Maybe you'll have more."

Liam took the bag. He flipped it over and studied the oddly compelling pastoral scene on the reverse. "It's Titan's. It's his twisted idea of a calling card. Dani got one. Senator Gregory, as well. I got one. There've been a few others."

Damn. "Despite the plastic, you probably won't have luck with prints. It's been handled quite a bit."

Liam shook his head. "It won't matter. We'll try, but Titan hasn't left any yet. Bastard's too smart." Liam tipped his head toward the second bag. "What's in there?"

"A note I received. The envelope, too. One line, typed. But this one's on our side. He or she has to be."

"What's it say?"

"'He who seeks to destroy your heart also seeks you.'" Dare flipped the bag over, displaying the triquetra on the reverse. "It matches my tattoo right down to the size. A tattoo I've never advertised, by the way. And, as you pointed out so succinctly, I have few friends. Certainly none close enough to reproduce it."

Again interest flared within the man.

"What's it mean?" But Dare knew. Everything Liam Brooks had revealed tonight confirmed his initial suspicions. Someone had been trying to warn him that he and Abby were in danger. Someone who knew what Abby meant to him, perhaps before he'd first felt Abby's essence. Whoever sent the warning had probably included the tattoo to ensure his attention.

Liam nodded his agreement.

Dare passed the second bag over, as well. "Do you know who sent it?"

This time Liam shook his head. "No. Dani received a similar warning, though. Hers came from a fortune-teller who warned her that 'Those who walk alone are the first to fall.' But I haven't been able to locate the fortune-teller to question her, much less confirm—" The guy's phone shrilled again. Liam retrieved it, checked the number and cursed. "Pike. Man's worse than a pit bull with a bone."

"Or an empath's leg."

Liam grinned. "I think I like you. Good thing. For a while there, I was afraid I was going to have to beat the crap out of you or arrest you. Think of the reception I'd get at home after that." His grin faded as he held up the plastic bags. "May I?"

Dare nodded. "Just keep me posted."

"Will do." The guy tucked the bags inside his suit jacket and turned to the door once more, then stopped. He turned back and reached into his trouser pocket, this time surfacing with his wallet. He pulled out a card and passed it over. Only it wasn't a card. It was a picture of a woman and a boy around five or six. Unlike that sketch, both faces were hauntingly familiar…and yet not.

His sister. His nephew.

Liam was right. The kid was a ringer for him at that age.

A knot lodged in the middle of Dare's throat. His hand actually shook. He memorized their faces and passed the photo back before he embarrassed himself.

Liam waved him off. "Keep it. I can get another. Hang on to it until I can arrange a visit. Oh—" He retrieved the sketch of Titan. "I've got another copy of this, too. Show it to Abby for me, will you? If she recognizes the guy, you've got my number. If not, I'll be calling you soon enough."

Dare took the sketch, shifting it and the photo of his new-found sister to his left hand. He held out his right.

As before, the true nature of Liam Brooks flooded him as they shook. But this time Dare was able to feel more than his sister and her son. Curious, he delved deeper until he felt an-other woman in this man's life. Another child. He also felt the keening loss that still surrounded their memories. The guilt. Guilt that belonged not to the man standing in front of him, but to Titan.

Dare tightened his grip momentarily and did what he should have done with Abby. He asked.

Liam agreed.

It took several more moments, and he couldn't quite get it all, but eventually he was able to ease the worst of Liam's pain and loss, leaving the good behind. He absorbed the guilt next, but left the ironclad determination. Not only was the man clinging to it fiercely, they'd all need it.

Liam withdrew his hand, thanked him quietly and left.

Dare was still standing at the open door, attempting to re-align his equilibrium, when Abby gathered up her nerve and left his bedroom. He opened his eyes as she reached the cen-ter of his living room and forced himself to see her through them, and only them. Sometimes it worked if there were but one or two others in the room, at most a handful. But with her, the attempt failed. Miserably. He could still feel her heart breaking along with his.

It gave him hope.

Like him, she desperately wanted to go back to last night. To this morning. To them. But she was scared. And as usual, he stunk at words. One touch, and he could show her. But he couldn't risk it. He wouldn't. She had been serious earlier.

She didn't want him inside her.

Though it nearly killed him to remain apart from her essence, he honored the request. That just left the physical need. His own body's reaction to the damp streaks still staining her reddened cheeks. The tears still clinging to her lashes. The single plump drop that spilled over and slid to a halt just shy of the corner of her quivering lips.

"You heard. You saw."

"I—" She stopped, then drew her breath in deep and started again. "I don't know what I saw. What to think. If I'm even sane. And if I am…I don't know what I feel. If it's really me, you know?"

He nodded. "I know. Abby, I know this is a shock. And God knows I could have handled it better."

"Then why didn't you?"

"Because you get to me, affect me, in ways no one else ever has. In ways I don't understand. Ways I can't control. When we're together, when we touch, I can't see past you. I can't *feel* past you. If you're not happy, I'm not happy. If you feel excitement, passion or joy, then I feel it. It's…"

"Frightening?"

"Yeah." Terrifying.

"I know."

She did. He'd felt that inside her all along. It was why she too had been fighting what was happening between them. She'd been scared to fall for him and find out he was just like Van Heusen. Only, what she got was worse.

"Honey, I know there's nothing I can—"

Terror slammed in. Hard. Deep. He stiffened as he tried to absorb it. *Jesus, Mary and Joseph.* What the hell was that? *Who* was that? He opened his mouth, but nothing came out. It was as if the words themselves had been torn from his tongue before he could form them. All he could do was feel the stark, roiling horror. Before he could recover, Abby had vaulted across the remaining yard of carpet and grabbed his arm.

"What is it? What's wrong?"

The second she touched him, the terror exploded within every receptor in his body. The horror consumed him. Somewhere amid the fiery depths he finally found his voice—only to have it rip free on a base curse along with half the carefully constructed mental defenses it had taken him years to erect.

There was only one explanation.

Abby was acting as an emotional conduit. And that meant the source was—

"*Brian.*"

"What?"

"Your brother. He's in danger."

He felt her own terror skyrocket, even as she tried to convince herself that, empath or not, he couldn't possibly know what he was talking about from halfway across the city. Part of him wanted to take the time to convince her, to soothe her fear. But he didn't have time. Brian didn't have time. He did the next best thing. Dare asked the one question he knew she'd answer. "Honey, I know you're furious with me, but you believe me. You trust me, right?"

"Absolutely."

"Then let's *go.*" With that, he grabbed her hand and hauled her out of the apartment with him.

# Chapter 11

She'd always wondered how she was going to die.

Earlier in the day, clinging to that cliff as that boulder had come crashing down, Abby was certain she'd been about to meet her maker. She'd been wrong. She was going to die right now—on the back of a souped-up motorcycle from Dare's racing days with her aching arms clamped about the man's waist, her eyes squeezed shut and her face pressed into the iron muscles of his back as they roared through the darkened streets of New York City, cutting in and out of bumper-to-bumper traffic with hair-whitening precision. If the next car didn't get her, her skyrocketing terror would.

Because Brian wasn't the only one in danger. Marlena and Stephen were in trouble, too.

Dare had figured that out, too—after he'd tossed her his cell phone and ordered her to call her friend's house as they tore out of the Tristan's stairwell and into the garage, her lungs still blistering and her legs quaking from a trip that would have taken a quarter of the time if an elevator had been available when she'd called for it. But it hadn't been. Neither had Marlena. Confused when she couldn't get her friend's number to ring, she'd passed the phone to Dare, only to receive the worst pronouncement possible as he fired up his bike.

Marlena's line had been cut.

A split second later Dare had jammed the phone into his pocket and swung her up onto the motorcycle behind him. A fishtailing trip through the garage, and they were on the street, sucking in the city's nauseating exhaust along with half the Upper West Side. Ten seconds later they'd come within kissing distance of their first city bus. She'd slammed her eyelids down then and shoved her face deep into the security of Dare's back, determined to suffer the remaining honking horns, whiplashing twists and turns and stomach-lurching bumps in ignorant darkness.

Dare had saved her brother twice already. Once she'd recovered from the shock of discovering that not only did empaths exist, but that the man she'd fallen for *was* one, she'd realized that Dare had done more than save her brother from that monster. Dare had saved Brian from himself. She still didn't understand it yet, but she would. For now, she squeezed her lids harder, held on tighter as she prayed Dare would pull off another miracle.

Five excruciating minutes later, he did.

Hope ripped in as the bike jerked to a halt, only to sear off as she opened her eyes to find not one, but three flashing police cruisers and an ambulance parked haphazardly in front of her friends' house—with Marlena herself barreling through the open door, off the porch and down the sidewalk. By the time Dare had removed the helmet he'd secured to her head at the Tristan, swung her off his bike and set her on shaking legs, Marlena had reached them. Marlena grabbed her arm, half guiding, half dragging her back up the walk as she babbled out the night's terror.

"He's upset, but he's fine. It all happened so fast. He came up the fire escape. By the time we knew, the phone line had already been cut. Thank God the guard and that cop were here. Who knows what that monster would have done? The guard's giving his statement and Stephen's with Brian in his room. He's upset, but he's f-fine— Oh, God, I'm repeating m-my—"

"It's okay. I've got her."

Abby wrenched her gaze from Marlena as Dare gently disengaged her friend's hands. Dare's dark, reassuring stare captured hers, calming her own blistering fears.

He nodded down at her. "Marlena will be fine. Go to Brian. She's right. Physically he's okay. But he needs you."

Maybe it was her overwhelming need to see for herself that Brian was in one piece or maybe it was the peace already smoothing Marlena's brow as Dare eased her friend to his side and guided her into the house. She didn't know. She only knew she was grateful to him again. She managed a shaky nod and bounded up the stairs. Seconds later she was standing in the doorway of her brother's room. Brian was lying on his side, huddled against the far edge of his twin bed, oblivious to Stephen's soothing voice as he methodically knocked his forehead into the wall over and over. Dare and Marlena were right. Physically he was okay. But emotionally?

Her heart broke on the answer.

Two steps in, her heart completely shattered as Stephen reached out to pat her brother's back—and Brian mewled like a terrified animal caught in the steel teeth of a hunter's trap. She vaulted across the room. Stephen moved aside as she eased herself down on the bed and tentatively placed her hand where his had been. "Hey, bro, I'm here."

No response.

Worse, he continued to rap his head into the wall.

But at least he hadn't made the god-awful whimper. She stroked her fingers through his hair, losing a strip off her heart each and every time that chilling knock reverberated through the room. "Brian? It's Abby. I'm here. I'm...home."

Sweet heaven, she didn't know what to do, what to say. Did he think she was still in Europe or did he remember her at all at this point? Dammit, where was Dare? She *needed* him. And not just for what she now knew he could do. She scrubbed the tears from her cheeks and turned to Stephen.

"What happened?"

"I'm still not really sure. Some cop showed up asking questions. The guard Dare left went ballistic. I thought they were going to go at it right there in the living room when Brian let out a bloodcurdling scream. We damned near killed each other trying to get up here first. Thank God those two were here." He shook his head, as if to clear the gruesome memory. "He climbed the fire escape while the guard was inside, and tried to come in through the windows. The brute was twice my size. I never could have taken him. As it is—" Stephen shuddered.

She followed his stark gaze to the double windows. The miniblinds were drawn, but she could make out the faint murmur of voices and shuffling forms behind them. Something about not being able to move the guy because he was past help. Some part of her probably should have felt guilty the man was dying, despite the fact that he was a murdering thug, but she couldn't.

All she felt was relief.

Unfortunately, horror still filled Stephen's face as he turned back. "I closed the window when I couldn't calm Brian enough to move him. It's...pretty bad. The EMTs and two of the cops are still out there. We called nine-one-one from the neighbor's but we couldn't reach you. I guess you were on your way. Abby, I don't know how you knew we needed you, but—"

"Sir?"

They both turned to the doorway.

A uniformed cop stood in the hall. Ironically, she recognized him from that night outside Avery Fisher Hall. Officer Ryder nodded to her first. "Ms. Pembroke." He turned to Stephen. "Mr. Kane, I know this is a bad time, but I really need your statement."

Stephen glanced at her. "You going to be okay?"

"Yeah." It was Brian she was worried about. "Could you please ask Dare to come—"

He was already there. Standing in the hallway to the left of Ryder, patiently waiting. No, she couldn't see him. But she could feel him. Not because he'd violated her internal space, but because *she* had reached out to him somehow.

The connection should have unnerved her. But it didn't.

She felt comforted by his presence.

And so much more.

Stephen squeezed her shoulder as he stood. "Yell if you need me."

"I will."

But she wouldn't. The only man she needed entered the room as Stephen and the cop left. Dare approached the bed and stared down at her brother. She could feel his tension and his uncertainty. His fear. It wasn't that Dare didn't know what to do. He did. He even knew she wanted him to do it.

But he was afraid to try.

She reached up and took his hand. "It's okay. You won't hurt him. You can't. What happened last time wasn't your fault. I know that. *You* know that."

He nodded.

"Dare, I trust you."

He lowered his frame down to the bed. She pulled her breath in deep, pulling Dare in even deeper as he reached up to smooth his fingers across her cheeks. He wiped the tears she'd shed from her skin, then cupped his hand to her cheek as he closed his eyes. Though the first soothing touch had been for her, she somehow knew this second was for him. To help restore whatever part of him he'd taxed as he'd helped calm Marlena. She only wished she could do more. His eyes still closed, he inhaled slowly, then opened them.

"I'm ready."

"Do you want me to leave?"

He shook his head. "Stay. Please. I'll need you again when I'm done."

She nodded and stood. There was barely room for Brian on the bed, much less all three of them.

By the time she'd moved into the center of the room, Dare had stood as well, but only to bend down and scoop her brother's quaking form into his arms. He settled them both on the bed, closing his eyes once more as he cradled her brother to his chest as gently as a newborn babe. She wasn't sure what she expected. While she knew now he'd performed this miracle for her several times, she was now on the outside looking in.

At first she didn't see anything.

But somehow she could feel it. Them.

The faint whispers of the acute emotions tearing through her brother as Dare brought them into himself.

She watched as Brian's initial confusion, anger and then outright horror played across Dare's face. The more his features tensed—the more Dare absorbed—the calmer Brian became. Soon her brother was lying peacefully against Dare's chest, his breaths gradually lengthening until they were no longer short and rasping but pulling in and out in a slow, steady wash. She had no idea how long Dare sat there, leaning against the wall, holding her brother in his arms. All she knew was that she'd been so very wrong. So was Dare. This extraordinary skill he possessed was not a curse.

It was gift.

A precious gift he'd shared with her and her brother.

God willing, Dare would give her another gift. The one of forgiveness. She never should have doubted him. She still had a lot to sort out, true. A lot of questions to ask and even more answers to understand, but she knew in her heart Dare had never bent her emotions to suit his own. If he could have affected someone's mind and changed it against his or her will, surely he'd have done it with his parents a long time ago. Instead, he'd put up with the worst kind of abuse a man with his gift could endure. The emotional kind.

But there was more.

She knew where that scar on his lip had come from now, the other one he'd gotten that same night Janet died. The scar he'd refused to discuss. Duane Randall hadn't split his lip; his father had. But the rent to his heart had hurt much more. Despite Dare's denial to Liam Brooks earlier, it still did.

She refused to add to it. She couldn't.

She—

"Sir?"

Abby flinched as Officer Ryder returned, stepping through the doorway before she could head him off. The opportunity already lost, she shifted her own stance, deliberately shielding Dare and her brother from the cop's view.

"It's okay, Abby. He can come in." Dare stood and settled Brian on the bed. He took a moment to draw the quilt up to her brother's chin as his soft snores filled the room. Exhaustion tinged Dare's features as he stopped beside her to murmur, "He'll sleep the night. But when he wakes in the morning, he'll be ready to remember everything. Until then, let him rest. Okay?"

"Okay."

He nodded, then faced the young cop. "What can I do for you, Officer?"

"I gave him your message."

Ryder crossed the room and raised both sets of blinds, revealing the backs of two more uniformed cops flanked by a pair of hunkered-down EMTs. It was then that Abby noticed Ryder had fetched an IV bag for the EMTs. Ryder passed the bag to Dare and lifted the window, then retrieved the bag. The two cops already out on the landing parted as the third slipped out, revealing a scene that caused Abby's stomach to roll faster than all the twists and turns she and Dare had taken on the bike combined. Somehow the thug had been thrown up onto the metal spikes that fenced the far side of the landing. Three had impaled him through his back. But that wasn't the most horrifying part. It was the body.

It didn't belong to that thug.

It couldn't. The man might be wearing a suit, but his torso was half the size she remembered. Nor did those limp arms and legs come close to the tree-trunk girth she'd seen. As the second of the uniformed officers raised the poor guy's head, Stephen's comment made sense: *Some cop showed up asking questions.* Not just any cop. A NYC detective.

Pike.

Abby swung around to Dare. "You knew?"

He nodded. "Marlena told me. Stephen and Pike arrived in the nick of time. Pike pulled the bastard off your brother and ended up getting tossed out of the open window for his efforts. The detective lost his gun during the struggle. Stephen recovered it, scared the bastard off, but it was too late. Pike had already landed on the spikes when he fell."

She stared into those dark, tortured pools of green. Though she already knew the answer, she couldn't help asking. Hoping. "They can't move him, can they?"

"No."

She nodded. "And your message? You offered to help him, didn't you? To give him peace in his final moments?"

"Yes."

Why didn't he go out there, then? Why wait in here with

her? Brian was fine now. Dare had assured her of that himself—and she trusted him more than her brother's doctor. But, again, she knew. Dare had already given her the answer in his penthouse. "It's up to him, isn't it?"

"It always is, Abby. Whether it's accepted subconsciously or not. Always."

They weren't just talking about Pike anymore.

They were back in that penthouse, back in her apartment, back in that police interrogation room and every other time Dare had slipped inside her. He hadn't violated her. Not once. Whether or not she'd been consciously aware of what she'd been doing, she'd welcomed him each and every time. "I'm sorry I didn't understand. That I accused you of—"

"It's okay."

Shame swamped her as she shook her head. "No, it's not." She pushed the humiliation aside. Now wasn't the time for her to wallow in her own selfish emotions. Dare had just led her brother out of yet another hell. The evidence was all there for her to see, just as it had been each time before. The haunting exhaustion still lingering in those dark emerald eyes, the Atlas crush to his shoulders. His dusky cheeks were flushed, too. And he was sweating.

He was running a fever again, but not because of some viral bug. Because of what he'd done for her brother. And for some reason touching her helped him.

She didn't wait for him to reach for her as he had after he'd helped Marlena; she reached for him. But as she drew him in, she heard the window sliding open. She turned in Dare's arms, dismayed as the cops and EMTs ducked silently through the opening and into the room, past her, Dare and her sleeping brother one by one as they headed out into the hall.

Ryder was the last man in.

She swallowed hard. "Is he...dead?"

The cop ignored her in favor of Dare. "He wants to see you.

Alone. He said you'd understand. You'd better hurry, though. He doesn't have a lot of time."

Abby released Dare's hand, hoping it had been enough as Ryder followed the subdued procession out into the hall and down the stairs. "I'll be right here."

Her heart in her throat, she sank onto the bed beside her brother as she watched Dare slip through yet another window. But this time he wasn't escaping to his penthouse. He was headed out to ease the suffering of the one man who, because of his mentor's word, had all but convicted Dare of the most heinous of crimes—a man who was about to learn the true measure of Darian Sabura for himself.

Sadly, for Pike it was too late.

God willing, it wouldn't be for the two of them.

Letting Pike go was one of the most difficult things he'd ever done—and Dare knew why. The twin reasons were roughly thirty feet away, on the opposite side of those French doors and down the hall, in the guestroom of his penthouse.

Abby. Brian.

The relationship they shared with each other. The complete, unconditional love and support they had for each other. He didn't need his empathic sense to know it was real. All he had to do was walk into his guestroom to see Abby sitting beside her slumbering brother, grateful simply to be near him again, looking forward to the moment when he woke so she could tell him she loved him and feel it in return.

Would he ever know that love for himself?

Dare turned, bracing his forearms against the balustrade of his balcony as he stared out over the glittering lights of the city. As much as he hated admitting it, Liam Brooks was right. He had no friends. Other than Charlotte, nemesis or not, Pike had been the closest thing to a friend he'd ever had. And now Pike was gone. But in the true form of relationships, however twisted theirs had been, he and Pike had been able to offer each other a parting gift. Dare's had been twofold. First, to put to rest the detective's fear that he was leaving behind a murderer to walk the earth as a free man. And second, the physical and emotional surcease he could offer Pike in his final moments as he prepared to meet his maker. Pike's gift had been equally as precious, at least to Abby and him.

Pike had given them a name.

The bastard who'd attempted to take Brian's life for the second time, but had ended up butchering the detective instead, was none other than Zeno Corza. Pike had recognized the thug from his early days working vice. It made sense, given the connection Liam and his FBI associates had been able to establish between Corza's elusive boss and the illegal-drug markets. From what Pike had been able to relay about Corza, the butcher's non-existent moral code and grisly fascination with knives were a perfect match for Titan's leave-no-witnesses-behind mindset.

Dare had called Liam with the identification shortly after Pike had slipped away, only to learn why Pike had been attempting to reach Liam at his penthouse earlier. Just before Pike had knocked on Marlena and Stephen's door, Stuart Van Heusen had woken from his coma. Dare was torn between sharing the news with Abby when she took a break from her bedside vigil or waiting until tomorrow. Abby had enough to worry about without adding on the fears that Stuart would accuse her of blackmailing his mother.

Or perhaps not.

He straightened as he felt the whisper of Abby's essence slipping around the edges of the glass doors and the blind-drawn windows that spanned the exterior walls of his bedroom. She was searching for him. He turned his back on the city and answered her call, guiding her down the hall and across the rug of his dimly lit bedroom with his heart. He lost her essence as she stepped directly in front of the French doors, only to be bathed in her serene beauty moments later as the buffer parted. She smiled softly, bathing him with her physical beauty, as well.

"Hi."

He returned her husky greeting with one of his own. "Hi."

"Mind if I join you?"

"Please."

Her warmth teased him as she crossed the balcony, resting her slender forearms within inches of his on the balustrade as they stared out at the city lights together.

"It's gorgeous up here."

He smiled. "I thought you didn't particularly like heights, especially after this morning."

She laughed softly and shrugged. "Who said I was referring to the city?"

His pulse thrummed. Because she meant it.

Unfortunately, though she'd accepted his offer for her and her brother to stay with him until Liam located Corza, he hadn't yet had a chance to explain why he hadn't been honest with her, much less see if he could get them back to where they'd been that morning before that boulder had come crashing down. Nor had she invited him to commingle his essence with hers. He missed it. He missed her.

Especially standing this close to her.

"How's your brother?"

She snapped her gaze to his. "Don't you know?"

Dare nodded. But he'd felt the need to say something. To try and fill the void between them. If he couldn't fill it the way he wanted to, he would take her voice.

She seemed to understand.

"Brian's still sleeping. I can't believe he didn't wake during the taxi ride. I swear every other car we passed blared their horn."

"He'll be fine in the morning. Understandably upset over what happened, but he will remember you."

"I know. I believe you. I'll just feel better when I see it for myself, you know? Hear his voice."

He did.

The silence settled in again. This time she was the one who desperately wanted to end it. Though he was fairly certain what she wanted to ask, he waited for her to form the words.

"What happened tonight, that…sympathetic feeling you got when you realized Brian was in trouble? That's what happened when you were fifteen, isn't it? With Janet?"

"Yes." And no.

He had no intention of burdening Abby with the latter. Though the connection he'd unintentionally formed with Duane Randall had been based in ugliness, it had been as unbreakable and inescapable as the one he'd forged with her brother during those moments outside Avery Fisher Hall. And as with Brian, that bond had lingered for a time. Tonight he'd felt what her brother had felt—Brian's overwhelming confusion, fear and horror. As to the maelstrom of emotions he'd felt emanating from Randall on that fateful night all those years ago? Dare blocked the memory before it could taint this moment with her.

Unfortunately, she tugged on another.

"What about your dad? Yesterday morning in the elevator, you told me you went to your father and asked for help, but that he didn't believe Janet was in danger."

Dare nodded.

"I was right, wasn't I? There is more to the story. You told your dad you were an empath that night. To convince him to help. But instead of giving you his trust and support, he gave you this." Dare held his breath as she reached up, closing his eyes as she pressed a finger to the scar on his lip.

He didn't answer. He still couldn't.

He could feel her heart breaking for him. For the boy he'd been. He wanted to tell her it didn't matter, that he was over it. But it did and he wasn't. He still carried the memory in his heart. The disappointment and disillusionment. But also the fear. The fear to ever tell another. After all, if his own father didn't believe him, who would? But she understood that, too. He could feel it radiating from within as she settled her hand on his shoulders. "No wonder you couldn't tell me."

He drew strength from her touch and opened his eyes. "For what it's worth, I was about to. But then Liam showed up."

"And he did it for you. I think there's more to it, though. I think you were hoping I'd eavesdrop."

Again she was correct.

Even if she couldn't feel his embarrassment, she had to have seen it, because he certainly felt it—searing up his cheeks. "Abby...you may have noticed these past few weeks, I'm...not terribly good with words."

She nodded solemnly. "That's true." To his disappointment, she dropped her hand from his shoulder and stepped back, though not far. "What about the limits and enhancements you discussed with Agent Brooks? Were those true, too?"

"Yes. I can't feel through glass. Sometimes emotions can spill around the sides if they're intense enough, but for complete peace, there must be no gaps in the glass."

"I don't understand."

How did he explain it? "Have you ever turned off your TV and lights, yet still heard a faint electrical whine?"

"Sure."

"It's like that. An emotional signature, if you will. One that never goes away. The darker emotions are harder for me to absorb, but even joy can cut if it's intense enough. The more people, the more emotion. So I climb. The adrenaline dulls it for a while, but it's not enough. For complete peace I need the glass. Hence, the shower. You may have noticed the glass in the ceiling. It's embedded beneath the floor, as well."

"And the police station? When your temperature shot up? It was because of all the negativity in that place?"

"Exactly."

He dreaded the next question. The next answer.

"And the symphony? It's like you said, isn't it? All those people, all that emotion… Even if it's the good kind, it's too much. That's why you didn't hear me perform. Why you'll never be able to hear me, not in public."

"Abby—"

"I know. It's not your fault." But the silence dipped in. He could feel her fighting the disappointment. Then searching. Brightening. "There are always private performances."

True. But would that be enough?

The violin was a huge part of who she was. How she expressed herself. The stage, the orchestra, the audience. She might be willing to accept his limits now, but what about six months from now? Six years? Would she grow weary of explaining away his absence to others and to herself?

She stepped closer, came within inches of him and lifted her right hand, slipping her fingers into the very ends of his hair. "Hey, I don't have all the answers. We're just going to have to see how it goes. Make adjustments along the way."

She was right.

He would simply have to accept what she was willing to share for as long as she was willing to share it.

He nodded.

Her mood lightened. He could feel her growing confidence. And something else. Something good. And very, very promising. "That last thing you mentioned to Liam, the part about touch. It's like tonight, with Brian and with Marlena? When you touch me, you feel exactly what I feel?"

"Yes."

She stepped closer. "What about right now?"

"I can sense your emotions, feel your inner self. But even this close it's not nearly as strong as when we touch." And not nearly as satisfying. "But there's something I didn't tell Liam.

With you, the touch is different. There's...more. More than there's ever been with another. Even when we're not touching." He now knew that day he'd first felt her had been especially intense because he'd unconsciously reached out to her across the lobby, mingling their essences without thinking, much less asking. "Abby, I don't really understand what happens when I'm with you, except to say you...complete me in a way I never knew I could be completed. A part of me seeks you out. Constantly. When you're not near or when I'm holding myself apart, I miss the connection. I miss you."

He felt her happiness well up, saw it fill her eyes. Spill over. He had to clench his fingers to keep from catching the tears. His hope burgeoned.

"I know. I know I told you to leave my mind earlier. But now that you're gone, I realize I miss it, too. I miss you."

"Are you inviting me back?"

Though his sense rejoiced, he forced himself to wait for the words, reaching up to capture a curl from the mass still tangled from their ride across town. He wrapped the lock about his finger and smoothed it, savoring the bittersweet sensation of touching her and yet not touching her.

Not as he craved to touch her.

Inside and out.

She inched closer, then all the way onto her tiptoes, rewarding his restraint a millionfold as she bathed his lips with her husky invitation. "You know, I never did take that shower. Why don't you give me a minute or two to get cleaned up, then come on in and touch me...everywhere."

She felt him before she could see him.

It had happened like that with him before. And yet, it had never happened quite like this. Because this time she knew what was happening—and she welcomed it consciously.

She welcomed him.

Abby tipped her face up into the closest spray of water, rinsing the last of the soap from her face as the cooler air from the bathroom cut through the shower's steam. Gooseflesh rippled down her backside. The chills lasted no more than a second because Dare had already stepped into the eight-foot hexagonal chamber and closed the door, sealing out the entire world—except her. Though she'd finished rinsing, she kept her eyes closed as she absorbed his essence.

Savored.

She smiled as she felt Dare respond by easing deeper into her mind and her heart, until he was mingling with a part of her she'd never shared with another man and never would. Only then did she open her eyes. When she'd entered the shower, she'd turned on all three of the overhead nozzles for the sheer decadent novelty of it. If she had it to do over again, she'd have used one. Though Dare stood barely three-and-a-half feet away, there was far too much steam swirling between, most of it obscuring his body from the waist down, darn it. She consoled herself with the hard, rippling beauty of his chest naked and dripping wet.

Her breath caught as Dare stepped closer and smiled. He was eighteen inches away now, so near she could feel the heat of his body within the warmth of the water raining down. Or was that her imagination? She didn't know. She was too busy attempting to restart her lungs as Dare shifted to the left, stepping directly in front of a spray nozzle to tip his head back and soak his hair. She stared at the dusky length of his throat, her own going dry despite all this water. The spell broke as he bent down, disappearing into the steam for a moment to retrieve the bottle of shampoo she'd used. Her breath caught yet again as he straightened and smoothed the shampoo into his hair. The voyeur she didn't even know she possessed crawled all the way to the surface, completely hypnotized by the sight of those strong, callused fingers working the shampoo into a lather. And when he smoothed the frothy suds down the ridges of his chest?

*Mercy.*

A slow striptease set to a sultry tenor sax couldn't have been sexier. She knew then the show was deliberate. He hadn't waited outside the room while she'd lathered herself.

He'd watched.

She felt his shameless smile.

Anticipation fired her blood as he stepped back into the gentle spray and rinsed his hair, turning as the last dollop of suds slid down his chest, directly over his tattoo, hanging at the thick edge of his pectoral muscle for a brief, tantalizing moment before slipping lower. She followed frothy suds down his abdomen, only to frown as she met more swirling steam.

He stepped closer.

He was barely twelve inches away now and for the first time, utterly exposed in all his masculine glory. He stood silently, allowing her to look her fill, daring her to watch the evidence of his increasing pleasure as he absorbed the sight of her naked as well. The voyeur returned—and she looked. Even so, her cheeks grew hot as his erection grew thicker, harder. Somehow she managed to tear her gaze up, only to lose herself in the dark, erotic hunger of his stare.

His heart.

His hands.

She started momentarily as those fingers finally reached out for her, shivering as he smoothed the tips along the tender flesh of her upper thighs and hips, slowly slicking them through the water droplets still spilling over her belly until he'd reached her ribs. She shivered as his fingers rasped higher and higher until he'd reached her breasts. Dare traced each plump swell in turn, up and around, and then back down. He dragged his fingers up once more, but this time he caressed her nipples, too, slowly and deliberately scraping his calluses across the tips.

Her entire body quivered in response.

A moment later she felt his whisper. "Close your eyes."

*Feel.*

All of it. All of him.

Let him feel her.

She obeyed, her lashes drifting down of their own accord, as she felt Dare lower his slick, sinewy frame to his knees. A moment later she shuddered as his tongue flicked out, tasting one nipple, then the other. She dropped her hands, instinctively clutching his shoulders. The thick, roping muscles bunched beneath her fingers. She could feel him holding fast to his restraint as she regained her equilibrium and began to caress his arms and upper back, teasing his body as he teased hers. He responded in kind, bathing her breasts with slow, hungry strokes of his tongue until they were swollen, licking the water from her flesh as he drank his fill of the pure, sweet pleasure flooding her. He lifted his head and bit down on her nipples, worrying them gently between his teeth. He soothed each in turn and moved on. She started as he stopped to tease the slight ridge of her ribs with the tip of his tongue, then sighed as he kissed his way down her stomach.

There he paused. Tarried. Tasted the tender flesh of her belly, his hungry mouth drawing lower and lower, until she was silently, wantonly urging him further. His smoky breath torched her womanly curls for a single, breathtaking moment. And then he was tasting from her intimate font.

Her legs buckled.

Even with the textured floor of the shower, she'd have slipped and fallen right then and there if he hadn't sensed her need and deftly adjusted his grip. And then he delved deeper, robbing the air from her lungs even as he plundered the piercing pleasure directly from her soul. By his own admission, Darian Sabura might not be all that wonderful with words, but he was an absolute maestro of touch. And she was the cherished Strad beneath his hands. He glided his palms over her water-slicked curves, strumming her body with nimble strokes as he seduced the sweetest of melodies from her inner core. She gasped and she sighed.

And then, he changed.

He turned passionate in his demands, fiery. Determined. The erotic rhythm increased as his clever fingers and darting tongue took over, plucking at the strings of her passion until she was all but writhing in his arms. Suddenly, she couldn't take the pace anymore. Any moment, she was going to shatter.

No! It couldn't end like this.

Not this first time.

While she knew he was absorbing every ounce of the pleasure she felt, she needed to feel his, too. She opened her mouth to tell him, but the words wouldn't come out. A dark moan escaped instead. It didn't matter. As always, Dare heard her heart. Listened. But as she felt his shoulders bunch, felt him rise to his feet, the worry set in.

Yes, she was ready. So very ready.

But was he?

One look into that emerald inferno and she knew. Dare was more than ready. He dragged his palms down, clamping them beneath her rear, lifting her up straight in the middle of the shower. She was still gasping as he parted her thighs, wrapping them firmly about his hips. He anchored her there, staring into her eyes as he drove deep into her body with a single, powerful thrust—all the way into her soul. She was dimly aware of him guiding their bodies out of the rain of water and across the shower, of sealing her spine against the icy wall. A moment later, she was lost somewhere between the slick chill of the glass and the rock-hard blistering heat of him as he drove into her again and again.

The music had returned.

It was growing. Swelling. But it was nothing compared to

the song in her heart. She could feel Dare deep inside her mind, merging with her very being, crooning along with her. And then he was commanding, encouraging, begging. He wanted her now. Needed her. And so she wrapped her arms tighter and gave herself up to the throbbing music, exploding in a whirling crescendo of passion, pleasure and *him*.

And then they were raining down.

Together.

Slumping against the glass wall of the shower, listening to the steady splatter of water as the spray gradually cooled around them. She barely noticed as Dare scooped her up into his arms, twisting the master control off as he carried her out of the shower and into his bed. It wasn't until he'd drawn the covers over them and drawn her even closer that she realized they hadn't even taken the time to dry off. She didn't care. She was already drifting deeper into his arms, into sleep, blissfully happy and completely in love.

Abby woke with two men on her mind.

Her damp head was still pillowed against the warm, firm chest of the first. Dare's solid, comforting arms were still wrapped about her back as he pulled the night air deep into his lungs only to blow it out on an utterly contented sigh.

That left Brian.

Had he even stirred?

Guilt bit in. The familiar pangs of worry followed. If Brian woke in a strange bed, in an even stranger apartment and she wasn't there…? Abby lifted her head as carefully as she could, gently disentangling the length of her hair from Dare's arms as she peered at the clock beside his bed.

Four o'clock.

She'd slept all day and most of the night?

She glanced down at the gorgeous face of the man now stirring beneath her. That was some mojo Dare possessed. And she wasn't the only one affected by it. Last night hadn't transformed her into an empath. The proof was in Dare's eyes. The weight of the world had left. Though she suspected it would be back, absolute peace filled its place for now. She trailed a finger through the sexy rasp covering Dare's jaw.

"Hey."

Sleep dipped his smile deeper than she'd ever seen it. "Hey, yourself. Where are you running off to?"

"Nowhere. I just—"

"—need to check on Brian."

She nodded. "Do you mind?"

"Absolutely." His smile deepened. "But it's purely selfish. And I will get over it—with your help." He reached up and caressed her arms, then teased his index finger beneath the edge of the sheet she'd drawn to her breasts. "I keep my T-shirts and shorts in the bottom drawer of the dresser. Hurry back?"

"You bet."

He nodded, opened his mouth again—but a deep yawn edged out whatever he'd intended to say. He murmured something about her working better than Mount Everest and sank back into the dark-gray pillows instead. He looked so warm and content, she was tempted to sink down along with him.

But she didn't. She couldn't.

She had Brian to check on.

Because of the man already snoring softly as she nudged her feet to the floor, her brother would be waking soon, ready to see her, ready to talk about what had happened outside Avery Fisher Hall. To deal with it. And to deal with the leftover wound of their father's passing. She intended to be there when Brian woke, grateful that she'd found a man who not only understood, but cared for her brother as well. Abby retrieved a worn gray T-shirt from the drawer, but left the stack of shorts untouched. Dare's shirt was so baggy when she pulled it on, and elastic or not, there was no way his shorts would fit. She headed for the bathroom and donned the blue shorts she'd worn climbing the morning before.

It seemed like a lifetime ago.

As she closed the door to Dare's bedroom and padded down the hall to his guest room, she realized it was. Unfortunately, another realization snapped in as she opened that door.

Brian was gone.

She blinked at the tangle of bedcovers, certain she was seeing things. She wasn't. Nor could she find Brian anywhere. Not in the guest room, its bathroom, the living room, the half bath in the hall or the kitchen. Not even in the room that looked to be Dare's office. Her brother simply wasn't there.

Dare. Shouldn't he have said something?

Unless he didn't know.

Mount Everest.

Somehow making love with her had drained Dare of his empathic ability. But for how long? It didn't matter. They weren't in the middle of the Gunks. They were in a New York City apartment building. A building with a doorman. Even without Dare's amazing sense, he could help her track down one sleepwalking brother. She was about to wake Dare so he could help her search when the intercom buzzed in the foyer.

Jerry.

She spun around, heading for the two-way speaker that matched hers as the doorman's hushed voice confirmed what she suspected. Brian had taken the elevator down to the lobby. Her brother was fine, though surprisingly he'd curled up on the lobby couch and fallen into a deeper sleep.

"I'll be right there, Jerry. Thanks."

Abby grabbed her keys from the foyer table and made a beeline for the elevator. If she was lucky, she'd be back before Dare realized she'd left. But first— She punched the button for her floor, singling out the key to her apartment as the doors slid open. If Brian was asleep, she could take a minute to retrieve the portable motion detector she'd purchased for her place. She should have thought of it earlier, but she'd been too rattled over the thought of how close that butcher had gotten to her brother—twice.

Heck, she was still rattled.

She had to be. It wasn't until she'd stepped inside her darkened apartment that she realized she'd forgotten to lock her door again that morning. Fortunately, her nerves would be returning to normal soon. With Pike dead, every cop in the city had joined Liam Brooks in his search for Zeno Corza. By now the brute was probably in jail or on his way there.

Zeno was neither.

Nor had she left the door to her apartment unlocked. Zeno must have jimmied it. Because a split second later, that same door slammed shut behind her, trapping her with the shadowy giant she'd seen beside that limo. And he was wielding that same gleaming knife.

Her father would have been proud, Dare, too, because she didn't think. She reacted, tightening her grip on the keys, slicing them up the way her dad had taught her, as the bastard's fist locked around her left arm. Abby screamed as the knife sliced across her right biceps. A second later the brute's bellow displaced her own pain as she stabbed her keys into his face, hoping like hell she'd taken out an eye. Either way, his grip loosened. She heard the knife clatter to the floor as she tore away from him and down the hall to her bedroom. She slammed the door shut, locked it and grabbed the receiver to her princess phone. She pounded out Dare's number.

Before the phone could ring on the other end, she dropped it as the entire bedroom door shuddered against its frame. Zeno must be throwing his body into it.

She had to get out of here. Now. But how, dammit? There was only one door.

And a window.

A window she knew led directly to the penthouse.

She'd have to climb if she wanted to live. Because that door was going to give way any moment.

Abby scrambled across the room before she lost her nerve, not even having to bother throwing the latch on the window. She'd left this portal deliberately unlocked. She shoved the window open and crawled through, terror ripping in as she stepped out onto the ledge. Two seconds later panic seared it off as her bedroom door crashed open. She forced herself to look up and not at the knife-wielding brute bearing down on her as she searched the building's shadowy facade for the hand- and footholds she'd practiced out on that cliff at the Gunks. But she hadn't made it all the way up that cliff, had she? Not on her own. Dare had been beneath her, coaching her and encouraging her every inch of the way.

Only, Dare wasn't beneath her now.

Zeno and his gleaming knife were.

And there was her arm. The one Zeno had already slashed. She was losing blood with every reach she made.

And weakening with each passing second.

# Chapter 12

Before Dare even opened his eyes, he knew something was wrong. No, he couldn't feel it. But that was just it. He couldn't feel anything, anyone. Brian, the building's inhabitants, the city beyond, but most of all, Abby.

And then he heard it. The phone.

A split second later white-hot terror pierced Dare's gut, jump-starting his sense. *Abby.* She was in danger. Dare shot out of bed and grabbed the jeans he'd worn the day before off his chair. He yanked both legs on at the same time, but by the time he hit midzip, the terror had disappeared. Completely, leaving the simmering crush of the building and the city behind. He could feel Brian again, too. Sleeping, but not near. And something else. *Someone* else. A bastard he recognized secondhand, but a bastard nonetheless.

Corza was in the building. Hunting Abby.

So why couldn't he sense *her?*

Ice-cold dread punched in along with the only two possible explanations. The first Dare refused to voice, even in his own mind, much less his heart. The second reason sent him tearing across his bedroom, slamming through the French doors with such force most of the panes shattered. He reached the balustrade of the balcony, automatically zeroing in on the window that led to Abby's room twenty-five feet below, praying he'd find her clinging to the side of the building.

He did.

He caught the shadowy waterfall of her hair, the faint outline of his shirt. He could feel her now, too. She was injured and frantic—because she was slipping. Dare's horror doubled before he could purge enough adrenaline from his veins to call out with his voice or his essence. *There.* Breaking the plane of the open window. He could make out the flash of that damned knife as Corza stretched his torso out of the bedroom window, extending arms twice the girth of Abby's slender neck as the bastard tried to slash her again.

She was out of reach. Barely.

And her grip was still slipping.

Desperate to keep the element of surprise, Dare clamped down on his bellow and whirled about, vaulting across the balcony and into his room. He tore through the master closet, grabbing the first coil of rope he touched. He reached for his stash of steel carabiners, only to remember the few he bothered to keep on hand were still stowed in the back of his Blazer in the parking garage, twenty floors below. There was no time to search for a stray, much less fashion a Swiss seat from the rope to go with it. Dare shot out of the closet, then the bedroom, uncoiling the rope and doubling it over as he reached the cement balustrade of the balcony. For the first time in his life, he'd be going down *with* a rope—because of Abby.

It was the only way to save her. As long as he could manage to tie the damned thing off and rig an emergency Dulfer-sitz in time.

Abby's sharp scream cut through him as he accomplished the task with shaking hands. The fresh wave of pain that shafted through her right calf speared straight through Dare's gut as he straddled the doubled rope before pulling the length up from behind his back, over his head and down across his shoulder. He snapped off a wave of silent assurance, hoping it reached Abby as he swung his legs up over the balustrade. But instead of bounding down the side of the building, he waited. Prayed.

The moment Corza leaned out of the window for another slashing pass, Dare loosened his grip. Friction ripped along his inner thighs and back as he played out twenty-plus feet of rope to end up on the raw end of a modified swinging rappel that sent the balls of his feet slamming straight down into those beefy shoulders with the full force of gravity and a massive dose of desperation behind them.

Corza lost his grip on the windowsill.

Before the thug could curse, Corza was well on his way to losing his life as he went pitching headfirst into the dark.

Dare didn't even look down.

Instead, he kicked off the now-empty sill and swung sideways, snagging a stunned Abby with his left arm and hauling her in close as they swung back toward the window together. Four feet from the window, Dare loosened his grip once more, playing the rope as he hooked Abby's legs with his. He jerked her calves up with his, slicing both their bodies through the open portal with a precision that surprised even him. He clamped down on the rope as they hit the floor, bringing them to a rug-burning stop just shy of a pair of worn cowboy boots.

"Impressive stunt, Tarzan. Guess you two don't need the cavalry after all."

Once again, he and Abby moved in unison, snapping their stares up to greet Liam Brooks. There they parted company as Abby dragged her wide-eyed gaze back to Dare's.

And promptly passed out in his arms.

* * *

Dare was still holding her when she woke.

Abby studied the naked muscles cradling her cheek, the familiar, rumpled sheets beneath. They weren't lying on the floor of her bedroom, however. They were back in Dare's penthouse. In his bed. She glanced up, losing herself in that dark, mesmerizing stare. A stare that was still missing most of the weight of the world. "What happened?"

He smiled. "You fainted."

She blushed. "That I remember." Sort of. She lifted her right arm, no longer wondering why her biceps and calf didn't even sting. She was in Dare's arms, after all. What confused her was the oversized bandage taped to her biceps and the one she could feel on her leg, rubbing into Dare's jeans. He'd managed to dress her wounds without her waking? "How—"

"Shock. I thought it best not to revive you until I got you up here and finished treating your cuts. Thankfully, neither required stitches. Then Jerry called up. Since Brian managed to sleep through all our excitement, I figured you'd want me to retrieve him first, spare him the confusion of waking to it. I carried Brian up and tucked him back in bed. He never even stirred. And there was still Liam Brooks, the police and most of all—" This time Dare flushed. "Most of all, I wanted to be alone with you when you woke."

That part she minded least. But what about Brian? She could see the first rays of day breaking beyond the French doors. Doors that were missing huge sections of glass, incidentally. "My brother's still sleeping?"

"Yes. And to answer the next logical question, it's nearly six." That wry twist she'd come to adore dipped in. "Amazing capacity you Pembrokes have for deep sleep."

She pinched his chest. Or rather, she tried to. The muscles were too thick and too hard. She settled for a bit of teasing herself. "Hey, we had a bit of help. And if I remember correctly, you passed out longer than me after our…shower."

He sobered instantly. "I know." Part of his gift must be rubbing off on her, because she could already feel the self-recrimination setting in. "Abby, I—"

"You saved my life. Again." She braced her forearms on his chest and scooted up so she could press her lips to his. "Thank you. Besides, if you ever decide to try going to another concert, we know how to prep you."

He nodded. Let the guilt go.

Thank goodness. Heaven knew he had enough inside him. Most of which wasn't even his. She changed the subject before he could drag another batch to the fore. "You mentioned cops? Liam?"

"Abby, I neglected to inform you of something. You were worried about Brian and I—"

She pressed her finger to his lips. "Just say it."

"Van Heusen woke. He's fine. Talking."

Stuart was okay? She was happy for the man, yes. Relieved. But what about— The sheet pooled about her as she scrambled to her knees. "The money. Oh, God, what did he say?"

To her horror, Dare frowned darkly. "Everything."

She sank onto her haunches.

"Sweetheart, it's not what you think. What either of us thought. There's…more."

"More?" Dare hadn't even told her what he thought Stuart had done. "I don't understand. I took the money. How much more can there be?" She licked her lips. "Did Stuart accuse me of blackmailing his mother?"

"No. And I wouldn't worry about the money. Van Heusen has larger problems. Starting with the fact that you're not the only woman Katherine paid off—is still paying off. Van Heusen impregnated a sixteen-year-old while he was in college. She had the child."

"Meaning there's proof he's not the unstoppable, lily-white mayoral candidate everyone thinks he is." Dare was right. Stuart had bigger problems than her.

He nodded. "Through Zeno Corza, Titan uncovered that proof. Used it against Van Heusen to rig a case years ago, before he'd developed his designer drug. Through Corza, Titan used that proof again two weeks ago when Corza forced Van Heusen to sneak into your dressing room at the concert hall to steal hair from your brush. But he had second thoughts. That's why he was trying to reach you. Why he was there that night."

She sucked in her breath. Her shock. Stuart had tried to help her that night? "But why would he give that monster my DNA in the first place? Why would they even need it?"

But she already knew.

Again Dare nodded. "Because of me. Liam was right. They only went after you to get to me. According to Van Heusen, Corza was watching the building. He saw me enter your window that first night. He assumed we were lovers."

And now they were.

It seemed the mystery had finally been solved. But she had no idea where the aftermath left her and Dare. Was that all they were—lovers? Or did Dare want more? Did he want what she wanted? Did he want forever? He had to know what she was feeling. That she needed reassurance. Hope. But he didn't say anything. She swallowed the lump in her throat when Dare turned to the nightstand. He held out a slip of paper as he settled against the headboard.

"What's that?"

"A gift. Take it. Please."

She retrieved the slip and unfolded it. "I don't understand." She gasped. "What—"

"It's a receipt stating you've repaid the loan Katherine extended you. See?" He tapped the barely legible signature. "Van Heusen signed it. Liam witnessed."

"But I didn't repay the money. You said not to."

He shook his head. "I told *you* not to."

*He'd* repaid her debt? A million dollars?

"Why?"

"Because you needed it." He shrugged. "I can afford it."

She was still trying to grasp that he'd written a check for a million dollars on her behalf. "Dare, how can I ever—"

"Thank me?"

She'd been about to say *repay,* but she nodded.

"By marrying me."

Shock ripped through her. The very best kind. But it was still shock. "Wh-what did you say?"

He cursed. "Sorry. I didn't mean it to come out like that. It's a question, honey, not a statement. And I swear to God, one's not dependent on the other. I just—" He stopped, muttered anther curse, then mumbled something about his lousy conversational skills and fell silent altogether.

Except he wasn't really silent. Not inside.

She could feel the uncertainty churning within him. The apprehension. The flat-out fear. But why? Couldn't he feel—

He couldn't. Adrenaline.

Dare was terrified she was going to say no. So terrified, there was enough adrenaline flooding through his veins that he couldn't read the answer bursting from her heart. From her soul. She leaned close and laid her left hand on his naked chest, directly over the tattoo that for years had represented his subconscious hope that he wasn't meant to go through life alone. Then she snagged his left hand with her right and tucked it beneath the shirt she'd borrowed two hours earlier, sealing his palm to her own bare flesh—to her own thundering heart—and let him feel her answer.

*Yes.*

The fear shattered. She felt Dare's joy surge into its place as he dipped his head to claim her mouth, only to stop a millimeter from her lips. He didn't have to glance at the door.

"Brian?"

Dare nodded. "He's waking."

She closed her eyes and swallowed her selfish sigh for the kiss and the shower that would have to wait. "I—"

"—need to go."

She nodded, returning Dare's teasing smile as the rest of the conversation played out. One he had all the right words for. "Do you mind?"

"Absolutely." His grin turned downright wicked. "But it's purely selfish. And I will get over it—with a lot of one-on-one help from you." He slid his fingers lower, slowly caressing the curve of her breast. "Hurry back?"

"You bet."

She swung her feet to the floor and stood before she changed her mind. But before she could turn, she caught the longing in that gorgeous emerald gaze, for something else entirely. She held out her hand. "Dare, would you like to join me and meet part of your new family?"

He took her hand and smiled.

"Absolutely."

\* \* \* \* \*

*Next month, look for the story of Hawk Donovan in*
*A TOUCH OF THE BEAST by award-winning author*
*Linda Winstead Jones*
*as*
**FAMILY SECRETS: THE NEXT GENERATION**
*continues!*
*Coming in September 2004*
*Available wherever Silhouette Books are sold.*

**Silhouette®**

INTIMATE MOMENTS™

Go on the ride of your life in

# Marie Ferrarella's

next novel from her thrilling miniseries

★★★★★

CAVANAUGH JUSTICE

## In Broad Daylight

**(Silhouette Intimate Moments #1315)**

When a child goes missing, it's up to Detective Dax Cavanaugh to find her. But he hasn't counted on Brenda York, the feisty teacher who's also looking for the little girl. Passion flares between them, but will they be able to rescue the child—and fall in love—before tragedy tears them apart?

*Available September 2004 at your favorite retail outlet.*

Visit Silhouette Books at www.eHarlequin.com

SIMIBD

# INTIMATE MOMENTS™

## Reader favorite

# Sara Orwig

### continues her tantalizing Texas miniseries with

## Don't Close Your Eyes
### (Silhouette Intimate Moments #1316)

Everyone thought
Colin Garrick was dead.

But this fourth Texas knight
is undoubtedly alive, and
he's come to Stallion Pass
with a mission...and a
warning. Colin had closed
off his wounded heart long
ago, but when a spunky
nanny gets caught in the
middle of his plans and sets
sparks of passion flying
between them, he'll do
anything in his power to
protect her!

### STALLION PASS:

# TEXAS KNIGHTS

**Where the only cure for
those hot and sultry Lone Star
days are some sexy-as-all-get-
out Texas Knights!**

*Available September 2004
at your favorite retail outlet.*

Visit Silhouette Books at www.eHarlequin.com                    SIMDCYE

**Silhouette®**

# INTIMATE MOMENTS™

invites you to pick up the next installment of

# Justine Davis's

**heart-stopping miniseries**

## REDSTONE, INCORPORATED

*When the world is your workplace, love can find you anywhere.*

# In His Sights

**(Intimate Moments #1318)**

Kate Crawford was the most captivating woman
Redstone securities expert Rand Singleton had ever
known—and a suspect in his investigation. But could he
uncover her secrets before she discovered his?

*Available September 2004 at your favorite retail outlet.*

Visit Silhouette Books at www.eHarlequin.com                    SIMIHS

If you enjoyed what you just read,
then we've got an offer you can't resist!

# Take 2 bestselling love stories FREE!

# Plus get a FREE surprise gift!

Clip this page and mail it to Silhouette Reader Service™

**IN U.S.A.**
3010 Walden Ave.
P.O. Box 1867
Buffalo, N.Y. 14240-1867

**IN CANADA**
P.O. Box 609
Fort Erie, Ontario
L2A 5X3

**YES!** Please send me 2 free Silhouette Intimate Moments® novels and my free surprise gift. After receiving them, if I don't wish to receive anymore, I can return the shipping statement marked cancel. If I don't cancel, I will receive 6 brand-new novels every month, before they're available in stores! In the U.S.A., bill me at the bargain price of $4.24 plus 25¢ shipping and handling per book and applicable sales tax, if any*. In Canada, bill me at the bargain price of $4.99 plus 25¢ shipping and handling per book and applicable taxes**. That's the complete price and a savings of at least 10% off the cover prices—what a great deal! I understand that accepting the 2 free books and gift places me under no obligation ever to buy any books. I can always return a shipment and cancel at any time. Even if I never buy another book from Silhouette, the 2 free books and gift are mine to keep forever.

245 SDN DZ9A
345 SDN DZ9C

| | | |
|---|---|---|
| Name | (PLEASE PRINT) | |
| Address | Apt.# | |
| City | State/Prov. | Zip/Postal Code |

\* Terms and prices subject to change without notice. Sales tax applicable in N.Y.
\*\* Canadian residents will be charged applicable provincial taxes and GST.
   All orders subject to approval. Offer limited to one per household and not valid to
   current Silhouette Intimate Moments® subscribers.
   ® are registered trademarks owned and used by the trademark owner and or its licensee.

INMOM04                                                    ©2004 Harlequin Enterprises Limited

# e**H**ARLEQUIN.com

## The Ultimate Destination for Women's Fiction

Your favorite authors are just a click away
at www.eHarlequin.com!

- Take a sneak peek at the covers and
  read summaries of **Upcoming Books**

- Choose from over 600
  author **profiles!**

- Chat with your favorite authors
  on our **message boards.**

- Are you an author in the making?
  Get advice from published authors
  in **The Inside Scoop!**

**Learn about your favorite authors
in a fun, interactive setting—
visit www.eHarlequin.com today!**

INTAUTH04

## *Silhouette*®

# I N T I M A T E   M O M E N T S™

# GHOST OF A CHANCE
### (Silhouette Intimate Moments #1319)
## by award-winning author
# NINA BRUHNS

Could the gorgeous man Clara Fergussen found in
her bed really be the infamous pirate Tyree St. James?
He'd been caught in a curse for the past two hundred
years, and had only one week left on earth. After
a passionate night in his arms, would Clara risk
everything to be with him—forever?

*Available September 2004 at your favorite retail outlet.*

Visit Silhouette Books at www.eHarlequin.com                        SIMGOAC

# Silhouette®

# INTIMATE MOMENTS™

**Presenting the fourth book in
the thrilling continuity**

## FAMILY Secrets
### The Next Generation

*No one is alone...*

## A Touch of the Beast
### (Silhouette Intimate Moments #1317)
### by award-winning author
# Linda Winstead Jones

Rancher, loner—horse whisperer? Hawk Donovan had always longed to seek the source of his mysterious power, and when a tip from a stranger opens the door to his past, he takes a leap of faith and begins to explore. To investigate the old fertility clinic, though, he'll first have to convince Sheryl Eldanis, the beautiful vet who has hidden the clinic's files in her attic, that he can be trusted. But as their search progresses, trust gives way to passion—and when they uncover the sinister information about Hawk's birth mother, they unleash a deadly chain of events that threatens Sheryl's peaceful life. Can Hawk save his lover from the danger he brought to her door before it's too late?

*Available September 2004
at your favorite retail outlet.*

Visit Silhouette Books at www.eHarlequin.com

SIMATOTB